Iron Curtain

Iron Curtain

A Love Story

VESNA
GOLDSWORTHY

Chatto & Windus
LONDON

1 3 5 7 9 10 8 6 4 2

Chatto & Windus, an imprint of Vintage, is part of the
Penguin Random House group of companies whose addresses
can be found at global.penguinrandomhouse.com

 Penguin
Random House
UK

First published by Chatto & Windus in 2022

penguin.co.uk/vintage

A CIP catalogue record for this book is available from
the British Library

ISBN 9781784744588

Typeset in 10.5/15 pt Nexus Serif OT
by Integra Software Services Pvt. Ltd, Pondicherry

Euripides, *Medea*, translated from the Greek by Martin Collier; Ivan Lalić,
'Places We Love' from in *A Rusty Needle*, translated from the Serbian by
Francis R. Jones and reprinted by kind permission of Carcanet Press,
Manchester; Milovan Djilas, *The New Class: An Analysis of the Communist
System*; Anthony Hope, *The Prisoner of Zenda*; Czesław Miłosz, 'City
Without a Name', translated from the Polish by the author with Robert
Hass © 2001, The Estate of Czesław Miłosz, used by permission of The
Wylie Agency (UK) Limited.; Anna Akhmatova, 'I am not one of those
who left their land', translated from the Russian by D. M. Thomas; Osip
Mandelstam, *Tristia*, translated from the Russian by Peter McCarey;
Nina Cassian, 'Lady of Miracles' from *Life Sentence*, translated from the
Romanian by Laura Schiff and reprinted by kind permission of Carcanet
Press, Manchester; Blaga Dimitrova, 'Butterfly on a Pin', published in
Scars (Ivy Press, 2003), translated from the Bulgarian by Ludmilla
Popova-Wightman

Printed and bound in Great Britain by Clays Ltd, Elcograf S.p.A.

The authorised representative in the EEA is Penguin Random House
Ireland, Morrison Chambers, 32 Nassau Street, Dublin D02 YH68

Penguin Random House is committed to a sustainable future for
our business, our readers and our planet. This book is made from
Forest Stewardship Council® certified paper.

To all my friends who, like me, grew up east of that line
from Stettin in the Baltic to Trieste in the Adriatic

Stronger than lover's love is lover's hate. Incurable,
in each, the wounds they make.

Euripides, *Medea*

When you go, space closes over like water behind you,
Do not look back: there is nothing outside you,
Space is only time visible in a different way,
Places we love we can never leave.

Ivan Lalić, 'Places We Love'

Prologue

The Curtain Falls

Live from Berlin, December 1990

'The walls are crumbling all over Europe. A year ago, this city was still divided by one. Many of those who wanted to escape life in the East, by climbing over or tunnelling under it, lost their lives. Concrete fragments of that wall are now sold as souvenirs, pathetic remnants of a former threat.

'From Tallinn to Tirana, from Belfast to Bucharest, people are on the move, free at last. We don't need visas any more and soon we will need no passports. We are witnessing the end of history. And this glorious city, where I am now standing, is both the heart and the fountainhead of this new world.

'In the past two years, small countries lying on what some wrongly see as the edge of Europe, but which are just as much part of the continent's glory as any lands to the west, have suffered agonies of social turmoil. Some have ended decades of repression with bloody revolutions. These countries are now queuing up to join us in the European Union. As an Irishman and, above all, a European, I feel their pain and share their hopes. We must offer them a hand of friendship, show that our world is better, that it was worth their sacrifice.

'I am honoured to receive this great poetry prize in the newly reunited Germany, a harbinger and, I hope, a leader of further unifications. Allow me to dedicate the honour to my sons, Nicholas and Philip.

'Their generation will grow up without the Iron Curtain, without the suffering it brought to millions, and in a new Europe without borders. I am speaking for them, and to them, this evening.

'Dear boys, your father promises you an open, unfettered Europe. I look forward to seeing you in Britain very soon.'

He stared into the TV camera as though straight into my eyes. His hair was tamed in a smart cut and his Nehru jacket was too obviously bespoke to be borrowed, but he seemed unchanged otherwise, every centimetre his dishonest self, spooling out clichés unworthy of the award he was about to receive.

I used to love this man.

I could not bear to witness the eagerness with which he glided in the slipstream of political power, a cultural opportunist performing like a circus dolphin. How well he did it, and how uncritically and enthusiastically his audience accepted him for what he wasn't. His skill was in striking the precise chord they wanted, to stroke their desire to feel simultaneously cultured and virtuous. I knew his power to seduce. I had been just as gullible once.

A crystal orb and fifty thousand Deutschmarks: that was the prize, they said. The performance was worth every pfennig. It was a betrayal of everything poetry should stand for.

I could not bear the sounds of Beethoven's 'Ode to Joy' rising under his words, deployed in that sentimental way that only the Germans seem capable of when they want to mask their own might. And I definitely could not bear to hear Europe mentioned once more.

I used to love Europe too.

I switched the television off.

Part One

East of the Iron Curtain

In a Far-Away Country of Which We Know Nothing

Membership in the Communist Party before the Revolution meant sacrifice. Being a professional revolutionary was one of the highest honours. Now that the Party has consolidated its power, Party membership means that one belongs to a privileged class. And at the core of the Party are the all-powerful exploiters and masters.

Milovan Djilas, *The New Class: An Analysis of the Communist System*

Chapter One

Victory Day

1981

It was a mediocre essay: threadbare insights into the details of the life of the poor in *Oliver Twist*, the kind you had to spew out in order to pass an exam, interleaved with a few adolescent aperçus of my own. I was passable, good even, as a student of the English language. Home tutoring and access to imported music and films helped, and of course I had attended our capital's sought-after English-language high school, one of the unisex 'Etons of the East', as it was waggishly nicknamed.

Literature was a different matter. I found analysing books, particularly the sort of English novels that graced the Communist curricula, too tedious. Teaching assistants treated me timidly, as though it was an honour to have me in their seminars, but my attendance record remained dismal.

I went to the end-of-year awards ceremony only because I knew that my absence would speak more loudly than my presence. I did not want to fight every battle against the system just to show my father that I was my own person. How do you rebel when even your rebellion is anticipated?

The Dean called my name. His articulation of my arguments was sharper than anything in my essay. The gold medal. Imagine my fury when I was summoned to the podium. Both the silver and the bronze winners looked stunned as the three of us were lined up for a photo.

'Great work, Comrades,' the Dean told the other two. 'Not quite matching the finesse of Comrade Urbanska's understanding, but well done nonetheless.' He managed to sound lovelorn as he pronounced my name.

I shut my eyes when the camera clicked.

I opened them to spot Misha and Lana, my boyfriend and his brat sister, smirking in the third row. They were there purely to embarrass me. Someone must have told them – but not me – about the prize. I dreamed of pushing Father from the top of the stairs back home, of breaking his bovine neck.

'Happy Victory Day,' Misha said in Russian when we met later that evening. His intonation was soft: Leningrad rather than Moscow.

'You speak too soon,' I said as he stepped towards me. I gave a snort, like a prize pony, then shoved him away. I was still fuming about the medal, not in the mood for fondling. Had I only guessed that Misha would be taken from me so soon – Russian-style, albeit not by the Russians – I'd have pulled him closer, held him better.

I was in my regulation black-widow student outfit – black shirt, black trousers, black plimsolls, kohl-rimmed eyes to match raven-black hair.

'The Juliette Gréco of the steppes,' Misha said.

He was dressed as faultlessly as ever: navy Converse, red-label 501s with button flies, a racing-green Lacoste polo, Ray-Ban aviators tucked into its neck opening, a wine-coloured cashmere cardigan draped over his shoulders. His Jim Morrison curls stood out in a city in which the police scooped boys up off the streets for savage shearing if their hair so much as touched their shirt collars.

My relationship with Misha achieved the rare feat of dividing my parents. My father, predictably, hated the little sissy. Mother's concept of manhood was broader, accustomed as she had been to tenors in powdered wigs and lipstick in her days on the operatic stage. My own take on Misha was, to begin with, very simple. I wanted a boyfriend, he was good-looking and good in bed. The local choice was limited. We weren't – certainly I wasn't, or not yet – in love.

He offered me a cigarette from a shiny black-and-gold John Player Special packet and, when I took one, he held up his cloisonné Dupont lighter. Click. He was a vacuous prat, I thought, and I was worse than him for being able to read his get-up, item by item.

Nothing on him – not the socks, not the boxer shorts, not the watch, not the braided leather bracelet on his wrist or the musky aftershave – was purchased locally. Even the bitter lemon he drank arrived in cans from Italy. Only the rare few around here had passports; fewer still could afford to travel in order to shop for fripperies; and a handful had foreign fripperies delivered to them.

I used to think Misha an immature snob for needing his Western façade to be so immaculate that even the briefest of walks required an hour's notice and a full-length mirror. I had misread its significance. It was an exoskeleton, a scaffold that held him together. It was not so much about worshipping the West – Misha knew the West too well for that – as about a refusal to belong to the East.

All Communist countries were supposed to be alike. Socialism was scientific after all, a repeatable experiment. But each one, including our own, bore the imprints of its past. Catholic, Orthodox, Protestant, Islamic; Byzantine, Ottoman, Habsburg, Tsarist Russian, Königliche Prussian, regicidal Serbian or even theocratic and tribal Montenegrin – centuries of tradition lingered into the Marxist dawn.

Kafkaesque, bureaucratic Prague or the déclassé but still bleakly Germanic East Berlin was very different from the quasi-oriental satrapies of Bulgaria or Romania, with the latter's sinister tales of secret executions, not to mention the terra incognita of closeted, deviationist Albania. The worlds that came before eventually seeped through the layers of fresh paint like bloodstains on the wall of an ancient torture chamber.

I preferred history to literature. However, there was little point in studying history here. We lived it every day but could only discuss it freely but furtively by night. Our own land melded both Latin and Phanariot ingredients in a soup of Slav blood. It had been ruled for centuries by despots and *sebastokrators*, men dressed in velvet and pearls and unused to opposition. Their fathers died in their own beds only when given a nightcap of poison. Their melancholy mothers – princesses imported at six or seven, from palaces as far afield as Sicily or Seville, to shore up an alliance or buttress a peace deal – spoke Latin and Greek and knew little of our barbarian tongue. They brought up their sons to expect the finest of everything, because an all-too-fleeting luxury was the only succour they could guarantee.

In addition to all that, we were a satellite orbiting the great mother planet of the revolution, the Soviet Union itself. Misha was the latest member of one of our illustrious, indigenous revolutionary lines. Of course, he was against entitlement and privilege. We all were; it was a matter of principle. But I am not speaking about principles here, I am speaking about DNA.

'We are the most talked-about couple in town,' Misha said. 'Comecon's Charles and Diana.'

That spring, it was our running gag. Both our mothers were mesmerised by the fairy tale that was the British royal engagement. While their husbands were nominally committed to executing monarchs wherever they might reign, the two wives followed royal families avidly in glossy foreign magazines, savouring palace intrigues from Monaco to Stockholm. Neither of them had anything better to do.

'My lady Di,' Misha appraised me in sing-song, pronouncing the name the way my francophone mother would: *maladeedee*.

'I can't wait to see you in uniform in a couple of months' time, dearest Charles,' I shot back, just to be mean.

In army matters, boys like Misha got off lightly, spending their two years of military service in the cushiest corners of our lovely land. Yet even so they sometimes suffered mental breakdowns, because their privileged locks were finally shaven to match other heads, or because coordination of every last detail of their outfit was no longer up to them.

Two years were still two years; no one could give that time back. And occasionally someone shouted, even at them. The fathers might well have encouraged the barking of orders. Rather like that notorious tradition of English fathers paying good money to send their sons to bleak and spartan public schools, it was good for character-building.

'It's four months away still, darling, not until September,' Misha said. 'Don't cry for me, Argentina.'

The tosser had the only LP of *Evita* this side of the Iron Curtain. We held *Evita* parties in his villa.

'Have you heard what's happening at the Youth Palace this evening?' he asked. 'Lana is already there, guarding two seats for us.' He took the jumper off his shoulders and threw it over mine, perhaps to break my coiffed and sartorial monotony of black.

The pavements under our feet were covered in acacia petals. Their scent was stronger than the ubiquitous diesel fumes, so strong that it reached through fastened windows and balcony doors at night. People went about their business in this confettied whiteness like swarms of bees.

It was the eve of Victory Day and a rehearsal was going on along the main drag as we emerged. The street echoed with the sound of boots falling on tarmac, kicking petals into the air.

'Present arms,' the drill sergeant shouted. Several hundred young heads turned right just as Misha and I were passing, their dark eyes glinting, bayonets sparkling. Wafts of boys' sweat and the felted wool of their overcoats cut through the perfume of the acacias. Their winter uniforms were too heavy for the weather. There was the inhuman, grinding sound of tanks on the move somewhere further up the road.

Misha grabbed my hand and pulled me back under the trees and into the park.

'Present arms,' he imitated the sergeant in stage whisper. I froze to attention and he lifted me up. I propped my chin against the top of his head. His curls tickled, so I tilted my head back. The sky was lit by a million stars. It seemed just possible, in that moment, to love both him and this place. He was mine and it was ours.

We skipped over rows of municipal flower beds and across freshly watered lawns, ignoring the warnings not to walk on the grass. The row of flagpoles in front of the Praesidium came into view, pale like giant birch trunks in the evening light. The flags fluttered redly some fifteen metres above our heads. I always hated the building; in its rejection of bourgeois taste, it seemed to me instead a celebration of ugliness and, in its massing of reinforced concrete, well beyond any scale that could be described as human. Even the paws of the stone lions at the entrance were as tall as we were. It was an expression of power, as brutal as the boot forever stamping on a human face that I had read about in the Orwell novel my father kept under lock and key.

That evening, unexpectedly, there was something magical about the animals; the granite they were carved from sparkled in the moonlight.

'Let's climb the lions,' Misha said. 'Let's sit up there. The guards have gone to bed.'

He gestured towards the massive bronze doors. Their patinated squares, produced by some Communist Pisano, illustrated the story of the revolution. The doors were wide open in daytime, with guardsmen in ceremonial uniform standing on either side, guns at the ready. One side was now closed, the squares shining faintly in those low spots where a human hand had touched them. Where the other side was open, you could see another door further in, made of thick glass, and, through it, the lobby. There, in the half-light, stood a soldier in battle fatigues with a machine gun. Unlike his chocolate-box colleagues in daytime, this one wasn't for show, but a reminder of the less-than-distant memory of the revolution that had eaten so many of its children. He looked in our direction but it was unclear whether he could actually see anything.

'The revolution never sleeps,' Misha said, undeterred. 'Let's climb up there anyway, please, Mimi. Let's be like those hippies who ride the lions in Trafalgar Square.'

'You are out of your mind,' I said and pulled him away. We ran towards the residential quarter.

That too was shockingly empty. I wondered if we had missed some edict. As we walked past shops and that socialist speciality of alcohol-free milk restaurants, all closed for the day, there was a sound of motorcycles. Eight outriders on heavy Ural motorbikes turned in from Odessa Square, followed by a line of black limousines – a couple of ZiLs, a couple of Mercedes and an old Chaika – then four strange white vans with security grilles over their windows. The flotilla trailed off towards the Praesidium followed by another cluster of Urals.

'Did you see that? Mercedes!' I asked, disbelieving.

'It must be my dad in that Chaika. That man is incorrigible,' Misha laughed, ignoring my question.

The comrades were fond of West German technology at home – sound equipment, kitchen gadgets, fridge freezers and even washing machines – but cars were different, a step too far, too public a gesture. I wondered which ministers were inside those two German vehicles. Were their capitalist conveyances a reward or a punishment? Were they being set up for a fall?

As the sound of motorcycles trailed off, I saw plain-clothes policemen, always so obvious with their ferrety features and their smart-casual mufti, stepping out of doorways and side passages here and there. Then people, ordinary citizens, began to emerge, slowly filling the street, going about their business again.

'Where were you two shaggers?' Lana hissed when we finally reached the Youth Palace. The auditorium was full, boys and girls squashed against each other and spilling out into the lobby at the back, yet she had somehow managed to keep two front-row seats for us. This was not Party privilege, this hogging of premium spots, this was Lana's genes at work – pure Darwinism – seizing, then defending, her territory. I could see as I squeezed into my seat that her win had not come without a fight.

There was a young woman onstage, seated at a low table that could have come from a primary-school dining hall. She was dark-haired and lean, and naked above the waist, with only a grey pleated skirt below. From where we sat, you could occasionally observe that she wore no knickers, but she wasn't showing off the fact. She stared ahead with kohl-rimmed racoon eyes, her left hand splayed flat on the table, a knife in her right, stabbing blindly between the fingers as fast as she could. Her nipples bobbed furiously to the rhythm of her hand movement, like two blackberries on a flat chest. All the while she sang an anthem of our wartime resistance movement in a hoarse, passionless voice. A couple of young men walked up to the front and unfurled a banner with the words 'Arise, Ye

Wretched of the Earth' inscribed in thick red paint, then just stood there, holding it at the girl's feet. The room hummed along, waiting for blood.

'That's us through and through,' Misha said. 'This bloody country. Always derivative, even in subversion. Marina Abramović did this same thing in Belgrade eight years ago.'

'Fuck Marina Abramović,' Lana said. 'It's easy to pull off this kind of stunt in Yugoslavia. That's a capitalist country with a little Communist make-up. Here it takes bloody balls. Shut up, Misha. Watch.'

Lana's eyes were wide open and welling with tears as she stared at the performer. I winked in Misha's direction. He flicked his tongue in mock cunnilingus. I am afraid I sniggered. We used to call girls like Lana sapphic and think of their sexuality as unnatural. They were treated in psychiatric hospitals. For all its revolutionary heritage, ours was a conformist culture. I thought myself advanced but I was as blinkered as everyone else.

'You watch yourself, Psycho,' I said to Lana.

I was bored. I got up, fought my way through the crowd, went downstairs to a smoke-filled lavatory and then sat in the cubicle, adding to the smoke. The walls and door were covered with obscene limericks and drawings: plenty to read, and more to enjoy than on the stage upstairs. Lavatory walls were, we sometimes joked, our free press. I peed, eventually. There was no paper. There never was. I had to waste another handkerchief. I liked the touch of silk, but it was a pity always to have to throw these things away.

When I stepped out of the cubicle and moved over to the row of dirty sinks, I noticed a man just standing there, next to a pillar, his head shaved, the back of it pressed flat against a mirror. He seemed to be waiting for me, unbothered by the fact that he was inside a women's lavatory. I started towards the exit as fast as I could, but he was faster. He grabbed my wrist and blocked the door with his foot. There was no one else around.

'Comrade Milena,' he said, 'I have been searching for you.'

Although he looked like a bald gorilla, his voice was educated, and unthreatening, but that did not mean he was not about to rape me. Socialism had done little to suppress our much older macho traditions, and a woman alone in a space such as the one I found myself in was all too easily seen as fair game. I tugged away, opened my mouth to scream. He let go, but his foot was still blocking the door.

'How do you know my name?' I hissed. Despite my father's fame – or notoriety – my face was not public property.

'I am here to tell you that you must leave this building, you and your two friends, by ten-thirty at the latest,' he said.

'Or?' I asked.

'There is no "or". I am to tell you that you must leave this building, you and your two friends, by ten-thirty,' he repeated.

'Goon,' I said.

'I am sorry to hear you say that,' he said and withdrew his foot. Someone had been trying to open the door from the other side. A girl I vaguely knew burst in and had difficulty hiding a smirk when the goon planted a light peck on my cheek before leaving. It was, like his use of my first name, an annoying attempt to pretend that we were acquainted. His cologne was sharper than car deodorant, but it did nothing to mask the smell of cheap tobacco.

'Fuck you,' I said. 'Fuck both of you!'

Misha and Lana waited in the lobby. Misha looked fed up. He must have dragged his sister away from the performance, for she kept glancing back. The young crowd inside was now humming the Internationale: you wouldn't think it possible to infuse humming with irony, but they achieved it. I could hear the shouts of 'Happy Victory Day' amid the reverberating noise. I had a vague feeling I should warn someone about something but I didn't know where to begin. I did not want to tell even these two about the goon. We left.

'Children! It's just normal rebellion.' I heard Mother's voice the following morning as I was approaching the breakfast room.

'Nothing wrong with a spot of—' Father stopped when I walked in.

They were already eating. My breakfast sat under a silver cloche. A napkin was wrapped around the handle, although everything underneath must have gone cold long ago. There was no reason to have our breakfasts served at the same time, other than as a punishment for what they thought of as my lie-ins.

'How was your evening, Mimi?' Father asked.

'Fine,' I said. 'We went to some boring arts event, then to Misha's.'

That was as much as I was going to say. Father knew what I was doing as well as or, given my hangover, even better than I did. I couldn't be bothered to try finding out what he and Mother were talking about, or what, if anything, had happened at the Youth Palace after I left. I guessed members of the audience were probably searched and warned not to attend similar gatherings again. I was sure their IDs were recorded; two strikes like that and you became a registered hooligan. That meant no place at the university and the catch-22 of unemployment. No one dared give you a job, yet social parasitism was itself an offence.

The fate of the artist was a different matter. There was no second strike for her, unless, like Marina Abramović, she was someone's daughter. Possibly not even then. Ridiculing the revolution, public nudity, banned songs: that performance went too far on several levels. Still, there are worse fates than whatever might have befallen her last night. This wasn't Stalin's Russia, and these weren't the 1930s. Those in power recognised that the problem with apocalyptic, irreversible punishments was that they could be inflicted on them and their own families as the wheel turned. My best guess for that girl was a psychiatric hospital, some drugs, maybe a little electricity, then silence. And you couldn't call that a pity, I thought. She was risibly derivative.

I remembered her blackberry nipples and felt a faint tremor between my legs. I hope I am not going psycho in Lana's way, I thought, and let out a small involuntary giggle. My father looked at me with a mixture of exasperation and concern, then recalled something and smiled at me.

'I heard about your essay, Mimi,' he said.

'Before I even started writing it?'

'Ha-ha,' he countered, his voice flat. 'Don't you get tired of always making the same jokes? You'll thank me when you get an academic post. Not that I had anything to do with your bloody medal yesterday morning.'

'Surely not,' I said. 'Our name bloody well helps, though.'

'Talking about names: that boyfriend of yours, young Kovalsky ...' He went on regardless. 'His father's a veteran of the Spanish Civil War, a National Hero, mother's a close friend of Margot Honecker, maternal grandmother a pal of Clara Zetkin.'

There was no need to recite common knowledge from the Communist *Almanach de Gotha* to Mother and me, but Father liked the sound of his own voice. His pronunciation of Honecker and Zetkin was baroque.

'Fine pedigree, but a bit of a ninny,' he went on. 'What's he studying?'

'Architecture,' I said. That was, nominally, true. I wasn't sure Misha was taking any actual exams, but his studio was a black-and-white temple to Mies van der Rohe. I could confirm that Mies had never tested his Barcelona couch for sexual comfort after designing it, but that was probably the last thing Father wanted to know.

'Architecture,' he echoed with an unexpected touch of distaste. I could have said ikebana.

'I don't need to ask if he is a Party member – not with that hair. Still, the army will sort the boy out soon enough, I expect, even where old Kovalsky has allowed the reins to slip. But I'd rather not have my only daughter wait to find out if that young *Beetus* comes good at the end. I have other options in mind for you, Mimi.'

Father was not above matchmaking. I shuddered at the thought of the kind of boyfriend he might consider suitable for me. Mother tee-heed. She knew how to pronounce Beatles, but wasn't going to correct him. Father took pride in not understanding a word of English, believed that its time as a lingua franca had passed.

'Good, good family. Excellent family,' Mother echoed with a delay. 'Lovely sister. Talented too. Music academy, I hear. And architecture is a useful subject. Our country needs its architects.'

That was as far as she dared go by way of contradicting him.

'Anyway, enough of that,' Father stood up and lowered the napkin on the table just as Dara walked in bearing a tray surmounted by my soft-boiled egg ensconced in its cup, a thimble vase with a cornflower alongside it.

Dara's role in our household was not easy to define. She had always been with us: her presence so taken for granted that I never wondered about its rationale. She was educated far too well to be one of our domestic staff, but she wasn't obviously involved in any of Father's official business, notwithstanding the fact that Communism ran in her bones like the names of English seaside towns in sticks of rock. I took her for Comrade Danvers to my Father's proletarian Maxim de Winter and, by extension, us: too taciturn to be one of the family, yet too obviously devoted to be an outsider.

We were not supposed to call Dara a housekeeper, let alone a maid, and she certainly wasn't supposed to cook my eggs to order. Another egg would have been sitting under the cloche, hard-boiled and stone cold, since six-thirty. That was the precise time when Svyatoslav, our cook, served breakfast every morning, New Year's Day and May Day included. Mother's alarm went at six; Father woke up under his own steam, God knows when. I knew that he considered every minute spent abed after five-thirty a sign of decadence. I often came down in my dressing gown at seven or seven-thirty, intending to go back to bed and have another three hours after he'd gone. I felt a touch of self-pity. My friends were allowed to sleep off their hangovers.

*

Dara liked to spoil me, but she also liked an excuse to see Father and Mother.

'Comrade Dara, a very good morning to you,' Father said.

'Good morning, Darina,' I added.

'Good morning, Mimi. Good morning, Comrade Stanislav. Good morning, Comrade Gertruda,' Dara said. She lifted a jug of juice from the table and topped up my mother's glass.

'Moroccan oranges are sweeter this year, Dara,' Mother said. 'So these must be Algerian, I assume? A touch bitter. Or did Cook neglect to peel them properly before juicing?'

'I'll speak to Comrade Svyatoslav, Comrade Gertruda,' Dara said.

'You better get ready, young woman,' Father said. He hated this kind of conversation. He would be happy subsisting on gruel, he always claimed, and I knew that to be true. Even the two years he spent in prison before the war seemed idyllic when he talked about them. Simple diet, cold showers, German-translation workshops with other political prisoners. Marx all the way.

'Why, it's Victory Day,' I said. 'No lectures.'

'Precisely,' he confirmed. 'You are coming with me. Go and get dressed while Dara and I speak to the staff. White shirt, blue skirt, black shoes, ponytail. None of that rubbish around the eyes, please.'

Mother tee-heed again as Father and Dara left the room.

'Last night,' I said, 'what happened?'

'I know nothing about last night. I watched *Borsalino*,' she said.

I took a sip of her orange juice. It was heavily laced with vodka.

Chapter Two

Swearing In

Misha had barely gone away to do his military service when he returned for a visit. It was not leave as such. He had been selected to take his oath of allegiance at the annual ceremony on the Manezh, the vast square next to the General Staff headquarters in the heart of our capital. The October Oath – the start of a month-long series of Communist festivities – was one of our country's biggest annual gigs, a substitute for the religious and royal festivals of former times. We may have been latecomers to socialism, but we marked each anniversary of the October Revolution with all the zeal of tardy converts. If you don't count early apostles of the Bolshevik faith such as Misha's dad and mine, the country as a whole, like so many of our neighbours, wasn't sure about Communism until well after the Russkies kicked out the Hun in 1945, when we found ourselves on a different page of the atlas.

'The gig is to be televised nationally as usual, but this year it will also be transmitted by the Soviets for the first time,' Misha explained. 'A huge honour for our little land, so we better not screw up. There are representatives from each major unit in the country and, for yours truly, two days at home.'

'What about those who have no place to stay?' Lana asked.

'You twit,' Misha laughed. 'Everyone else is staying at the Kronstadt Barracks. Even I am allowed to return to my home base for forty-eight hours only. Being the son of Yuri Kovalsky brings some advantages,' he added, turning to me. 'Although the compensations are never a match for Father's bullying.'

We were hanging around, passing time in the blue salon on the ground floor of my house: boring, but the safest way to alleviate the all-pervasive ennui in our city. We all knew about the consequences of decadent public gatherings such as the one in the Youth Palace.

The rain was lashing against the French windows and huge cedars swayed in the darkness of the garden outside. Further below, you could just about spot the lights of the city. We lived on a high hill, in one of several belle-époque villas requisitioned by the Party in 1947. Our place felt cavernous even when fully occupied, with all of us, plus the staff on duty, inside. Mother was three floors higher, in what she still called the nursery, sleeping, I assumed. She was gripped by depression at the start of each opera season – October blues, she called it – and this year it had hit her particularly badly. I hadn't seen her in days. Father was in Egypt, representing our government at the funeral of Anwar el-Sadat.

Misha was unrecognisable. Although he was trying to carry on as usual, he was subdued, and as unkempt as one can be in uniform. His army shirt was unbuttoned to the navel, his boots unlaced, his peaked cap with a red star on the floor next to him. His shaven head looked strange, split in two hemispheres – his face still tanned from the summer, the skull ghostly white with dark dots of hair follicles, like the test of a sea urchin. There was the pathetic beginning of a moustache above his upper lip. I'd seen better growth on thirteen-year-old boys. He paused his drinking only to smoke. His eyes were empty. I glimpsed a small tattoo on his arm: 'IX 1981, PA', for People's Army. Although it was common for new recruits to acquire such markings on their brief permitted outings in our godforsaken garrison towns where there was sod all else to do, it was so unlike Misha that it seemed, for a moment, like the date-stamp that butchers put on animal carcasses in a slaughterhouse. I put my hand on his shoulder, felt the bone under his skin, but he moved away. I would have thought it impossible to lose so much weight in such a short time.

Lana had brought a friend along, a tall, long-limbed woman from the provinces, with a narrow face that could have been a painting by El Greco made flesh. Her name was Alycja and she was allegedly a talented harpist. She sat on the floor next to Lana and held her hand, saying nothing all evening, just gawping, as though she had never seen the inside of a house – as opposed to a two- to three-room state flat – before. A little private decadence always gave our social gatherings a frisson, but in this case you soon forgot that the woman was there.

I ran the back of my hand over the top of Misha's skull once or twice, felt its sandpaper surface. Each time he shifted to avoid my touch. I changed a few LPs on the record player before I too lost the will to live and simply sat there, my legs across the arm of a chair, smoking.

Then Misha suddenly decided that we should play Monopoly. It took ages to explain the rules to Alycja, and further ages to help her buy her properties and make her understand the concepts of banking and ownership.

She claimed to have no problems with the English language, but she stared at each card as though it had been printed in Armenian. Good English was, after all, pretty much the prerogative of our circle, the *jeunesse dorée* of the capital; people like Alycja had to learn what they could from dated textbooks and tape recordings.

Alycja nodded to indicate that she understood what she was supposed to do, then made a nonsensical move. She seemed happiest while staying in jail, watching the three of us doing the rounds and taking loud slurps from her first-ever can of Coke.

'So different from Voke,' she said, referring to the domestically produced carbonated caramel concoction that was the only substitute available in our ordinary shops. 'And way too sweet,' she complained, but she carried on drinking and blushing whenever she failed to suppress a little burp.

Lana too had seemed bored since the start of the evening. She indulged Misha and went on with the game but she had even less of a competitive spirit than Alycja. She declared herself bankrupt and went away to riffle through my record collection, while Misha and I still owned all of the London stations, both utilities and almost every property, collecting cards even for places that meant nothing to me. Alycja aside, we'd all travelled to the West. Lana and Misha knew London well; I had yet to visit.

Misha had managed to amass a multicoloured pile of banknotes without trying. He carried on drinking, first vodka and Coke, then just vodka. I am not sure why I continued to play, but I did. I wasn't going to let the bloody drunk win if I could help it.

*

'This is sooooo boring,' Lana sighed as Misha got up to go to the lavatory, unbuttoning his flies even as he stood up. The rough, ugly fabric of an oversized pair of khaki boxer shorts spilled out of the opening.

'He must hate that,' I said when he was out of the room.

'Hate what?' asked Alycja.

'The uniform. The underwear. Those awful lace-up boots,' I said. 'The fact that nothing fits. So shoddy. The cloth so scratchy it gives him eczema.'

'So, soo boring,' Lana repeated, not paying any attention to what I was saying. 'I should have gone to the cinema. *Air Crew* is still on at the Astoria. I always end up following my brother like a poodle on a leash. You'd have thought he'd want to be with you alone, Mimi. What's wrong with your sex life?'

I ignored both the impertinent question and Lana's sarcasm, although she'd cut closer to the bone than she knew. Our sex life used to be the best of Misha and me. I had expected him to come rubbing himself against me like a randy chihuahua as soon as he arrived, but he had barely touched me. I now admitted to myself that it was worse than that: he was avoiding my touch.

'They put bromide into soldiers' tea,' I said to Lana. 'Either that or he is even more depressed than the rest of us.'

Alycja glanced at me blankly. She was reclining on the sofa, drawing invisible figures-of-eight on the side of Lana's thigh with her index finger. It was long and white, like some obscene cheese stick, just right for the harp business.

'Seriously, Lana, do you think Misha's OK?' I asked. 'He's only been away for three weeks, yet I no longer recognise him. What will he be like after two years? You would have thought they'd take it slowly at the start, give the boys time to adjust.'

'Oh, on the contrary,' Lana shrugged. 'The deep end, they call it. In fact they are treating poor Misha more harshly than the others. He was on lavatory-cleaning duty twice in this last week alone, because he failed some stupid endurance test. Daddy's orders, he assumes. No cushioning – make a man out of him. And they are forcing him to eat meat. He told them he was vegetarian but they don't even know what that means. They think chicken is vegetarian, so they don't allow him chicken. Bacon for breakfast, sausage for lunch: urgh! You know the kind of sausage I mean. Reconstituted old boots, off-cuts from veterinary treatment: your guess is as good as mine. Misha makes himself puke whenever he can. But he'll be fine … It's just his hair.'

'What's just my hair?' Misha stepped back into the room. He was holding a revolver in his hand.

Alycja let out a squeal, like a toy someone had trodden on. She looked at Lana and me. No one moved.

'I have an idea. Let's go for something better than Monopoly, something to perk us all up,' Misha said. 'Let's play Russian roulette; it must be the only Russian thing I could face right now. One man, one woman, a dyke on either side.'

'Not the only Russian thing. You forget vodka,' I was about to say. There was an empty bottle on the floor, its neck pointing towards me.

He did not seem drunk any more.

I will never be able to explain why we went along with it. All three of us, like three bunny rabbits hypnotised by the sight of a stoat.

We watched him put a single round in the cylinder.

'It's a sissy's take on the game, this,' he said. 'Five empty chambers – just one chance to have your brains splattered. It should be the other way around, the true Russian way.'

He spun the cylinder.

'Ladies first,' he said and, holding the muzzle, proffered the grip.

I was astonished to see Alycja reach for it. I was still struggling between the urge to stop the madness and the desire to find out what would happen, and I was still convinced that only Misha would ever be lunatic enough to pull the trigger in this situation when the harpist pressed the muzzle against her temple as though she could not care less.

The long finger moved. The hammer clicked on empty. Alycja stood up, dropped the gun and raised her arms into the air. She looked euphoric, although she still wasn't saying a word.

Lana planted a disgustingly wet kiss on the girl's mouth. She picked the revolver from the floor, then sat down again. I heard another click, now almost inaudible against the lashings of rain outside.

Then Lana lowered the gun into her lap, still holding it loosely in her hand.

'You were meant to spin the cylinder,' Misha said.

'I am not doing it again,' Lana said flatly and shrugged her shoulders.

Misha took the weapon from her hand, spun the cylinder and handed it to me.

'Is this army-issue?' I asked, examining the gun, buying time. It looked old. And I didn't think they would let a rookie leave the barracks with a weapon – Kovalsky or not.

Neither did I think the cartridge inside was live, but I wasn't going to risk finding out.

'Are you blind, Mimi?' Misha said. 'It's my dad's Nagant.'

'C'mon, we're waiting.' It was Alycja, finally saying something. Her voice was a high-pitched croak. I did not have her down as a total fruitcake, but there she was, proving me wrong.

'I'm not doing this,' I said.

I could feel the bullet at the other end of the muzzle. I just knew it was there, with my name on it.

'C'mon, Mimi,' Lana said. 'Don't be a spoilsport.'

'Ah well,' Misha said. 'While you are deciding …'

He grabbed the pistol back from me and put the muzzle on his temple. Everything went silent. I could hear not only my heart, but the sound of the blood it pumped through my arteries, the pulsating waves of it, spreading. I stood up, turned away to face the door and yelled, all at the same time. I sensed the cartridge gliding along, then I heard it: the shot, then the crunch of the bone, in separate units of time. Surely that must be impossible?

Misha took the bullet. My bullet.

Alycja and Lana screamed but I was out of the room already. I heard Misha's brief whine, then just the girls' screams continuing. I rushed across the hall and into the vast conservatory at the back of the house. Branches of cedars whipped the glass roof like wet sails. I am not sure why I hadn't registered the howling of the wind before. The front must be much more sheltered, I thought. It was still raining.

I heard Dara running out of the kitchen, then practically falling as she rushed into the blue salon.

'You idiot kids,' she yelled with a kind of animal sound. 'You idiots.' Then, after a beat that seemed an hour long: 'Is this what I fought for? Is this what I fought the war for? Mimi! Mimi?'

'He took my bullet,' I said, when she found me in the conservatory.

'Don't be an idiot, Milena,' Dara said. 'I've called the police.'

Her face was distorted by anger rather than shock. She must have witnessed worse scenes in her time, I thought, than splattered brain and bone.

'That boy,' she said. 'That idiot boy. It will kill Comrade Kovalsky.' Then, again: 'Is this what I fought the war for? It will kill Stanislav too. In his house.'

It was the only time I heard her calling my father by just his first name.

Mother slept through it all. Or so she claimed the following day, citing the strength of her Chinese tranquillisers as an explanation. Three police cars and an ambulance van arrived, no sirens, no flashing blue lights, merely the crunching of tyres on wet gravel. Dara must have explained there was no emergency to attend to.

Chapter Three

The Fallout

1984

> Cadres decide everything.
>
> Joseph Vissarionovich Stalin

After Misha's death, everything changed. Or, quite possibly, nothing changed, but I did. There was the slow fallout, then silence. It took a while – two years and a bit – to recognise that I was a different person.

In the immediate aftermath, Father cut short his visit to Egypt, then bellowed at me for days. He threatened to despatch me to his back-of-beyond native village for good, or let me be taken to a correctional facility if the comrades so decided.

'One of our female gulags perhaps?' I asked him to clarify. It was meant as a joke, but I didn't repeat it after I saw his expression. We reached an unacknowledged truce.

Perhaps for the first time I grasped the reality of his position. He had rushed back from an official visit abroad not just to manage the situation, but also to avoid finding himself cut off, unable to return. Exile was the worst of all possible punishments, and the comrades would have known that. Father was one of those people who would prefer a cyanide pill to an old age in some Western research centre, doling out dissident opinions, with or without Mother and me. He had nothing but pity for the political whitebait who had willingly chosen such destinies.

The moment when his plane landed must have been tense. He was now shouting because he wanted to protect me and Mother, but also because the country and its future mattered to him as much as the two of us did – perhaps more.

The comrades were not known for sympathy, not even of the 'There but for the grace of God' (or his atheist equivalent) variety. There was no room for God or his mercy in their world. Father was all-powerful, but he also lived on standby, waiting for his own fall from grace, and he was too astute to ignore the possibility of it happening. Yet I now also knew that there was no fear in him, just as I saw there was no fear in Dara when she found Misha's body; and, as I finally discovered, that there was no fear in me. I was Daddy's girl, and by virtue of being Daddy's, I was Dara's girl too: we were made of the same mettle. It was a pity that, unlike Father and Dara, I had to travel so far in order to find a cause; even more of a pity that my cause was to be vengeance.

Meanwhile, Mother – who panicked at the sound of a falling leaf – lurked in distant corners of the house, complaining of migraine, keeping the blinds drawn, waiting for the storm to pass. Cowardice has its Darwinian compensations. She displayed the best of the survival instincts that had seen her through decades of marriage. Although she maintained that every event on Earth was engineered by some hostile deity to make her – and only her – more unhappy, she also knew when not to draw attention to herself. In the end, it was Yuri Kovalsky who must have helped things move on behind the scenes, perhaps because he preferred not to dwell on the details of his son's last evening on Earth. It took place in my father's house, but it was his own weapon that killed his son.

'The children played a stupid game,' Kovalsky said. 'These things happen,' he went on, although we all knew they didn't. Decadence and deviance might be prevalent among the bored children of the higher *nomenklatura* across the socialist bloc, but what had happened was extreme, especially for our country.

His face turned grey with grief as the timeless feelings of a father competed with the bleak duties of a modern Party man. I felt more sorry for him than for Misha's mother: she had the option of heavy sedation, of not having to appear in public. Wives didn't expose themselves to the public gaze, not even to enjoy the glow of good news.

'Silly children,' Comrade Yuri said. It was the secret session of the Praesidium, and my father supported him.

'Children will be children,' Father said, echoing Kovalsky's words, although he well knew they wouldn't. Not any more.

It sounds like a banal solipsism, but it was much more than that: an expression of solidarity.

Mother reported all this back to me. I assume that Father supplied the outlines, but that she did the colouring in, as usual. She was dubious about the need for any display of loyalty to Kovalsky, however secret the session. Solidarity was not one of her virtues.

Of course none of this was public. After what could barely be called an inquest – that, too, conducted *in camera*

– everything was hushed up. Had it been possible to pretend that Misha had never existed, we would have gone along with it, but too many people had known him to make that pretence viable. We all went to state schools, even the President's stork of a daughter who otherwise kept herself to herself inside her own turret in the Residence, although some state schools were infinitely better than others. If there was a problem, then connections, not fees, secured places. There was no alternative to state education in our egalitarian society, unless you wanted to risk being frozen out – in every sense of the phrase – in some boarding school in the USSR.

So there was finally, as there had to be, the briefest of notices in the newspapers, two or three lines ten days after the funeral. The matter, and Misha, were laid to rest: the son of Comrade Kovalsky, a tragic accident while on leave from army service, blah-blah-blah-blah.

Misha's biography was slight. Not even his closest friends could say much about his achievements. They published a picture of him in the papers, looking like the innocent that he had been long before I first dated him, in middle school perhaps: a neat fringe cut diagonally across his forehead, white shirt, Pioneer scarf. The editors must have had to go that far back to find a presentable image, for neither the curls nor the shaved skull he had blown open would have done. I felt sorry for them. How terrifying making that choice must have been.

Of the many unwelcome aspects of Misha's end, his suicidal impulse was perhaps the greatest taboo. Our children didn't kill themselves, particularly not the lucky children of our greatest revolutionary leaders. There was just too much to live for: the hard-won freedom we enjoyed, the most beautiful country on Earth, its rich natural resources, our glorious future in Communism.

I never saw Alycja again and I barely saw Lana in the run-up to the funeral. We may have been in the same audience for one or two public events, but I would not have blamed her if she looked away. I know I did. I assume she thought me responsible for Misha's death: not for the way our game went wrong, or for the fact that he took what was supposed to be my bullet, not even for the missed opportunity to re-enact, with me, some melodramatic Communist take on the joint death-pact of Mayerling.

I don't think Lana ever thought of what happened that evening as Misha's suicide, but I imagined that she blamed me for Misha's end in some wider, more metaphysical way. Misha did not love me enough to want to live, and this must have been my fault. Had he loved me, he would not have dragged her and Alycja along with him that evening; he would not have carted his father's gun around. Had he loved me, it would have been only the two of us, making passionate love, stealing every moment of his short leave.

I imagined that, in Lana's mind, the blame for Misha's death lay not in his general nihilism, not in some final straw delivered by the army, or in alcohol or drugs. It lay in me. I was guilty of not being lovable, of not making her brother want me sufficiently for that desire to lessen the burden of whatever else must have troubled him. Lana blamed me for not making her brother happy, although the idea that Misha could ever be happy was an illusion to end all illusions. I could just as easily have blamed her and her bloody parents.

In fact Lana had never bothered to find out if I cared for Misha. Not before, and certainly not after that evening. I did care, perhaps not in the 'in love' way she would have wished, but that was not relevant. My loss was immaterial, although I felt it keenly. The point was that her brother did not love me, and that was my fault. There may have been some truth in it, I began to think eventually, when still unloved and in a very different place. It may indeed be that I am not lovable.

'You are a cold bitch, Milena,' Lana whispered into my ear at the funeral. She had leaned away from her mother, Misha's mother, in whose arm hers was locked, to deliver the aside out of hearing. It was supposed to be a family funeral, but the entire Praesidium of the Central Committee was lined up next to us, dark coats buttoned, ranks closed, although there were no cameras, and although the cemetery was otherwise shut for the day. Their own families stayed away; no need to give other children ideas, I suppose.

'Thank you,' I said, loudly enough, clearly enough, as the mahogany casket was lowered into the grave and the guns of the guard of honour clicked in readiness for the final salute to mark Misha's weeks-long military career. 'Thank you, Lana, for finding the right words even in the depths of your own sorrow.'

I didn't believe in an afterlife, not for a second, and yet, when the guns fired, I had a momentary vision: Misha, leaning to look into the concrete shell of his own grave, out of uniform, his curls restored.

'So long,' I said; then he vanished.

There was an embargo on any reporting. The story was too dangerous to be handled even by those trusted hacks who, since the so-called democratisation of the early 1970s, had been producing an anodyne semblance of investigative journalism, even occasionally exposing abuses by middle-ranking officials, in order to create the illusion of a free press. Still, there were too many witnesses to the immediate aftermath of Misha's death to keep the affair secret. Details leaked and, as the days passed, the rumour mill churned out more and more improbable versions of that evening.

The four of us were found at the scene naked. We were high on heroin. There were needles, strewn everywhere, people said, although none of us had ever, to my knowledge, experimented with hard drugs. Small packets of hashish occasionally found their way to us from Afghanistan, with whose government the country was enjoying friendly relations then, but stronger stuff was, so far as I knew (and I suppose I should have known), non-existent in our socialist state.

Not that hard drugs were the worst of the rumours. There were others in the room, conspiracy theorists claimed, shadowy people, Westerners, spies, diplomats, Freemasons, and these people had escaped well before our police got there. Misha was a pervert. Just look at his sister. Just look at his hair.

It was Soviet spies who were there and vanished, others countered. Dara was working for the Soviets, everyone knew. She was the person who had cleaned up the scene. Misha's death was a warning to Kovalsky. A warning to Urbansky too, though at least Urbansky's child – spoiled brat that she was – wasn't a degenerate like Kovalsky's. Those kids were simply too decadent. If you can't control your own family, how can you run the country?

Instead of dying out gradually, the stories got wilder and wilder. Whenever Stanislav Urbansky went abroad there were orgies in the house, revels that my mother, a descendant of a well-known reactionary family, orchestrated and took part in, like some experienced madam of a brothel. No, wait. Comrade Stanislav was part of the same ring, too, his enemies alleged. It was impossible to be ignorant of so much debauchery going on under your nose. He had married Gertruda against the best advice of the Party. He thought that he could change her, but instead she had corrupted him and their daughter. Now the house was bugged: even Comrade Urbansky was not to be trusted.

How did I know all this? I had so-called friends in the Party's Youth Palace circles. There were enough malicious souls there to pass on every improbable take on Misha's death in minute detail, directly or via intermediaries, and all under the pretence of sharing a great joke or sniggering about those primitive yokels who assumed that even Misha's Ray-Bans might have acted as transmitters of Western propaganda.

The suggestion of phone-tapping was the only rational supposition in all the wild imaginings, but that was hardly new, and those doing the tapping were our own people. Since I had emerged into adulthood, I had reckoned on the possibility that someone could hear my every word, but, before Misha's death, I chose not to care. After it, I stopped using the phone. I practically stopped talking too.

Father was a workaholic, so he was not there to notice my silence, but Mother felt it. She hung forlornly in the doorway of my room, waiting for me to respond to the latest innocuous remark that she attempted to make in an effort to cheer me up, or so she claimed. I ignored her. I knew there was no getting away from my parents – not inside the country. We did not take off to bedsits at eighteen, like so many teenage students in the West, but remained rooted at home, at least until marriage, heirs to our conservative peasant past, and victims of a housing shortage that condemned most of my compatriots to life sentences in tiny but hard-to-get flats. Still, even I had a right to be left alone; or so I, with naïve arrogance, thought. Was it a sign that toxic Western individualism was seeping into our seemingly closed system?

I wanted Mother to shut up and Father to stop preaching, on those rare occasions when the three of us lunched together. I wanted to forget Misha and his stupid, pointless death, for which I both pitied and resented him with more passion than I had ever felt when he was alive. The feeling took a long time to blunt. The thought of life's energy draining from his body sucks the air from my chest whenever it hits me, even now, but I've learned how to dodge that bullet most of the time.

I stopped going out. I studied extra hard and I graduated extra fast. I squeezed four years' worth of exams into less than three. And the high grades I received, post-Misha, were earned: that was new. It wasn't because I started to care about my subject, or because my degree classification mattered in the least; it was because I needed work to take me out of myself. I even started reading books the way impoverished people must always have read them: to escape. As I said, I changed.

I disappointed Mother by not going into diplomacy. She had dreamed of me abroad, heading one of our old-world embassies in a capital city big enough to be glamorous but not so big as to be dangerously political: Copenhagen, Lisbon, Dublin, even Prague at a push. Czechoslovakia was not as depressing as other fraternal states, she thought. She was unwilling to accept that I was not the diplomatic type, that I had blotted the copybook long before Misha's brains had flecked her silk wall hangings.

I could have taken any job I wanted after graduation, but translation appealed most.

'Had I known you were going to become a translator,' Mother said, 'I'd have suggested you study a melodious language. French, or Italian. Even Spanish would have been so much better than English.'

'It's not that kind of translation, Mummy,' I said. It was pointless to argue with her about English. In the end, I too wished I hadn't studied it.

Father did understand. The more mundane my work, the better, I told him, and he engineered the job description exactly as I wished it, an entry-level post at the State Institute for Maize Research. I spent an entire year after graduation translating scientific papers about the hybridisation of corn. Yield, resilience, nutritional values, genotypes: not exactly Coleridge, but active, purposeful boredom can be healing.

Maize hybrids were, I found out, an area of research in which my country led the world. After all, even our people had to eat something, and maize porridge was filling. There was a never-ending line of maize-breeding studies to translate into, and out of, English. I often carried work home and laboured over it late into the night.

I was given specialist dictionaries and my own typewriter very early on. These machines were individually registered by the state, their specific quirks making any attempt to carbon-copy samizdat traceable, but I was trusted with one and it tick-tocked away long after Mother and Father had gone to bed. At first my parents seemed delighted and anxious in equal measure, perhaps fearing that I was heading for a breakdown of some kind.

Months passed. I became something of a maize expert and they got used to having a solitary, hard-working daughter.

Chapter Four

Unseasonal Weather

The take-home, paper-based aspect of my work was the most blissful thing about it. I accepted interpreting assignments reluctantly, and only when the director insisted. He was a friend of Father's. This didn't need saying, but he said it all the time anyway.

The Institute hosted delegations of maize producers and seed developers from all over the world. The Russian language was always in greatest demand, but English came a close second, and they were short of English-speaking staff. Two of the small team of English interpreters had vanished a month or two after I joined. There were rumours of defection and, as usual, their exact opposite – allegations of unspecified transgressions followed by banishment to remote villages.

In spite of my reluctance to undertake such engagements, I discovered that I possessed an unexpected talent for consecutive interpreting. I could hold my nerve and remember what was being said without taking notes. The self-confidence founded on my membership of what we were never allowed to call the 'new class', and my privileged exposure to Western music and media, helped a lot. There were men – they were almost all men in maize production – who could not pause in their rambling speeches, so that I had to deliver gunfire interjections in the tiny gaps afforded by their exhalations of cigarette smoke or intakes of breath. They visibly resented the fact that my versions of their speeches sounded far too succinct, but those from the East knew better than to be anything other than flattered about having Stanislav Urbansky's daughter as their interpreter, and smiled unctuously as we met and parted.

We toured the labs. We traipsed up and down the same display rows of maize. We signed deals, and then, to celebrate, took our guests to the Metropole, where foreigners enjoyed the world-famous shashliks while the Institute executives ordered platefuls of tournedos Rossini and chateaubriands. I tended to push a sliver of red pepper or a spear of tinned asparagus around my plate. It was easier to blame the fact that my work never stopped than to keep explaining that I was vegetarian, and that – yes – this meant I didn't eat chicken or fish.

My compatriots, or at least those among them who had heard of vegetarianism, tended to see it as a religious cult. Consuming meat, as much of it as possible, was a mark of worldly success, showing how far one had progressed from our forebears' diet of bread, beans and cabbage, with perhaps a garnish of lard. Their ideal meal was simply a repetition of the all-too-occasional wedding feasts of their ancestors. Even failures strove to cook with animal fat rather than vegetable oil. I knew that many of my bosses at work, like most of their generation, would be visibly shorter than their lanky offspring, exhibiting during their lifespans the straitened circumstances in which they had grown up. If I tried to clarify, to explain that I ate dairy products and eggs but not flesh of any kind, they would think me spoilt as well as deluded.

Although I was busy interpreting, I sometimes overheard remarks which suggested that my feeding habits explained a lot about me. My thinness, my paleness, my irritability, even my lack of a boyfriend, could be cured by devouring a large steak. The executives I interpreted for were men, and those remarks were telling of our manhood. I was neither particularly thin nor pale, and the lack of a boyfriend was none of their business. I found my singledom, if anything, quite liberating. I was also less excited by offers of free food than either the locals – who had grown up in homes where they had rarely, if ever, sated themselves on rich food – or the freeloading foreigners who were enjoying an exotic treat at our expense and without ethical qualms.

Not eating left me freer to concentrate on my work. I flattered myself that a fair share of our precious hard-currency earnings came as a result of my efforts. Maize may not have been what I had studied English for, but I was, almost, becoming interested in the corn trade.

After Misha's funeral, Lana and I managed to avoid directly setting eyes on each other for two and a half years. This was an astonishing fact. Our capital city functioned as a series of overlapping but self-sufficient villages, and Lana and I inhabited the same one. It helped that people like us didn't exactly walk the streets.

Then, out of the blue and as though some unknown statute of limitations had expired, she telephoned, several times in as many days, trying to get hold of me. Because I always happened to be out at work when she called, she spoke to Mother, each time adding a new detail to an initially hesitant message.

She had been appointed head of cultural programmes at the Youth Palace. Young, female – everything our regime wasn't: a reason in itself for her appointment to manage this showcase. The Palace, in spite of its association with youth, was an important organisation, and the position would have put Lana, who could not organise her own breakfast, in charge of a considerable budget. She was lucky there was no such thing as accountability in 'really existing socialism'. So long as you spent the money on what you were vaguely supposed to spend it on, no one was bothered about even sizeable deficits.

The hazards of Lana's post were all political. You never knew which performer – and when – was going to go off the rails and deliver an attack against the government, instead of a patriotic poem or song. The fate of the Marina Abramović wannabe whom we had seen self-destructing onstage was still a murmured-about mystery. And the Youth Palace, contrary to its name, did not deal only with young artists. Even old hands – poets residing in luxury state housing, with dozens of state-funded publications to their names – were not safe. They slipped, sometimes inadvertently, and were then removed from the public eye in perpetuity, pulling Lana's predecessors down with them. The post was offered for four years, but most incumbents left early.

I had heard that Lana played it safe, scheduling people exactly like her, giddy girls and boys, self-styled *littérateurs* who wrote and performed gobbledegook. If they slipped, you wouldn't know it. *L'art pour l'art*, they called it. After months of harmless surfing on such apolitical whimsy, Lana was encouraged to organise an international poetry festival. The government liked to put on an occasional show of openness, while proudly taking to the global – or at least the European – stage played well to the base nationalism that still stirred with surprising force beneath the internationalist veneer of socialism.

One of the invitees was British: Jason Connor, the recipient of the Shelley Prize for his debut collection. No one I knew had ever heard of the prize before – it wasn't exactly the Nobel – but it sounded important enough. And Shelley's heart was on the left.

The laureate was twenty-seven, Marxist in politics and handsome in person, Lana told Mother, in an effort to win her over to the cause of conscripting me. She needed an interpreter with a bit of polish for this twentieth-century Shelley. He was the only bona fide Westerner at the festival. She could not bear to embarrass the Youth Palace by handing the Brit to some clunky in-house yokel, however solid their English. Arab and African socialists could get those off-the-peg linguists: racism was alive and kicking behind the socialist façade.

Mother loved the idea. I would not even need to take any leave, she said: Lana had already checked with my superiors. It would be the briefest of secondments, just four days. No one wanted the Englishman lingering around longer than was strictly necessary.

I am not sure why I gave in. The man sounded like a Western version of Lana's *l'art pour l'artistes.*

'So long as I don't have to speak to Lana Kovalska,' I told Mother.

The opening of the festival was set to coincide with the first day of spring, but the temperature had dropped from fifteen degrees Celsius to minus seven the night before.

Twenty-five centimetres of unseasonal snow fell while Jason Connor was in the air above Europe.

He walked through the arrivals gate in a yellow T-shirt and a pair of faded jeans, with a tatty little canvas backpack on his shoulder. His plimsolls, once presumably white, were now the colour of a urine sample. He was tall and slim, with a handsome narrow face and a mop of copper-blond hair. His long limbs dangled as he walked. He looked foldable, like something you could stash away at the back of a kitchen cupboard. He brought to mind marionette puppets made of bottle brushes.

He shook my hand, then the festival driver's, then stared out through the airport windows in bewilderment. The snow was relentless. A row of cars parked outside the terminal building had thick white toupees on their roofs. Just as well, I thought, for, if you ignored the shiny official Volgas and ZiLs that moved too fast to acquire a snow cover, my compatriots' vehicles were beige or grey – socialist beige or socialist grey, indistinguishable from each other – the colours of a depressing Sunday afternoon.

'Have I gone back in time?' Jason Connor asked. 'Three months, or thirty years and three months?'

'Witty,' I said. 'I do hope there is a coat in your little backpack.'

'Nope. *Niente. Nada,*' he said and opened his arms wide as though I was about to frisk him. 'An Aran sweater and a couple of books. A sponge bag and a change of underwear too,' he rushed to add, when he registered my expression. He saw immediately that this was more than I wanted to know. 'I do brush my teeth,' he exacerbated the effect by trying to explain, 'but I carry hand luggage only. Hand luggage only is a matter of principle for me, even on transatlantic flights.'

'But you do have some cash with you?' I asked, thinking of stopping somewhere in town to get hold of a cheap anorak. He didn't look like the sort of man who would expect fine tailoring – which was just as well, because the nearest half-decent tailor was in Budapest. I realised, even before I finished it, that my question might be misinterpreted, that Jason Connor could conclude I was asking about hard currency for my own private purposes. He wouldn't know it, but handling foreign money was a criminal offence. Everyone needed it sometimes but no one was allowed to have any officially. It was one of the ways the state controlled you: by making sure you had to break its laws.

He was not troubled by any such hints. He pulled out a scrunched-up five-pound note from his pocket and waved it like someone about to hang out a piece of wet washing.

Thus our very first afternoon had to involve a complete change of programme. My charge had no cash, the festival was not offering an allowance for winter clothing, and I certainly didn't feel like spending my own money on an ill-prepared poet.

I phoned home from the airport, planning to ask Mother for advice, but they said she was busy. I was put through to Father and, when he heard about our Western guest's predicament, he came to the rescue with more relish than I expected. He believed in the superiority of our state over Britain, that original but now forlorn cradle of the industrial proletariat. Here was the proof. Rather than kitting them out in proper suits and decent leather shoes in which to represent their country, the imperialists despatched their poets abroad in rags. They had no shame. He offered, half-grudgingly, half-smugly, to lend the young man one of his coats. He had a collection, in sizes that went slightly up with the years, but all in the same severe cut.

'Mother and I are about to go out. She has been getting ready since three p.m. The first night of that new *Vassa Zheleznova*, remember?' Father said, too flatly for me to discern what he thought of the play. 'If you come here, Dara will help you find a suitable garment.'

Jason Connor emitted a loud whistle when he entered our hall. The house had that effect on people, even high-ranking visitors, but I did not expect the same reaction from a Westerner. I had agreed to bring him in because I knew Dara was the only person he would meet. I promised the driver that we would take ten minutes.

'We don't own this place,' I said curtly. 'We only live in it.'

There was no virtue in chit-chat and I was not about to give the Englishman a guided tour. I waited while Dara took him away. She spoke very good English, but when she noticed that I was about to disclose the fact, she squeezed her eyes and gave the briefest shake of her head.

I listened to them walking upstairs, Dara giving her guidance in less-than-perfect French, her few words as hard as pebbles.

He looked as thin as a rake in Father's black overcoat when he eventually re-emerged, even with his Aran sweater still on underneath. The plimsolls, with their flashes of para-keet green, looked ridiculous with the coat, but Jason's feet were four sizes too big for Father's footwear. Dara had also produced a pair of knee-high ski socks and a sheep-skin gilet: both mine.

'That woman is scary. Is she your aunt or something?' Jason said, pirouetting in front of a wall-length mirror next to the hat-and-coat stand, convinced that Dara could not understand.

She nodded a silent *au revoir* and walked away without suggesting otherwise.

'I promise to give all this back to you at check-in on Wednesday,' he added when he saw that I wasn't about to enlighten him on Dara's role. 'The coat is not my style, but I love the folksy touches on the rest. Your people here have me down as English in the festival programme, but I am of Irish peasant stock, you know, at ease in this kind of tunic. If indeed tunic is the right word. I don't want to offend.'

'You can keep the socks and the gilet,' I said. 'Be my guest. And call it what you will.'

It was hilarious that he assumed my faux-Russian jerkin to be locally made, but if I admitted that it had come from the Paris workshop of Yves Saint Laurent, he might never take it. I hadn't worn the item since I committed to black. I had unpicked the label long ago, because – unlike Lana and Misha – I believed that only peasants were preoccupied with brand labels.

There were few worse epithets than 'peasant' in our society, despite – or because of – the fact that we had been until very recently an overwhelmingly poor, agrarian country (now, perhaps, we were just poor and part-industrialised). If you picked at almost anyone's genealogy, including mine on my father's side, you would uncover recent peasant ancestry. We were connoisseurs of snobbery, and I am sorry to admit that I was worse than most.

That is why I chose to ignore Jason's Irish-peasant spiel. You did not need to listen to him for long to understand that it was a narcissistic affectation, the reasons for which I could not fully grasp. He sounded as English as they come. Irish hostility to Britain made Ireland a reasonably popular country over here, allowing for the comparatively low standards of our official affections for the West, that is. Our attitude to the troubles in Northern Ireland was equivocal. We were – selfishly – nervous about being seen to encourage citizens to take up arms against their government, especially that of a fellow European state with which we had correct, if frigid, relations, but essentially the troubles were seen as a manifestation of British imperialism. The organisers would gladly have billed this man as Irish if that was what he was, I knew: the background briefing about him would have run to a sizeable booklet even before he was invited.

I was sure, if I asked, that he'd love to explain, but I wasn't that interested. In our country, unless you were seeking political advantage or your position was threatened in some way, you didn't go around bragging about your humble roots, and you certainly wouldn't lay claim to another nationality.

Nor did I want to suggest that his Wednesday departure was tentative. The snowfall was growing heavier and the weather threatened to close the airport forever. Flights were being diverted as far as Odessa.

Chapter Five

Performance

Jason Connor's outfit may have been underwhelming – his jeans tucked into my woollen socks looked like a folk-dancer's breeches, and he wore my gilet like a fleece, inside-out over his T-shirt, hiding its fine embroidery – but his performance was stirring, even electrifying. His poetry was unexpected. The local scene was modernist, the verse free, and only the old farts bothered to rhyme, yet he had somehow reinvented the sonnet, making rhyme and metre seem sexy and sophisticated. I forgot, while his reading lasted, that he looked like one of those homeless buskers I'd seen on my Western travels. My country allowed neither homelessness nor busking.

I watched him from the audience. He read in English, while the translation was projected above the stage. The surtitling was Lana's masterstroke, devised to prevent unscheduled improvisation. Foreign performers had been asked to send their reading weeks in advance, allegedly to provide enough time for the best possible translation.

Such planning made my work easier than I had expected. I did not have to join Jason Connor onstage either during or after his performance: that would have been additionally inconvenient for all sorts of reasons to do with my family. And there were no Q&A sessions. This had not been our tradition, even before Communism. Public analysis of verse smacked too much of a school class, while personal questions were not considered to be in good taste. Why would you want to ask a poet anything? A poem that passed muster should speak for itself.

After the reading, he and I were guided out of the auditorium and instructed to take our seats at an enormous table covered in green baize. There were no piles of books to sign or sell, but a queue for his autograph had already formed anyway – a long, orderly line that bisected the lobby of the Youth Palace. Girls at the front clutched Jason's collection. They were dressed in faded jeans, baggy sweaters and scuffed Doc Martens. They might have been mistaken for impoverished students but I knew these fellow daughters of the *nomenklatura* all too well. When they wanted an English book, they got it. The less privileged queuing further behind held notepads, festival programmes, newspaper pages, that evening's ticket, anything half-suitable to be blessed by a Connor signature. Scarcity gave everything and everyone Western – impoverished poets included – an unimaginable value in our world.

The girls at the front swooned but kept a disciplined distance while Jason signed his name and drew a shamrock next to it each time. Some waited for me to translate their thank-yous, while others spoke English as well as, or better than, me. As these exchanges continued, our minder tapped his breast pocket with a cigarette box, then disappeared somewhere to smoke. I knew already that he judged 'my poet' harmless enough because he had told me so on the way to the venue. In fact Jason and I were allowed to take the car to dinner alone after the event. There were barely two hundred metres between the hotel and the Youth Palace but all participants were sent a vehicle to fetch them. That was, I guess, one way of making sure they arrived.

The queue for Jason's autograph was considerably longer than that in front of a fellow poet from the Soviet Union, although the Russian was, in terms of reputation as well as his country of origin, the star turn of the evening. He was also much more elegant than Jason. I could see that he was better looked after too: we cared about such nuances of protocol. A vast double door separated the lobby, where Jason's table was positioned, from one of the loveliest bookshop spaces in town – a venue more suitable for a great poet from a fraternal socialist country.

The Youth Palace was formerly the Royal Cavalry Club, and the bookshop had once been its officers' mess hall. Its Art Nouveau tiling was among the finest in Europe. The chandeliers had survived two world wars as well as one or two putsches, to sparkle like the day they left the Baccarat workshops – at least on special occasions, like this evening, when someone had decided to overlook the energy restrictions, which stipulated that any lighting device with multiple bulbs could use a maximum of one individual twenty-watt bulb at a time. While Jason had a plain table in the lobby, the Russian poet sat at a richly carved desk, next to an elaborate flower arrangement, ready for the photographs that no one but the official photographer dared take.

The Russian also had piles of books before him to sign, sell or give away as he chose, whereas Jason was provided with none. He assumed it was his fault, that he should have brought copies from London.

'Oh dear, no,' I said. 'Certainly not. It would be outrageous to expect an author to lug his own books.'

'I am used to it,' he said.

'Aren't you a member of the Writers' Union?' I asked.

'The writers' what?' Jason asked back.

'Or do the poets have their own guild?'

'Their own guilt?'

'Royal Something-or-other?'

'Royal Society of Literature, you mean? I am most definitely not a fellow and I can't imagine *them* sending any books anywhere. Publishers, yes, perhaps, but not poetry publishers. Tristan, my editor, couldn't quite believe that your lot was paying for my air fare and my hotel. I tried to touch him for a cab to Heathrow. Whoever takes anything other than the Tube to the airport is mad, he said. So much faster. And I paid for the ticket.'

The street lights had gone off at ten, as usual, and the night sky shimmered above our heads while we crossed the central square to Jason's hotel. A late dinner was about to be served to festival participants. Since the minder was no longer with us, I had dismissed the driver too: not every interpreter had my authority. We paused under the bronze horseman in the middle of the square, watching as the rest of the festival car pool drove slowly around us like some surreal carousel, only to line up in front of the vast entrance of the hotel. The approach was marked with a strip of concrete planters containing early-flowering petunias drowned by snow. The huge red star above the hotel door shone brightly – truly essential electricity supplies were always maintained.

'It's a one-star hotel then?' Jason said.

'I am afraid I'll have to report that,' I said.

He froze. 'It was a joke. A childish joke,' and he moved to grab my hand as he pleaded.

I stepped back. I could see a look of horror on his face. *That* was funny.

'So was mine,' I said.

It took him a while to relax back into companionable silence.

He and I had known each other for just over a day and although we had not spoken much, Jason already felt like a familiar presence beside me. Perhaps it was the coat. That vague scent of tar soap and pine needles was there in every garment Father owned, right down to his wartime uniform in its moth-proof case at the bottom of his wardrobe.

Snow crunched under my boots. Jason progressed in brief slides, like someone on inadequate ice skates. His feet must have been wet and freezing in those plimsolls.

We heard plainchant from a little church in the far corner of the square. Our bronze horseman, his head covered by a snow *ushanka*, was pointing towards it with a raised sabre, as though he was about to gallop across and cut a slice, like a birthday cake. The building was a millennium and a half old at least: one of the earliest churches in Europe. It had sunk deep into the ground – or rather the ground had risen to swallow it.

As we approached, the top of Jason's head was almost level with its dome. The walls were so thick that its narrow windows looked like gun slits. Candlelight flickered from inside, refracted through stained glass like the bursts of coloured sparklers.

'Could we step down to see this? Please. Pretty please,' Jason said.

In spite of my so-called authority, even I was not supposed to improvise late-night detours, especially not to places of worship, but I could not refuse a pretty please.

'Five minutes, not more, or they will send a search party,' I said.

We pushed at a heavy door and stepped into a space that was humming with monks' voices. I was taken aback; I had no idea so many people still chose this way of life in our country and I was surprised that they were allowed to. Dozens of beeswax tapers had been lit and placed on metal stands dotted around the walls. It must have been the eve of some religious holiday.

The interior smelled like an apiarist's hive, and it looked and sounded as though we had walked into one. The faces of saints stared at us from rows of frescoes, wide-eyed inside their shimmering golden haloes. The towering iconostasis was like a darkened honeycomb, each cell displaying a sacred image. Jason shivered as though the hum of the chant was electric.

I am afraid I was a bad tourist guide. I knew little about our Orthodox Church, or indeed about any Church. I had studied bits of architectural history at school, but no ecclesiastical mumbo-jumbo.

I turned back to look for the frescoes of the founders that I expected to find painted to the side of the main entrance, as described in our bland, atheistically-neutered history-of-art lessons: images of medieval rulers, holding a scaled-down model of the building they had endowed. And there indeed they were, a Tsar and his Tsaritsa staring down at the waffled footprints of Jason's trainers on the stone slabs, and the fat exclamation marks of my sturdier footwear. The trail was drying fast, as if to suggest that this man and I were never going to find our way out of this maze of superstition.

The Tsar was holding up a miniature replica of his building like a peace offering. On his left stood the saint to whom the church was dedicated, a young shepherd surrounded by his flock. He wore a white fleece and a pair of tattered teal breeches that looked exactly like Jason's outfit. His wild, uncombed hair was like Jason's too, the same tinge of copper-blond, and even his long face was uncannily similar.

I raised my hand to point this out but there was no need to do so. Jason was already staring at his twin, painted fifteen centuries ago. High above the shepherd, in the teal sky that matched the breeches, a white star shone in its own golden halo, as bright as the stars above the square outside.

'You Celts,' I said, suddenly realising. 'All Europe was yours, wasn't it?'

Jason reached out and pressed my lips shut with a frozen finger.

Back in the hotel, the international poets had already polished off their mezes and were digging into cabbage rolls and mashed potato. Bottles of Zubrovka bison-grass vodka, a gift from the Soviet delegation, were doing the rounds. Each carried a single sweet blade of the grass harvested in Byelorussian forests. The meadowy spirit was rumoured to have been Brezhnev's favourite tipple.

I joined the crowd. Jason had rushed straight upstairs, supposedly to take off his wet socks and deposit my father's coat in his room. He was taking his time. I had two shots while I kept his place at the table, munching a pickled carrot in between. I did not fancy dining on mashed potato and bread, the only other foodstuffs I could eat.

Finally he reappeared wearing a startling East European peasant shirt with a collar embroidered in red-and-white cross-stitch. There was a round of drunken applause when he was spotted. The garment fitted him as though tailor-made, but it also highlighted his foreignness, his unbelonging.

'A gift from that Byelorussian poet,' he said, as he took his seat next to me. 'The woman who performed just before me. It was waiting in a parcel at the reception desk. She left, they told me. A bit sudden. She seemed interesting. I was hoping to get to know her.'

I was more surprised by the pang of jealousy I felt when he said that than by the Byelorussian's disappearance. With her blond halo braid, she was good looking in a buxom Slavonic milkmaid sort of way. When she stood up to read, and the surtitles of her own poetry started rolling, the woman delivered a nineteenth-century poem instead. It was an innocuous pastoral ditty whose nationalist significance would not have been manifest to Jason, even had he been able to understand the words, but its author was on the list of proscribed poets. Most of the people in the room knew that. The Byelorussian language was almost indistinguishable from Russian, and everyone around here understood some Russian. Other than a death wish, I have no idea what had possessed her.

I noticed the exchange of glances between Lana and a couple of men sitting at the end of the first row, the moment the Byelorussian began. I knew their type well. Although they were dressed in jeans and roll-neck jumpers and were supposed to blend in, they might as well have been in uniform.

One of the men nodded. They let the woman finish her recitation. She and Jason shook hands as he climbed the stage for his turn and then I saw her leaving with her interpreter and the Soviet cultural attaché. I felt almost sorrier for the attaché than for her. She had chosen her act, but he had probably lost his posting this evening; his jaw-clenching display was not going to save him.

I was more impressed by her gumption than by her intelligence. As an act of protest, her recitation was pathetically opaque. As a gesture of indiscipline, it could destroy any career she had in mind, and much more. Her act had shortened her visit, and she was not likely to travel again. In the end she might actually become a milkmaid, I thought.

I had noticed her in the lobby of the Youth Palace when Jason and I arrived, standing with her small entourage and waiting for her act. She was dressed in her embroidered shirt, so similar to the one Jason was wearing now that it might, in fact, have been the same garment.

She was staring at Jason like a hypnotised puppy, and I wondered if she was deciding on her little act of insubordination just then. He might have been the first Westerner she had ever met, and he was an attractive specimen. I felt an unexpected twinge of possessiveness. It wasn't nice of me, I admit, but I did not regret the fact that she was probably at the airport already, perhaps even on her plane to Minsk, or on the first one of several trains that she would have to take – in some goon's company, no doubt – if the airport was still closed.

*

Jason must have felt ravenous to want to consume six parcels of sour cabbage with their enclosures of grisly meat and rice. He cut each one in half and then demolished it in two disgusting bites. Grey mince fell like grit off his fork into the bottom of his bowl. He mopped up pools of watery tomato sauce with slabs of bread on which he attempted to spread blobs of margarine before I explained that it wasn't really spreadable. He downed a shot of vodka after each bite. I stopped counting at six. At least the vodka was first class.

When the Russians started singing *Ochi Chorniye* – 'Dark eyes, passionate eyes; Burning and beautiful eyes! How I love you, how I fear you ...' – Jason joined in loudly from the opposite end of the table, although it was obvious that he knew neither the tune nor the lyrics. They sent two further bottles of vodka our way.

'Saffron vodka for the beautiful interpreter and Moskovskaya for our young Shakespeare,' they said. I ignored the compliment. It was that stage of the evening when every woman was beautiful, I knew.

After several Slav melodies, one of the Russians stood up and shouted at 'our Shakespeare' to sing an English folk song. Jason paused to think about the request, then launched into a croaky rendition of 'Yesterday'. The Beatles. I wanted the floor under my seat to open and swallow me. It was difficult to imagine a choice of music that would make Jason seem more uncool than the Soviets, yet here I was, listening to that choice and obliged to smile.

Three poets – two Russians and a Bulgarian – joined in and kept in tune but several notes lower, applauding loudly at the end. Their interpreters – all women – stared ahead, their blank expressions matching mine. The

minders, gathered together at a table in the furthest corner of the dining room, seemed delighted with the
goings-on. I didn't think they would begin to understand
what was wrong with 'Yesterday'; it was fine so long as the
Soviets were happy. The column of smoke around them
was so thick it looked like a dry-ice display.

Jason took a bow. I tugged at the sleeve of his ridiculous
Byelorussian shirt, urging him to sit down. This was
against the interpreters' code, I knew, but I did not want a
repeat performance. Or worse. He might start singing
'Yellow Submarine' next, ask me to translate all its puz-
zling ambiguities. He fell into his seat and grabbed my
hand under the table to signal that he understood what I
wanted of him, then held it there. I didn't move.

'Michelle, *ma belle*,' a Romanian metaphysical poet
shouted, then looked at me and winked, determined to
complete my mortification.

Then a Cuban poet stood up, turned to Jason and
proposed a toast to Anglo-Soviet friendship in pidgin
Russian. I could not be sure if this was another mischief-
maker or another idiot. His Spanish-language interpreter
rolled her eyes visibly. The Russian interpreter looked the
other way; it was none of her business. I was forced to step
in. I worried that my Russian, obligatory at school and
then quickly and deliberately forgotten, was little better
than the Cuban's. Speaking perfect Russian, the language
of our ultimate masters, implied its own humiliations
too. Jason Connor was blithely leading me into a nightmare of embarrassment.

'*Dziękuję ci*,' he responded without rising to his feet
when the toast was translated, then downed another
vodka, all the while holding the glass in his left hand.
I could just about tell the words were supposed to be

Polish – God knows why – but I was glad that his delivery was so slurred that it sounded like 'Thank you, sir'.

'*Gracias, camarada*,' I shouted at the Cuban and managed to look sillier and more drunk than either of them. The whole gathering erupted into laughter.

I was furious at being made a fool of. Jason was still holding my hand. He squeezed it and nodded in the direction of the Russian corner where, under a shroud of alcoholic mist, one of the poets was trying to kiss his interpreter. The young woman kept dodging, like a practised boxer parrying blows, but she knew better than to protest. Everyone else pretended not to notice.

Jason leaned towards me.

'The Russians can do as they please,' I hissed and freed my hand before he got any closer. 'You can't. You are English.'

'But I love you, you know,' he whispered into my ear. You could have brined a carrot with his breath alone.

I stared at him. I did not expect this turn of events.

'This isn't vodka speaking. I have quite fallen in love with you, Milena. And I am Irish, not English. I explained that to you already.'

I too must have been more tipsy than I thought. I found his 'quite' both English and funny rather than irritating. We'd known each other for a day and a half, but I had already learned to expect claims of Irishness every time I referred to England. It was as though he'd rather be anything but English, keeping the language but jettisoning the nationality and any affiliation with the country where he had been brought up. When I'd enquired about his Irish connections the day before, he went on about the Connors at great length, yet it turned out that his experience of

Ireland added up to a drunken weekend in Dublin and a reading in Cork.

'Quite,' I repeated and the word sounded ridiculous. It had no exact parallel in our language. That it could mean both 'to the utmost' and 'only moderately' seemed itself, well, quite English. My anger had subsided but I wasn't allowing him to get any closer. I pulled my chair away.

Chapter Six

The Day After

We had nothing lined up for the day after his appearance. Jason was meant to have left the country. The weather could not make up its mind. Icy winds kept lashing out, then the sun would break through and kick-start a great thaw, only for the temperature to drop again and the surfaces to freeze. Layers of snow teetered on layers of ice in a perilous *millefeuille*.

I decided to take him shoe shopping. This was less taxing than it sounds – particularly when the suggested alternative was a three-hour guided tour of the National Museum. There were some twenty shoe outlets in town, about two per municipal district, and they offered a choice of four models of men's shoes: black and brown; a winter and a summer version in each colour. The aim was to decide which non-style Jason disliked least and then identify the store that had his size in stock. Dara explained the process. I had never set foot inside any of these places, let alone put one of their ghastly shoes on it.

Our minder did not protest when I dismissed him for the day. The official part of the visit was over, he had no instructions and Jason was clearly benign. Few men of his ilk liked shopping. As the hackneyed-for-a-reason joke of our region put it, if they pretended to pay him, he would only pretend to work, yet no one could question the necessity of my suggestion. Jason's plimsolls looked as though they were made of wet newspaper. They would not last another day. His footwear had ascended to a matter of national pride. We could not let the Englishman return home barefoot.

Misha wouldn't have been seen dead in any of these, I thought when I saw the options on offer, before the irony of the expression hit me. Jason Connor loved them all. He wanted to buy all four hideous pairs. I had to remind him that he wouldn't be able to squeeze them into his excuse for a rucksack.

We started with three centrally located shops, including the premier store, its elaborate cornices and glazing a faded relic of the *ancien régime*, even if its dingy stock was exactly the same as elsewhere. There were no customers in any of them. Five or six assistants loitered by each till: women of all ages dressed in starched blue sales uniforms and wearing regulation white lace-ups, mandatory for all professions that involved standing at work. Overemployment, providing pay and in due course pensions, however pitiful the amounts, was certainly better than the capitalist scourge of unemployment. The workers' state also took podiatry seriously, placing it ahead of bourgeois notions of elegance, even if it wasn't always so gentle when it came to its subjects' physical well-being.

Jason made the sales assistants' day – their decade even. They rushed about, fussing, opening dingy and sometimes dusty boxes, proffering different sizes of the same model, measuring his wet feet again and again, laughing shyly when he said he was size eleven and I translated without bothering to convert to our local sizing.

You wondered what had become of their notorious surliness. They clustered behind the Englishman to watch his reflection in the mirror, suppressing giggles while he turned his feet left and right, preening like a peacock, doing a balletic demi plié and repeating 'very nice, very nice indeed', 'thank you' and an occasional '*merci*'. There were no more '*dziękujęs*': he had been warned.

I had expected the shoes to be cheap, but the low prices still came as a shock. A pair cost next to nothing, even at the official exchange rate. I insisted on paying. Jason refused. He produced that same scrunched five-pound note out of the small fob pocket of his jeans. I declined to take it. We had a brief tussle. I won the day by saying that I was not allowed to handle hard currency, that accepting his banknote could land me in prison.

He couldn't know that I had a wooden box full of Deutschmarks and US dollars – thousands in each currency – hidden under my bed, in so far as anything could be hidden anywhere in our house. Good Communists that we were, confident of the ultimate triumph of the proletarian revolution and the defeat of capitalism in its imperialist incarnation, we all still valued the so-called hard currencies of our bourgeois adversaries.

I was driven by a deluded sense of privacy rather than a need to conceal valuables. We were in no danger of being burgled, and no one would have been surprised to discover my stash. Each year my birthday present from Mother came in a thick pink envelope with a kitsch card, which she had inscribed with 'A little something for my baby', and yet she never allowed me to spend my own money when we travelled together.

'It will come in handy later,' Mother would say, never explaining the eventuality that she had in mind.

'Is he your boyfriend?' an indiscreet saleswoman asked when I went up to the till to pay. She nodded in the direction of Jason. It was an impudent question, not least in her use of the informal *you*, but she wouldn't have known it; a legacy of our peasant heritage was a perceived right to intrude publicly into the affairs of others. Besides, although even the fact that I was allowed to accompany an Englishman without further supervision would have signalled a degree of privilege, the shop was scarcely used to visits from red princesses, as some called us.

I did not want to prolong the experience but I needed the receipt before I could pick up the box from her colleague at the opposite end of the empty shop. She was taking ages to write it, deploying her years of trade-school training to list the size and colour as though there was a chance of mistaking the order amid the non-existent throng of customers.

Jason was standing next to a cluster of plastic stools, pointing at a pair of summer sandals and then at me. They were ladies' slingbacks with a blue-and-white polka-dot pussy bow at the front, and a white heel so solid that I had a vision of kicking his shin with it. The stores were sizeable enough to warehouse footwear for all seasons and all professions. I thought that Jason must be making fun of the pathetic attempt to add a pretty touch to what was obviously intended as working women's summer wear, but he seemed to love the sandals too.

I handed him the box containing his purchase with a shove in the ribs. He opened it and sat down on a stool to put on his new footwear.

'You are so lucky here,' he said. 'In the West, the illusion of choice is killing us all. Engendering anxiety and competitiveness instead of nurturing workers' solidarity; a distraction from rational discourse,' he continued, in apparent seriousness, while he laced up his newly acquired pair of sturdy black derbies with their clunky toecaps and thick, poorly glued soles. He then held up his wet plimsolls and an assistant rushed to offer a box for them. He shook his head.

'A bin,' I explained.

Another woman ran towards us holding a waste-paper basket. Jason dropped his plimsolls into it with a watery splat.

'Western rubbish,' he said to the girl. I did not bother translating. She could interpret his facial expression for herself, but she wouldn't understand the comment anyway. As we walked out into the snow, I turned back to adjust my hood against the wind and saw her fishing the plimsolls out.

At the hotel reception there was a blue envelope for Jason and a note from the state travel agency. Snowploughs were back in action and the runways were clear. He had been rebooked on a flight to Vienna with Austrian Airlines the following morning, and then on to London, business class. They must have been keen to get him out of the country as fast as possible to incur that kind of expense.

Only a snowstorm could stop flights now and it was not expected, the hotel receptionist said when I discussed Jason's room bookings. On the contrary, the meteorological bureau suggested that the temperatures would start rising steeply in the coming hours. The news seemed to make her sad. She was clearly enjoying Jason's enforced stay; his comings and goings made her work less mind-numbing.

'A big thaw,' I said, and turned to Jason.

He had opened the envelope and was inspecting its contents. I expected to see check-in documents or transfer vouchers, but instead he showed me two tickets for Janáček's *Jenůfa* at the National Opera that evening.

'Do we have to?' Jason asked. 'I'll be packing tonight. I hate opera. Have never been to an opera in my life. I don't want to start going now. And I'd much rather spend my last evening alone with you.'

We had a strong tradition of cultural conscription. Our National Opera House might have remained select in spite of its heavily subsidised tickets, but even the remotest of village schools took entire classes to productions in their regional People's Palaces. I was taken aback at the notion that he had graduated without ever seeing an opera.

The packing excuse was feeble, and his personal preference irrelevant. Although Janáček and his grim tale of infanticide were not the best choice for an opera novice, the tickets might just as well have come with Party orders inside the envelope. Allowing a Westerner a whole day off was not an option. I was surprised they had given us so long for our shoe shopping.

There was a further note instructing us to turn up at the opera house an hour ahead of the advertised time. Professor Jaroslavsky from the People's Academy of Music would talk us through the history of the production. Dress code: formal.

'Ah well, at least I now have the right shoes.' Jason sounded resigned when I translated the instructions. I followed his gaze downwards. He may have been trying to wiggle his toes; it was impossible to see under the reinforced toecaps.

In order to avoid another dreadful hotel meal, I decided to dress Jason for *Jenůfa* by heading to my home and raiding my father's wardrobe one final time. I tried to cheer him up with a promise of Oscietra and *blinis* from our household stocks. Jason had no idea what I was talking about.

Only when we were already on our way did I remember that neither my parents nor Dara would be at home. Father had left for an international congress in Tbilisi the moment the airport opened, and Mother was at Minerva Terme, her favourite spa, some two hundred and fifty kilometres from the capital. She was staying at the eponymous grand hotel her family had owned before the Second World War, which was now, like everything else, in state hands. Older members of its workforce had known her as a little girl: it was home from home, home more than home. When Father was away, she often disappeared there to wallow in its world-famous medicinal mud baths, just as her own mother and grandmother had done in decades past. Dara had asked for two days off to visit her younger sister, a semi-mythical creature no one had ever seen.

Jason cheered up and forgot about *Jenůfa* when we mounted the trolleybus. This was a deliberate introduction to local colour for my Marxist guest. I guessed that the experience would be sanitised as it was well outside what passed for a rush hour, when huge consignments of workers were shipped in and out from the innumerable grey, stubby fingers of residential tower blocks that seemed to hold the older parts of the city in their grasp: cemeteries of architecture, Misha had called them. And the trolleybus line we were taking was one of the less popular ones anyway. It didn't end in a satellite settlement, but in a sparsely inhabited, wooded inter-war suburb, parts of which were effectively out of bounds to non-residents.

There were only five or six other passengers on board, reading books or staring out at the snow as we got on. They must all have heard us speaking English, but only one, an ancient man in an astrakhan hat, turned to look. He gave me the briefest of smiles, then buried his head in an enormous volume that resembled a medical encyclopaedia of some kind.

I never travelled by trolleybus and I was surprised to realise that people made a point of looking away, anxious not to find themselves in an inappropriate situation. A man and a woman speaking English and hanging off the straps, rather than taking two of the many available seats, could possibly be described as deviants courting trouble: to be avoided.

The novelty of using our public-transport system was making us both giddy with laughter, all the more for having to stifle it. You never realised how quiet our public spaces were until you breached those silences.

At least I knew that you had to buy a ticket at a kiosk before you entered the vehicle, and I worked out how to validate it by punching it in a little yellow device that sat like a snail on the handrail by the door. It was just as well, as a ticket inspector appeared out of nowhere after a couple of stops and moved straight towards Jason and me, his notepad ready, as though he was expecting to impose a high-penalty fare.

Someone would have been following us, I had no doubt, and at a more discreet distance than the officially assigned minders who were there, purportedly, to help with festival arrangements. It may have been the driver of the white car that remained at a steady interval behind the trolleybus, or one of the passengers inside the bus, perhaps the woman with the orange scarf who was most conspicuously staring away. I had neither illusions nor problems about being tailed; it came with the territory.

I'll account for this unauthorised excursion to my own home when Father comes back, I thought. I was sure he wouldn't mind. He had at least three dinner jackets that he could no longer button up, although his was the solid figure of a bread- and potato-eating peasant rather than that of a bloated bourgeois. He despised these items of clothing with their reactionary overtones, but accepted, grudgingly, that they were required for state occasions, even if a tailcoat, redolent of the depictions of capitalists in Bolshevik propaganda, would have been a sartorial step too far. Whenever a new jacket was made to accommodate his changing shape, the old one was mothballed and kept in the enormous walk-in wardrobe that came with the house, never to be worn again. His impoverished childhood had rendered Father unable to throw out so much as a handkerchief.

Our house was in limousine land, a rarely walked ten-minute walk from the trolleybus terminus. First there was an innocuous little space called the Square of 29 February 1944, clearly a second-tier revolutionary date that passed me, and most of my compatriots, by. It was adorned with the statue of Nepomuk the Great, around which the buses circled back into town. Then a guards' hut marked the turning into a lane that was private in all but name.

The three villas it led to stood well apart from each other, tucked behind several screens of mature trees. The buildings belonged to the Party or, de facto but not in bourgeois property law, to three of the most senior members of the Party's Politburo. Hidden in the woods even further back lurked the presidential palace, home of our leader, who wanted to enjoy luxury and security for himself and his emerging dynasty without being gawped at by the public, as our historical monarchs had been in the old palace in the city centre.

While a skeleton staff would be on duty, I didn't expect to engage with anyone at home. As well as the driver, there was usually a cleaner and a cook, and often also one or two of my father's many assistants, hand-picked severe young men with doctorates in Marxism-Leninism. 'Servants' was a term we studiously avoided. I used to think this was ideological, an avoidance underpinned by our care for the dignity of labour, but I was to learn on my travels that it was a Western affectation as well. I wasn't going to start explaining all that to Jason. I pulled the chain by the front gate, waiting for it to sound somewhere inside.

'You said your parents weren't at home,' Jason said, staring at the large façade, taking it in during daylight for the first time. 'Don't you have your own key?'

Indeed I had the keys in my bag but I couldn't remember the last time I had used them. Even as a little child coming back from school, I was taught never to sneak in, as if that were possible.

I waited a while but no one responded. When I fished out the bunch of keys, it took a moment to remember the right one for the gate, and Jason watched me try a wrong one first. I was relieved to find that the lock was still the same.

*

I am not sure why I led Jason to my father's walk-in wardrobe and why I encouraged him to try on Dad's wartime uniform, when he had simply noticed the case with its special zipped cover and asked what it was. It was some form of bravado, a wish to prove to this man that I was my own person, although he had no reason to think otherwise and I was yet to acknowledge that I was little better than the hotel receptionist and the women in the shoe shop; that my desire to impress him stemmed from his attraction; and this, in turn, not merely from his easy charm but from his rarity value.

Foreigners, at least the occidental varieties, were scarce in our country. The few who ever dwelt among us became objects of curiosity and constant talking points, while our capital's embassy quarter functioned as a zoological garden of caged foreignness. Encountering a good-looking, educated visitor from the West – not some dowdy academic or plodding trade unionist on a fraternal tour – had the alluring qualities of a fairy tale.

Even stepping into the room had been an act of sacrilege: what exactly was I doing? I thought that my impulse to disobey had died with Misha. Indeed, I had come to despise my old self for the hypocrisy of biting the hand that fed me while continuing to be fed so generously.

Yet as Jason unzipped the bag and took out Dad's jacket and trousers, I surprised myself by feeling and responding to a familiar thrill, like a seasoned swimmer diving into a pool after a period of idleness. Jason must have felt it too. I watched him hesitate, then act in what may have been a combination of innate exhibitionism and a sense of realising a unique opportunity. For a Westerner, this might be a bit like trying on Felix Dzerzhinsky's jacket, I thought. Or Mao's. I had no idea who Jason's Marxist heroes were.

I knew the West reasonably well, better certainly than most Western people knew my world, but I couldn't easily guess what a Western man might feel in this room, which belonged to one of the only fellow countrymen of mine of whom many Westerners had heard. They would surely be bringing a thousand prejudices to it. For me, the space was in some ways the essence not of the East, which was an abstract and shifting category, but of Europe itself as you might find it anywhere between El Escorial and the Winter Palace. Whatever offshore island he came from, British or Irish, Jason was a poet, sufficiently different himself to intuit that essence. They called us Eastern, but that was a wilful denial of something vital in the continent's soul. Our regime was an offspring of the Enlightenment, however contentious our variant might be. We were as European as France or Italy, more European than penitent West Germany.

Something in the atmosphere changed. Jason took his own clothes off, with a surprising lack of inhibition by the staid standards of our country, then started pulling Dad's trousers on over a pair of gingham boxer shorts. His hands were shaking. I wondered if any excitement on offer in the West rivalled the joy of this particular transgression.

The whiteness of his body in the semi-darkness was less shocking than the sight, moments later, of him – so evidently a Westerner – wearing the field-grey jacket made famous in a million photographs of my then-youthful father standing next to his best pal, the President, in their partisan days. It was an iconic image that graced every public space in the country, and – in the West – every last hostile article about it. Dad was vain enough to keep albums of any Western press cuttings he could get hold of, and he was particularly proud of those antagonistic to him personally. *The New York Times, Daily Telegraph, Le Figaro, Frankfurter Allgemeine Zeitung*: he had been profiled in them all. The more unfavourably they described him, the better. If it came from capitalists, invective was as sweet as honey.

Time magazine gave the photograph one of its legendary covers and went to the trouble of colouring it, I expect to make the red stars particularly lurid. They got the shade of the coat wrong – too green – but the cut was unmistakable. The framed image, *Time's* red border for once uniquely appropriate, was hanging on the wall behind Jason.

The coat hadn't been worn in years. It no longer fitted Dad. He had retained his youthful figure, people often said, but that was true only by comparison to other Party leaders, up to and including the President himself, who had all more visibly relieved the stresses of their decades in office through indulgence at the table.

The uniform suited Jason so well it could have been tailored for him. The stand-up collar looked as though it was meant to be worn with that Byelorussian *rubashka* that Jason had taken off at first and then, changing his mind, picked up again from the damp tangle of crumpled clothing at his feet. While the jacket covered the shirt, there was that exotic hint of red from the embroidered edge around the neck.

Only the khaki cap sat awkwardly on his tangled curls, but that could have been part of the charm too, a puerile, motion-picture version of a guerrilla: a preppy mate of Che. I wished I had a camera, then I wondered, as we were probably being filmed anyway, if I would ever see those reels.

Four summers earlier, I had ridden pillion on Misha's motorcycle from one end of the country to the other. We broke every speed limit in existence and finally got ourselves arrested just inside the northern frontier. We were held in a fly-blown provincial police station for a couple of hours. Misha was handcuffed because he refused to produce his internal passport. We both possessed documents with a code that opened every door – a real *passe-partout* – but Misha was beginning to feel ashamed of showing it. I failed to grasp his reasons at that stage but now see them as the first signs of some developing unease. He hissed that he would leave me if I produced my papers, and I desisted at first. The day was hot and I grew thirsty. It was stupid to pretend that we were not who we were, I said. Misha refused to speak to me on the ride back. Father had the police mugshots on his desk before I returned home.

Dad's medals sat in a row of plush red boxes on their own shelf. Leather tubes with rolled certificates stood guard behind them, each bearing the red wax seal of the Praesidium. Jason reached for the nearest case and opened it. He was about to complete his outfit.

'No,' I screamed. 'Don't even think of touching those.'

Dad earned his decorations for acts of suicidal courage against the Germans. No one, not even I, made fun of that.

The enamel glinted expensively, red and white and blue, on its red silk ribbon, with its touch of the fine pre-war craftsmanship that had lingered for a while after the triumph of socialism. Those late-1940s medals were much more impressive than the cheap mass-produced ones they were awarding now.

Jason covered my mouth with his left hand, still holding the box with his right. I bit his finger. He gave a little yelp, snapped the box shut and put it back, next to the others.

'I found it,' he said.

'Found what?' I asked.

'Your boundary,' he said. 'I was beginning to think you had none.'

We paused. He came closer. I could smell the cedar oil that Dara used as moth-repellent; a faint whiff of old tobacco buried in the twill.

'Sorry I bit you,' I said.

I was split, body and mind. One was already acknowledging desire; the other calm, wondering about the next move. Perhaps that's what Lana had meant all that time ago when she called me a cold bitch: that I could be two things at the same time. Losing your head was an alibi that people used to abandon responsibility for their desire.

What would it be like, sex with a Western man? I thought. I hadn't had a lover since Misha died. I will have this one, I decided, and Jason sensed both my hesitation and my decision. He took the jacket off and slung it over the line of grey suits on mahogany hangers, then offered his hand. I reached for it and took him back into Father's bedroom.

He was a good lover, a tender lover. Not better or worse than Misha: different. I had no others to compare them with. Jason was like me in his ability to monitor himself even as he seemed possessed by lust. That felt a bit unnerving, a bit new.

'Do you like this? Is this OK?' he kept asking, pausing. Misha never asked anything, never gave an indication that he could pause. Perhaps asking a question would imply either that he was not passionate enough or that he did not know what he was doing – hardly in keeping with our notions of patriarchy. And most of the time Misha had been so quiet that you could hear the gliding of skin on skin. It was perhaps born out of the same old sense of being monitored, but I was used to that silence.

With Jason, sex was a conversation. The foreignness of the language made it different too, the fact of speaking English in an intimate moment. I said *darling* at one point and the word made me feel that I was auditioning for a film role. Did native English speakers say *darling* to someone they barely knew? If not *darling*, what? My English classes had not covered this situation.

And then we were done.

'Wow,' Jason said, looking at me from his press-up position, his face flushed, a second before rolling over to his side, coming to rest next to me on a scratchy blanket, his hand possessing the curve of my hip. Father's metal bed looked as though it was salvaged from a field hospital, and it probably had been. There was a matching side table and, on its scratched surface, a battered tin ashtray and a glass containing a candle and a box of matches.

The oddity of such spartan furnishings in this richly panelled room was not something I had contemplated before. I was so used to the contrast that it seemed apt, even beautiful: as though Dad was camping in a palace. Mother's suite next door was as elaborately ornamented as a wedding cake, and hideous.

'Just wow,' Jason repeated.

'Wow' is a silly little word, unbefitting a poet. I am not sure what it was about anyway: my pale body still marked by its post-coital blush, our lovemaking or something else altogether. We weren't naked, just thoroughly unbuttoned. Nakedness came later. In England.

'I love you,' Jason said. 'I have been smitten from the moment I first set eyes on you at that ghastly airport. We were meant for each other, Milena. I took the snow as a sign. You looked so fierce, your beauty so out of time, like a young Maria Callas.'

I did not believe in destiny. No one is meant for anyone.

'Oh, shut up, Jason,' I said. 'You said you didn't like opera.'

I couldn't tell if a late-1940s dinner jacket worn over an embroidered *rubashka* counted as formal dress, but an unconventional outfit was not going to save us from seeing the wretched *Jenůfa*.

Professor Jaroslavsky's similarly ridiculous tuxedo was covered with a dusting of dandruff, which failed to obscure its appalling cut and lopsided lapels, making him resemble some cruel caricature of a person for whom classical music is more important than all material things. He kept brushing the white flakes off as he spun his interminable introduction to Janáček. His narrative was too specialised and too taxing on my English, and I was already distracted.

I was in an erotic dream in which *Jenůfa* did not figure. Images of the afternoon kept recurring unbidden, blocking reality. It was an experience so intense that I only wanted to repeat it. I tried to follow the drift of the lecture but I could not focus on interpreting.

Old Jaroslavsky could tell I was having problems. He kept pausing to wipe the thick lenses of his glasses in order to allow me to catch up. Whenever he noticed that I had lost his thread, he intervened with fragmentary French and German, the languages of our cultural old guard, which confused me further. I started talking non-sense, punctuating the flow with the words Janáček, *Jenůfa* and opera. Jason did not seem to notice, either. He was as lost in his own thoughts as I was in mine.

'You are extremely lucky to have an opportunity to hear *Jenůfa* in its original Czech,' Jaroslavsky enthused. 'The Kostelnička is performed by the great Magdalena Jakubova this evening. Our Czech comrades lent us their famous diva to help celebrate the eightieth anniversary of the opera. You will never ever forget this day.'

Of that, at least, I was already sure. Jason raised his eyes, as if to scrutinise the ceiling, smiling. I enjoyed our new, unspoken intimacy.

The old man followed Jason's glance, then explained, not missing a beat. 'It is the work of that legendary crafts-man, Ashot Tamayan. Eighteenth-century. Tamayan trained in Yerevan, Vienna and Paris.'

He turned towards me and waited for me to interpret.

'The plasterer, Tamayan,' he repeated when he noticed that I had no idea what he was talking about now. 'The plasterwork.'

He raised his fat, hairy index finger towards the ceiling. His hand was two-thirds covered by the greying cuff of his shirt. I looked up and saw a multitude of naked cherubs holding onto a ring of roses, while floating in the air like hummingbirds, their tiny willies drooping towards us.

'Are those snakes?' Jason asked. He was ignoring the cherubs, focusing instead on the oval relief inside the ring. It looked like a mass of apples and ropes, but it was hard to tell from so far below. I felt dizzy as I interpreted.

'Snakes, yes, or more specifically one snake,' Jaroslavsky said. 'The composition is supposed to represent the Garden of Eden. But back to *Jenůfa*: we have just forty-five minutes before the performance and so much still to explain. Comrade Milena, please, let us continue.'

'And the choir of angels below? Not the cherubs, I mean, but those proper, adult angels,' Jason interrupted again. 'Why are they all standing on clouds if they have wings?'

Chapter Seven

The Thaw

Ruritania is not England.
                    Anthony Hope, *The Prisoner of Zenda*

The temperature rose by twenty degrees overnight. We moved from minus two to plus eighteen. I knew the moment the thaw started: I couldn't sleep. I had no regrets about what we had done – on the contrary – but I felt relieved that Jason was leaving, so that I could deal with the aftermath of our lovemaking on my own, having heard the last of his silly declarations of undying love. I did not believe him. I was not a teenager. Nor did I need to be loved to make love.

At about two-thirty a.m. there was a single gust of wind so strong that it shook the house. I heard an almighty whoosh, as though the trees were about to take off, then the sound of someone manipulating the pulleys of our heavy external blinds. Dara must have returned while I was at the opera. The clack of wooden slats being lowered in one room after another continued for a while.

I put my slippers on and followed the sound of the blinds. I found Dara in my mother's bedroom, a space so heavy with the scent of Shalimar that I sometimes felt headachy even before I reached it. I followed Dara through the connecting doors into my father's chamber. She paused and turned to me when she saw that Father's French window was open, the silk curtain wet and caught in the railings of his balcony. The air coming in from the outside was warm, and the snow was falling off the roof in big, slushy chunks. Father's blanket, which had half-slipped off the bed, chose to complete its trajectory while the two of us looked at it.

'I will have a word with the hygiene team,' she said. 'Comrade Urbansky could have returned, found his room like ...'

She paused.

'Like the aftermath of an orgy, you mean,' I said.

She looked at me while stretching the blanket back over my father's bed. I tried, rather ineffectually, to help straighten it. I noticed that she was fully dressed under a thick checked housecoat. I wondered if she ever slept, if the robe was a telltale sign that she kept her own little flat in the basement unheated. I couldn't remember when I last went down there. Mother referred to Dara's quarters with a mock shiver as 'the colonel's lair'.

'And why aren't you asleep, Milena?' she asked. 'I thought you had work to do in the morning. Aren't you supposed to be escorting that Englishman to the airport? Comrade Gertruda will be back around midday. You'll probably spot her car at the terminal.'

'Yes,' I said. 'I can't wait to be rid of that silly man. Life back to normal – maize, et cetera.'

'I thought you liked English poetry.' Dara shocked me by saying this in English. She had helped, sometimes, with my English-language study in the past, but she had never used it for private conversation before. In part, perhaps, because the word 'private' had no real meaning in our world.

Another gust shook the house and several large icicles slipped from the roof with a sound like glass breaking. She pulled the shutters in, then closed the window.

'If Winter comes, can Spring be far behind?' she said. It took me a long moment to realise it was a quote.

'Oh, Dara, Jason Connor is hardly Shelley,' I said.

'I am glad you recognise the poem at least,' she said.

'I got an eight for an essay on Shelley and the French Revolution,' I said.

'You are showing off now,' Dara said.

Her sense of humour may have been odd but her English accent was better than mine. Although she never talked about it, everyone knew that she had spent five years at a girls' boarding school outside Bristol. This was in the thirties, before the People's War of Liberation. Her father was a diplomat, serving the old regime. Shot himself in 1941, when the country capitulated to Hitler. Dara was by then already red to the bone-marrow. Boarding made her a Communist, she said to Mother and me once.

'Thank God for England,' Mother replied. 'Where would we be without it?'

By the time I arrived to collect Jason from his hotel, the snow had melted away. The town was even greyer and uglier all of a sudden, with dark patches of damp like sweat-stained armpits beneath the eaves of the poorly maintained buildings. There were streams of muddy water everywhere, and only a few dirty scraps of white in the verges remained, as if to prove that the pristine glow of the preceding days wasn't a dream.

I sorted out Jason's paperwork at reception, then waited for him in the lobby. He now needed only to hand back his temporary city permit in order to have his passport returned, and that was it. Our minder waited outside with his colleagues; his job almost done. There was an all-pervading smell of fried eggs and boiled wurst coming from the dining room, a sound of chairs being shuffled around by underemployed waiters.

I could hear the heavy fall of Jason's new shoes on the marble landing two floors above. I saw that the young woman at reception was beaming in anticipation. He had that effect on my compatriots.

He emerged in his T-shirt and jeans, exactly as I had seen him the first time, his backpack on his shoulder now plumped up by the addition of my gilet and the *rubashka*, I assumed. He carried my father's coat, the dinner jacket and trousers – three heavy black garments – over his arm. He looked like someone who had just emerged from a period of mourning, en route to a dry cleaner's.

'I guess I won't be needing these for the airport,' he said. 'Can we leave them in the boot of the car while you see me off? I do hope you will be seeing me off?'

He pronounced *hope* and *seeing me off* with special emphasis, and I tried to avoid his eye, buttoning up my father's coat unnecessarily. I realised that what I now had to do was going to hurt us both.

A porter rushed to help, took the clothes off Jason's arm, then stood next to us, waiting for instructions. I asked him to hand the clothes over to the minder and nodded towards a trio of men waiting outside the revolving door. One way of soaking up excess labour, I suppose, was to have every notionally working person shadowed by another working person.

'The comrade in the brown coat,' I explained. 'Blue scarf. Shaved head.'

The moment the porter moved away, Jason stepped closer to me. Too close.

'Have you brought your passport as we agreed?' he whispered. I now saw that his eyes were rimmed with red and wide open. Standing so close to me, he looked like a demented bush baby. He had had no more sleep than I had.

'You must be mad,' I said, without making any effort to lower my tone. I had uttered the phrase several times in the past forty-eight hours, and I was beginning to mean it.

The previous night, during the second interval of *Jenůfa*, when Jaroslavsky disappeared to the lavatory for the third time, I rolled my eyes upwards and joked that prostates squeeze Bolshevik and bourgeois bladders alike. Jason interrupted me, as if in a kind of panic, to spill out a plan he had been hatching during the first two acts.

I was to bring my passport to the airport. He had a hundred pounds hidden in his rucksack, and another hundred in local currency, a sum he had received from Lana Kovalska for his reading. He reckoned that was enough to buy my plane ticket to London at the airport. He also reckoned his flight would be empty – no problem getting a last-minute seat. I did not need a visa for the UK, he explained.

I knew that well. The new, simplified visa arrangements had been established in a bilateral agreement with Edward Heath in the early seventies, when the President had visited Britain with my father. The perennially devious British were trying to wean us away from our Soviet masters, while we, with our masters' acquiescence, were raising our profile as a satellite and showing that good things did not only accrue to renegades such as Yugoslavia and Romania.

Before their State Dinner with the Queen, a paradoxical treat for the men who had pledged to do away with all bourgeoisies, aristocracies and monarchies, the two had met the Prime Minister and signed their deal, well aware that the opportunities were scarcely equivalent. In theory, my compatriots could get a British visa on entering the UK, and vice versa for Britons at our border – with both governments naturally retaining the right to refuse entry to undesirables. The procedure had been further simplified, but at the British end only, just that January: all entry visas were abolished, meaning that – irony of ironies – my compatriots were free to travel to the UK as they pleased. It was a gesture of friendship by the Thatcher government: a snake making an offering to a rabbit.

Jason called himself a Marxist. He hated the Tories and he hated Margaret Thatcher even more than the rest of her party, but this bit was OK. She had paved the way for my elopement. I was to come to London and marry him. I had to. It was as simple as that. A sort of loving kidnap. Then ... happily ever after.

Jason stayed silent and sulky all the way to the airport. I provided a running commentary, prattling on about the influence of Le Corbusier on our suburbs and then, as the city trailed off and an unbroken vista of ploughed land opened ahead, about maize production. The fields we were driving through were blacker than coal and among the most fertile in the world. And I knew so much about hybrids.

I wanted Jason to take my hand, to squeeze it and show that he understood how difficult this was, but he refused to engage. I looked at him. He looked out of the car window. I tried to touch his fingers; he withdrew his hand.

'You must be mad,' I repeated as we approached the airport building. 'We didn't agree anything.'

My English lover, my one-afternoon stand, had dipped not just into me but into my world and was now returning to his, unaware of the extent of the gulf between these two, precisely because his journey was so unbearably easy. If you were British, I read somewhere, you could go as far as India or Australia to find yourself. I had laughed at the Western notion of the self as something to be searched for, even as I envied the possibility of being able to travel so far looking for it, while still being able to return.

Last-minute tickets and impulsive marriage proposals were possible in Jason's world, but not an option in mine. I didn't have the time or the will to start explaining that, while I might not need a visa to enter the United Kingdom, I still needed an exit visa to leave my own country, and that was a much more complicated proposition. He would not understand. They were not exactly impossible to get, those exit visas, but if you were not on a guided tour, it took weeks and involved complicated vetting procedures, even for people like me, people with the best possible connections. If Stalin's daughter could defect, anyone could, the government assumed, not unreasonably.

In this context, Jason's offer to buy my ticket was irrelevant – touching but naïve. And who would have the heart to explain that his nominal hundred-pound performance fee was worth about ten pounds on the black market?

Only Lana Kovalska could be idiotic enough to pay her guests in cash on their last day. Cash it had to be, for we had no functioning banking transfers outside the country, but she should have given it to her poets on day one and then taken them to the state souvenir shop. Like this, the money would never be spent and, in theory, domestic currency could not be taken out of the country (indeed, why would anyone in their right mind want to take it?). It was possible that Lana had been so instructed. There was no harm in having an excuse to search and bully people while bidding them farewell.

'I don't need a passport to enter this building. And that is as far as I am going today,' I said clearly, without lowering my voice. Our minder was going through the terminal's revolving door a few paces ahead of us, checking his watch. He so obviously failed to turn – as anyone would, hearing my tone – that I wondered if he really had no English.

'And that's your last word?' Jason asked.

'That's my last word.'

'You don't love me?'

'That's my last word.'

I glanced at the split-flap display on the departure board. It was showing the full twenty-four-hour schedule: flights to Vienna, Moscow, Warsaw and Tripoli. I knew that Vienna was the only flight that day with more than a handful of private passengers. Thirty or so people waited to check in, several of them with carefully roped suitcases large enough to contain all their worldly possessions. For our people, travel was a serious, much-premeditated business.

There was a small family group among which, as Jason and I approached, I recognised an acquaintance from university, a thin mournful girl who had lent me her copy of *Middlemarch* for the Victorian Literature exam. I passed the exam but never finished the novel, my guilt assuaged by assuming that the English never read any of our own nineteenth-century novels. The girl was too stuck up to find such reasoning funny when I returned the volume, but she now greeted me with what, by her standards, was a high-energy wave.

'Where are you off to, Rivka?' I said, faking cheerfulness.

'Tel Aviv,' she said. 'Nice to see you, Milena.'

She did not reciprocate the question, but she did stare at Jason. Her father – a well-known surgeon – pulled her closer by pretending to hug her.

'It will be lovely by the sea at this time of the year,' I said and moved on.

I knew better than to chat. My country had been selling its Jews and Germans for some years now and everyone gossiped about it; they were allowed to emigrate in exchange for hard currency. The Soviets and the Romanians were doing the same. It was fair, people argued, because their education had cost us dearly, and because Germany and Israel had more money than they knew what to do with. Moreover, those two countries believed that someone was German or Jewish even if that person came from a family that had been living in our country, or elsewhere, for centuries. Let them pay.

This transactional approach made me sad nonetheless, because it made our people invent German and Jewish roots. And even where the roots were real enough, I believed these Germans and these Jews were our people – as much ours as I was. I rowed with Mum and Dad about it. I could sense that they were uncomfortable about defending one of those compromises that members of any regime have to sign up to. At least, in the case of the Germans, there was the permanent scar left by the wartime atrocities and economic damage they had inflicted, and not a few of our own ethnic Germans had sided with the Nazi invaders. In the case of our Jews there were not even those excuses; singling them out instead preyed on ancient prejudices. Now, seeing Rivka and her little sister, in their matching coats with velvet collars, I felt the kinship even more strongly.

In the business-class line there was just one elderly man in a grey Trachten jacket with green trimmings, wearing a felt hat with a pheasant feather that twitched as he moved his head. The man was agitated for some reason, so it twitched quite a lot. He was white-haired, red-faced and blue-eyed: the type that made you want to crack jokes about the war. He was speaking Russian to the woman at the check-in desk – bad Russian with a strong German accent – and I wondered where he had picked up the language.

'*Achtung. Achtung*,' I said to Jason, trying to cheer things up.

He wasn't in the mood. I was standing right by his side but, as the pheasant feather moved on, he immediately stepped towards the check-in desk himself. His body language suggested that he didn't want me to follow. He didn't need an interpreter any more. He took his documents out of the front pocket of his pathetic rucksack and proffered them as he approached the woman. She straightened her back and smiled. Her lipstick was so red that her lips somehow stood apart from her face, mirroring the red aeroplane badge on her uniform toque. I stayed back and watched them.

When she had completed the paperwork, she handed it back to Jason with an even bigger smile. He was clearly the main event of her week.

He moved on, fast, as though in danger of missing the flight, although there were still three hours before the scheduled departure time.

'You are so lucky to have been upgraded,' I said to Jason's back as I walked behind him. I was trying, and failing, to keep up in those last twenty or thirty metres before I lost him forever.

'Your foreigner is in a hurry,' the minder said. He was following me following Jason. 'Let him go. Your job's done.'

I waved the man off. He surprised me by getting the point and walking away.

'I don't want to part in anger,' I continued, speaking to Jason's back, now a touch more loudly. I noticed that his rucksack had a University College London badge and several ink stains on its pocket. 'Surely even you could not believe that I would be ready to drop everything and leave the country just like that; it's simply not possible. It's so easy for you. You have to realise that you're in a foreign country and we do things very differently here. Why this mad rush to go through? You'll probably never see me again.'

He turned, finally acknowledging my presence.

'I know you think I am an idiot, Milena,' he told me. 'You said as much. I suspect you regret what happened yesterday afternoon. With every atom of my being, I hope that you are not pregnant. It breaks my heart to leave you in this God-awful place. I love you. I don't think I'll get over you any time soon.'

Then he stepped back, closer to me, and lowered his voice. 'And in case there is something else about your reluctance to come with me now, something that I can't understand but which may change: that Welsh chap from the British Council Library who came to my reading, Huw. I know he knows you. When you're ready, find him and tell him that you would like to borrow my poetry collection. I have a friend at the British Council in London, someone who helped organise this whole wretched gig; I will ask him to tell Huw that that's a signal. Huw will be able to contact me without your people knowing. He'll be able to help. I suspect he has done this sort of thing before. But do it soon, Milena, please. Don't keep me waiting.'

He reeled off his speech, then turned back again and strode ahead, not waiting for a reply. I watched him proceed across the glistening marble floor. There was the international border ahead and, above it, our flag and that portrait of the President and my father, dressed in the uniform that Jason had worn the afternoon before. The two men looked so young, so handsome and so hopeful. If he had observed the image, Jason did not turn to indicate it.

'Workers of the world, unite,' said the slogan below in a plethora of languages, starting with Spanish for some unfathomable reason, and ending with several rows of ideograms.

I watched him offer his passport to the border-control officers and answer some questions while two men in uniform flicked through it, first one, then the other. I watched him take my gilet out of his rucksack. I watched one officer put his hand down the rucksack and rummage through it. Then a third man emerged from the side office, said something and Jason followed the three into this side room. At no point did he turn back.

The minder came up to me again and asked for permission to leave the airport.

'Do as you please,' I said without turning. I kept my eyes fixed on the closed door. I wanted to see Jason come out of that room. 'Feel free to take the car. I don't want to keep the driver waiting. Our family car will be out there soon, collecting my mother,' I added and glared at him.

He nodded at the mention of my family and walked away. I stood and watched the door with growing panic for another ten, twenty minutes, wondering what to do, whom to call. The border police had their own interpreters if they needed them. Whatever the reason they took Jason into that room, I could no longer be of any help; I could only stand and wait.

After an eternity I spotted the blond head through the vast glass window that separated the departure hall from the boarding area. He walked into the tiny duty-free shop, then, five minutes later, came out with a bottle of something. It was only at that point that he looked in my direction. I knew he could see me still standing there. I waved. He did not smile. He did not wave back, or acknowledge my presence in any other way. It was as though we were, again, complete strangers to each other.

Chapter Eight

The Spa

I was bleeding. There was a shortage of sanitary towels in the country. No chemist had any in stock. All imports of foreign luxuries had stopped and you were lucky if you could find even the scratchy home-produced sausages of grey cotton waste encased in a flimsy net manufactured by our own Krupskaya Female Hygiene Factory. They soaked through before you could say 'period'. If we had had the same problem with any product that men depended on, the authorities would have taken steps to import quantities of it in order to avoid unrest, but women just carried on.

As recently as March I'd received pink boxes of tampons from Italy without having to ask. The stock in my bathroom cabinet replenished itself. I now faced an empty shelf each morning. I am not sure where and why this particular supply chain broke down, and I dared not ask. Someone must have noticed that, between late March and June, I had not used any, just as they must have guessed that I now needed them again. When the last of the small reserve vanished, I knew that the failure to restock was a way of punishing me.

I was forced to soak face flannels in the bidet, wash them by hand and dry them on the radiator before rolling them into makeshift sanitary pads. The cleaner had clearly been instructed to ignore my efforts. She came into my suite daily to wipe and polish every surface, but she never acknowledged that my bidet was full of a pink, sweet-smelling soup in which face flannels floated like squares of honeycomb tripe.

Only a week earlier I had been driven to Minerva Terme or, more precisely, to the vast health complex attached to it. Its world-famous medical team had developed an elixir of youth, a preparation made of young women's placentas, which was then injected into older women's cheeks. No newspaper had ever mentioned the treatment, yet the news had clearly spread. Women enjoying privilege, the only fully convertible global currency, arrived from every corner of the world, Communist and capitalist alike. The price of treatment for international guests – those with capitalist passports – was astronomical. The comrades' wives, including highly placed wives from fraternal countries, had theirs free of charge. It made their faces as smooth as the embalmed visage of Lenin in his mausoleum.

My journey had nothing to do with the price or the effect of these procedures. I did not need an elixir of youth; I needed a termination.

Abortion was the only reliable method of contraception on offer in our workers' paradise, and it was freely available. Other options existed for me, of course, but I had been living chastely at the time of my unexpected encounter with

Jason, and in any case these other options always involved people knowing – not an enticing prospect.

Nobody cared that abortion was actually post- rather than contra-ception. Feminism didn't really get a look-in. Instead the balance between the workers' sexual needs and essential birth control (almost no one had more than two children; not only was that the convention, but accommodating more would have been difficult in our tiny state flats) was achieved in a completely functional way, the surgical procedure exemplifying scientific socialism.

In Romania they had outlawed abortion in order to boost the birth rate. Whole classes of women had to undergo regular gynaecological checks to ensure they were not hiding their pregnancies. Ours was a civilised state. If you were over eighteen, the procedure could be completed promptly in a local clinic, without needing anyone else's consent. No part of that proposition applied to me. I had had a pregnancy test, but my father knew the result before I did.

The initial conversation was more than terse. Mother and Father were having breakfast. I was sipping ginseng sweetened with royal jelly. Father did not bother to introduce the topic. He wasn't going to discuss my sex life or to enquire what I was planning to do. There was only one option – and so it wasn't really an option, he said, as precise as ever, not looking at me but at the soft-boiled egg in front of Mother, as though he was expecting a reply from the yolk. He was not so much against the procedure – what else could you do? he said, clearly pained – but against doing it locally. As the recent beneficiary of just such an ethical transgression at my expense, he knew that respect for patient confidentiality was not something you could count on in our health service.

His facial muscles twitched. Unlike Mother's, his was not a face used to expression, yet I had pushed him to the edge of making one.

'Before you know it, the whole town would be talking about my daughter bearing my grandchild,' he said, squeezing his lips tight as though he had been offered a sip of hemlock.

Sex and parents. The supreme awkwardness of the topic was probably the same the world over. Who knows whether Father played the field when he was away from home? There were surely opportunities, although I knew his dry puritanism was not an act. Nonetheless, the public – and even for me, as the closest outside observer, the private – edifice of my parents' marriage was as solid as socialism. It had to be.

My compatriots certainly screwed around – the range of alternative and affordable forms of amusement was limited. Even so, public affairs, desertion, what was still called illegitimacy ... all these happened but were seen as shameful. Beneath the carapace of socialism, ours remained a traditional society. We were not a forgiving lot.

I wanted that abortion, of course I did. Any other options were unthinkable. The concept of single motherhood was not recognised as a possibility, at least not in neutral terms. That was why the word 'grandchild' sounded strange on Father's lips. Until that moment I had imagined what was growing inside me to be just a miniature pale seahorse, part me, part Jason, but ultimately destined to be nothing. Jason would never know.

The procedure itself would not be a big deal, I assumed, although not from experience. Misha had known better than to make a girl pregnant, and he had been my only other lover. My university acquaintances had had abortions in sufficient numbers to be unfussed about keeping the procedure secret. It was no more shameful to have one than it would be to take a contraceptive pill, had the pill been available.

But these carefree girls did not have my father: to dictate, to organise everything and then to carry on as though neither party would ever mention the fact again, while preserving the knowledge for some unspecified future use like a vial of poison, until you thought it would have been easier to have had the details published on the front pages of every newspaper.

Thirteen weeks at most, Dr Petroffsky said. His wiry grey hair was only half-contained by the small white cap that made our clinicians look like aliens in some science-fiction movie, and his matching coat was unbuttoned to show a medal ribbon bar on the lapel of his grey suit. The medals made me feel embarrassed, and angry with Father. His motto may have been 'only the best for my girl' but I did not need a National Hero to carry out the curettage. And I had told Petroffsky the exact date of conception – I could even have specified the hour – but he chose to ignore me and instead demonstrate the superiority of his medical science over my pathetic certainty. He pulled a strip of white card out of a beaker of my urine, like a stirrer out of a cup of linden tea, and was holding it, with its double blue line, in front of my face, confirming what I already knew.

'Just my luck, Comrade Doctor. You do remember that extreme cold spell in March ...' I said, as if to suggest that

I was fertilised by snow, like Danaë by golden rain. 'And it was only that once.'

The unexpected whininess of my own voice struggling to fill the conversational void was humiliating. I couldn't care less about Petroffsky's opinion, yet I sounded as though I was trying to convince him that I wasn't a slut. He wasn't listening anyway. I was stripped and wrapped in a hospital gown even before I had entered his consulting room, and he was now buttoning up his coat and then tying an apron over it, while guiding me to climb the parturition table and instructing me to push my bare feet through the cold metal stirrups.

The hospital gown opened under me. I wasn't offered the dignity of a cover. A nurse stepped forward with a razor, a brush and a white kidney dish full of soapy water. She proceeded to shave my genitals, right up, touching me brusquely but as intimately as only both my lovers and perhaps, long ago, my nanny had ever touched me before, yet not once looking into my eyes, not even when she said, 'All done. Ready?'

It sounded like a question, but she turned to Petroffsky before I could say anything.

'The patient is ready, Comrade Doctor.'

There was a shortage of latex gloves, and I had brought some with me, as patients were expected to, but I now saw that they were the wrong size. Her hands were far too big. The cuffs had cut into her wrists, and her fingers holding the dish looked like a row of those small Nürnberger sausages that we sometimes obtained from the hard-currency shops. I tried not to think about the curls of pubic hair floating in the suds. You couldn't grow up in this country without learning not to see what you didn't have to see.

She took the shaving kit away and came back wheeling a hospital trolley with a row of steel instruments arrayed as though it was some gruesome dessert cart. They came in strange shapes. Some looked like scoops borrowed from an ice-cream parlour, others seemed more sinister, like weird symbiotic tools, all-in-one knives, spoons and forks. On the shelf below there was a pile of worn grey towels, as if to acknowledge, for the first time, that the procedure might turn out not to be as routine as Petroffsky had claimed.

I was offered no anaesthesia, not even the local kind. No woman had it, I was told. The doctors said the pain was to be suffered for our own good, to minimise the risk of uterine perforation. I bought – or at least rented – the argument, but, in hindsight, I am not sure how I'd have been able to tell if my flesh had been ruptured as opposed to being scooped away.

I tried not to think about what was going on inside me, tried not to worry that I might faint and impale myself on a curette. I tried to look past my thighs and focus on the ceiling and the goings-on there. It was covered in a vast fresco that contained clusters of cherubs hovering in the sky. Their chubby little faces, framed by minute wings, seemed menacing. The wings looked like ears: they, too, were listening.

And why had our ancestors wanted to paint so many winged babies everywhere? The hospital was a historical, protected building, purpose built as one of the earliest medical facilities in this part of the world. Although thousands of foetuses must have been aborted inside it since the war, it was scarcely designed for the operation I was undergoing. These ceilings were painted at a time when abortion was murder, and doctors no one's comrades.

'All done,' said Petroffsky, taking his bloody gloves off with a snap. 'That wasn't too bad, was it?'

I stood up from the table, feeling as though my pelvic bones would never join up again, yet the nurse suggested that I'd be ready to travel back to the capital later the same day. She did not reckon with Gertruda. Mother had booked us into her usual suite in the spa for three days of rest and recrimination. I'd have preferred a shift down a coalmine, even in my bleeding condition.

Seventy-two hours later we were back at home and Mother remained more determined than ever to sort out my life.

'It's two years since you graduated, Milena,' she said at breakfast, watching me shift from one buttock to the other. The awful sanitary-towel business was leaving me sore. There was no comfortable position.

She pretended not to notice. Her face was covered in blue gunk and her head was wrapped in an enormous towel. She had left wide, clear circles around her mouth and her eyes. They made her look permanently startled. The gunk was drying and cracking along her worry lines. I feared that bits of it would drop into her fermented *kasha*, like stucco falling off an old façade. She was taking spoonfuls of the buckwheat porridge, then lifting a glass in its elaborate silver holder and sipping some hot green-flecked, urine-hued liquid. It smelled strongly of vinegar. Her breakfasts seemed designed to create a cordon sanitaire around her.

Father was there too, and although it was a Sunday morning he was already fully dressed: suit, tie, white shirt, a copy of the Party newspaper on the table in front of him. He was eating a ham sandwich or, rather, attacking it in huge bites, then gulping them without chewing.

The noise – his gulps, her slurps, the rustling of paper – was unbearable.

'Thirty-six chews for each mouthful, Stanislav, please remember,' Mother said. 'The process of digestion starts in the mouth. You'll thank me for the warning one day.'

He paid her no attention.

'Two years,' she turned back to me.

'Yes, and?' I was halting, unsure where the conversation was leading.

'Yes, and? Is that all you can say?' She sounded incredulous. 'Two years in that awful Institute. All your friends are married. Soon you'll be the only one left, living with your parents – an old maid.'

Misogyny was as prevalent among our women – certainly those of my mother's generation – as it was among our men. It took its own form, with a relentless, caustic, judgemental focus on younger women's looks, prospects of marriage and hoped-for fecundity. To all of this, any concept of self-fulfilment was secondary.

I wasn't sure whom she meant by referring to my friends. I had cut myself off from the last of them when Misha died. He and I were part of a small circle. Outside it, I found people either fawned or displayed barely disguised hostility, and frequently both at the same time: need and hatred, together but distinct, like oil and water.

'I am twenty-three. What on earth are you talking about, Mum?'

'I don't mean to say that you shouldn't be living with your parents. On the contrary. You and your future husband, whoever he turns out to be, poor man, I expect you both – *want* you both – to live here with Daddy and me. There is no house better than this in the city. Konstantin's palace, for example, is too cold, too vast, all those guards everywhere, all milling about like flying ants. And those hideous turrets. What I mean to suggest is that a woman's fertility starts declining rapidly at your age and, even before this recent disaster, your eggs—'

'Truda, for heaven's sake.' Father stopped reading when she mentioned the President and slammed his newspaper on the table when my eggs were brought to it. Thick flakes of ham flew out of his mouth. One pink particle landed on Mother's cheek and stayed there, pink on blue, the hues of our old royal flag. I wasn't eating anything, just sipping my coffee. I did not dare ask Father where he was going, dressed up like that. Not to church, his recently exclaimed oath notwithstanding, that was certain.

'Well, you married at thirty-three, Mother, and your own fertility was phenomenal,' I said. I was born six and a half months after their wedding day.

'Yes, but times were different.' She ignored my sarcasm. 'There was the war, and then my voice-schooling. I had had barely five years onstage when I met your father.'

'Met,' I smirked. 'Eyes locked across a crowded room.'

Father had summoned her after watching her in a performance of *La Traviata* – the way other men order dinner in restaurants, Mother had told me once, when he had upset her about something. The summons was not as astonishing as the idea of him listening to Verdi. I found it impossible to imagine Father at the opera.

'Just that once,' he said, as though he was reading my mind. 'But that does not make what Truda says any less true, Milena. You sit at home for months with your agricultural papers, then all of a sudden ... you meet a man – a foreign man, a totally and utterly unsuitable foreign man – and what happens? No self-respect, no morals.'

I slammed my cup on the table, wiped my mouth with my bare hand.

'Fuck you both! At least he's a true Marxist, unlike the two of you,' I said, as Dara came in carrying croissants and a bowl of butter whipped with cinnamon and honey. She gave me a tight-lipped smile.

Father finished his sandwich, gulped down his black tea in one go, then claimed the excuse of an event at Army HQ. He was meeting a delegation, he said. The word 'delegation' was a code word; you could ask no further questions.

'I am off to church,' I said to Mother, the moment I heard his car drive off.

Her face mask broke into a craquelure.

'Church? That's all we need. I recommend the Museum of Atheism. Opens at eleven. Cure yourself of any God business before it takes root.'

'Atheism is a matter of faith and a religion too,' I said, leaving her to her *kasha* before she could add another word.

There was a monastery at the foot of the hill, below our house, its old buildings the wounded survivors of many wars and revolutions. I had passed it a million times but had no idea about its services or opening hours. I wanted a walk to get away from my parents, and anyone else who might be listening in on them and on me, and I am not sure why I remembered this cluster of domes as a possible destination, although perplexing my mother, as I had just done, was tempting. If you excluded a visit to the Sistine Chapel on a shopping trip to Rome, the only time in my conscious memory that I had stepped into a functioning religious building was that first evening with Jason.

The monastery church was almost empty, merely a few old women clustered in front of an ancient priest. They looked like a gathering of haystacks: he in his many-layered glittering robes, they wrapped in dark shawls draped over immense skirts and aprons. One of the women was kneeling. As I entered, she moved forward on her knees, then bowed down even further to kiss the priest's feet. I saw that he was wearing rubber galoshes under his robes. He rested his palms on the back of the woman's head and said something. I stood inside the door, waiting for the next thing to happen. The candle-punctuated gloom beneath the dome was perfumed with molten beeswax and incense. I could hear the flapping of birds' wings in the bell tower.

After the priest made the sign of the cross, they all, including the woman still on her knees, turned their heads towards me. The smallest among the haystacks approached and asked if I wanted to buy candles.

'Yes, please,' I said and followed her to the counter on the right. There was a pathetic display of goods: cards, calendars, prayer beads, paper images of saints glued on wood, an array of candles of different thickness and, incongruously, a couple of jars with wooden crosses suspended in honey.

'How many?' the woman asked and then, noticing my hesitation, pointed at a two-tiered candle-stand in the opposite corner. 'The upper tray is for the living. The lower for the dead,' she explained.

'And the unborn? Where do they belong?' I asked. She did not seem to understand.

She waited for me to explain, then grasped what I was saying, at least in part.

'Oh, I am so sorry, dearest. Believe in God's mercy. Your body is strong and you are young. You will bear sons to your husband, worry not.'

She raised her hand to touch my cheek but I stepped back, pretending to fumble for coins in my purse. I asked for two candles, then lit them: one below, one above. I stood watching while the lights flickered and the wax melted. I felt the woman looking at me from her pathetic sales counter as the blood seeped out of me. I longed for Jason and I wondered what to do with that longing: to own it and act on it somehow, or ignore it and starve that flame of oxygen until it died.

Chapter Nine

The Lake

I spent the summer alone by Lake Antai, in one of the holiday residences for Politburo members and their families. My parents never used the place. They hated its luxurious Art Deco simplicity. The whiteness of its walls and its stark chrome fittings were too spartan for my mother. That should, in theory, have suited my father, but didn't. The residence was too comfortable, its minimalism too obviously blended with opulence for his taste – precisely the aspect that I found soothing. There were far too many Gothic Revival horrors in the capital.

Our villa was originally built for an industrialist in the early 1930s, close to the holiday homes of other plutocratic supporters of the former monarcho-fascist regime. Pleading for their lives, his family donated it to the Party just fifteen years later. It did them little good: the industrialist was shot and his family forced into imprisonment, followed by an impecunious exile. The house would have been taken anyway.

The home of his dreams still shimmered like a mirage above the lake. Its grounds and those of the adjoining villas seemed permanently deserted, except for an occasional waiter who carried a tray into the deep shade of the pergolas. The fragile cups, jugs and teapots they served my tea in had survived the war, by a miracle. They were, equally miraculously, not stolen by the retreating Germans or the advancing Soviet liberators – surely spared because of the very simplicity of their lines. They had been designed by the same Swiss architect as the house itself.

I spent hours pretending to read in a deckchair shaded by the pergolas. The further Jason Connor receded into the past, the more often I thought of him, and I hadn't expected that. At first I tried to explain away those thoughts as the hormonal aftermath of pregnancy. I missed our conversations, his English, that carefree way in which he said what he thought or what he wanted, which made him sound like a creature from a different planet. I missed his body in spite, or because, of the fact that I had only possessed it once. I wanted to touch it again, and I told myself that this was to test my memory of it: was it really as lanky, and as luminescent in its northern paleness, as it was beginning to seem?

I felt no remorse about the abortion, but its circumstances made me feel more claustrophobic than before. Although our fatherland had always seemed like an extension of my father, I hadn't resented this so much in the past. There were advantages. I didn't need to summer at Lake Antai to know that I, a humble translator, would not find the level of comfort and protection that I enjoyed in my own country anywhere else, at least as long as my father kept his position – never a foregone conclusion.

However, comfort and protection came at a price, and that was now especially stark. In the aftermath of Dr Petroffsky's intervention, it had begun to seem as though I no longer enjoyed so much as a millimetre of trust.

When I came down to the lobby that morning, for example, the major-domo threw an anxious look at my jogging outfit and asked if I was planning to run the full circle around the lake. Rain was forecast for eleven, she said. I am certain I was only imagining that she had received a call from Father instructing her to ensure that I was back before eleven, but imagining it was enough.

I tried to console myself. Just look at the beauty of all this, I thought, as I descended towards the water's edge, picking up a trot. The lake was as still as glass under the morning sun. The only thing that moved were wisps of mist rising from its surface, evaporating as quickly as they formed. The air was fresh and scented. I'd need to be a billionaire in the West to enjoy this combination of luxury and solitude.

And I knew what I was talking about. I'd experienced the capitalists' miserable four- and even five-star hotels, bodies packed like sardines around pools and in spas, their pitiful attempts to secure a piece of beach by covering it with a towel or a lilo, the smell of others' sweat and suntan lotion, the voices. It was no accident that their advertising always showed scantly peopled facilities and attractions – as though that could ever be viable. I had metres of sand, translucent water, a cloud of silver spruce on one side of the lake and a thousand shades of deciduous green on the other, the fruits of the arboricultural interests of our former royal family, all to myself.

So what, if someone watched over me every minute? People are watched in the West too.

I ruminated in circles, with less and less clarity as the summer faltered. I perused the villa library, which seemed to have been thoroughly weeded out but never updated.

Except for a new Lithuanian edition of *The Condition of the Working Class in England*, inscribed illegibly to my father, the most recent volume was a novel by Romain Rolland published in Paris in 1935. Inside, there was a card with a photo showing the author with Stalin. Impossible to tell whether it was tucked into the book by one of our people to show Rolland's credentials or, in a piece of historical irony, left there by the previous owner of the villa.

I read the complete works of Turgenev, very, very slowly. I started, and gave up on, *War and Peace*. I felt glad that I had studied English literature, in spite of what it had led to. I went to evening concerts where some of our best musicians played for an audience of half a dozen. I slept, often from nine till nine and again in the afternoon. I took massages and swam. I ate the freshest of fruit as it ripened: cherries, then raspberries, then melons and watermelons, then peaches, then grapes, and finally the first apples of autumn. At the neighbouring villas a scattering of other guests came and went.

In late August I sent for translation work from the Institute. I was, officially, no longer on holiday. The mist in the mornings took longer to clear. The evenings grew colder and yellow leaves floated on the surface of the lake. I floated with them, looking back at the hillsides.

'Enjoy it while you can. It takes just one substantial rainfall,' the head gardener said to me one morning, 'then the air temperature will fall below twenty and stay there until next April.'

'And the water is already growing cold,' I responded. 'The surface is still fine, but you feel the cold layers rising up from below.'

'I took a swim late last night—' He stopped midsentence. Staff were not supposed to.

'Are those raspberry canes?' I asked, to help him out. I had observed him, perhaps around eleven, eleven-thirty, doing laps in the moonlight. I had been woken up by a splash and stepped out on the balcony to see a white head circling in the water, overalls and a pair of sandals left on the pale crescent of a little beach.

He was lucky there were so few guests. Lucky that our villa alone had a balcony above the treetops. Somebody else would have alerted housekeeping, I thought, feeling virtuous that I wasn't that person. Then I felt guilty for feeling virtuous.

At least we were no longer living through the early years of socialism. These days he might lose his job but not his liberty or his life, for such an offence.

'Canes, yes. They were great, the raspberries this year, weren't they?'

When the weather cooled permanently, I started going to the Russian *banya* before my own evening swims. Although it had originally belonged to our residence, the *banya* was now shared with the neighbouring villas. My father had allowed that, in an act of generosity towards his close colleagues, knowing perhaps that he and Mother would not use it more than once every three or four years.

It was an ornate space, an exotic edifice where the Swiss architect had unexpectedly indulged a dream of oriental Russia such as only a Westerner could nurture. It consisted of a sequence of four rooms lined with marble tiles, the colours of which ranged from pale rose to dark red, according to the set temperature of the room. The chambers were filled with increasing amounts of steam, and each was, usually, empty at that late hour, when the few remaining lakeside residents were dressing for dinner.

The final room was usually so steamed up that you could not see more than half a metre or so ahead, and so hot you could not stay in it for longer than five minutes. There was a font, permanently filled with snow brought from the mountains, just outside it, where the *banya*'s heavy door opened onto a conservatory with a turquoise plunge pool at its centre. This pool was filled with sparkling mineral water kept at four degrees Celsius. You grabbed the snow in handfuls and rubbed your body with its crystals even as you dashed into the water, while your skin reddened and tingled with cold. Once you overcame the initial pain barrier, it was an addictive routine. I often repeated the run several times in a session.

I had grown used to being alone while doing these repeats of hot and cold, but this time I noticed the outline of a large woman on a bench in the far corner of the hottest room. She was inhaling and exhaling loudly. I heard her breathing even before I saw her. Although I was naked, but for a tiny apron covering my genitals, as was the custom in the *banya*, the woman seemed to be wearing a black bathing costume and a white swimming cap. Her face was a circular carnelian blur, framed by pale rubber.

So far as I was aware, only three other women were staying in the villas at that late stage of the season: one with a husband, two alone. I vaguely knew them all, women my mother's age, acquaintances rather than friends. And, likewise, they would have been aware of me. The only true friendships these people sustained came from within their own extended family clans, and my mother had none. Because of her own father's blighted past, her relations had either vanished or been warned to keep away.

I was trying to guess which of the three women this was. I conjectured that it was a Politburo wife. The Politburo did not consist entirely of men – we were supposed to be an equal society and the Party had to demonstrate that equality right up to the top – but its female members worked twice as hard as the males. You would not catch them huffing and puffing in the *banya*, other than on major national holidays, and probably not even then if there were parades and state-sponsored events to support and show up at. There had to be a woman on each platform, and there were so few women in the Politburo that their engagement diaries must have been full to bursting.

'Good evening, Comrade,' I said. It was better to break the silence than to feel the woman's stare probing my soul. I intended to stay only as long as was necessary to make my departure seem unprompted by her presence. I was hoping that she wasn't planning to disrupt my evening routine by making a habit of using the *banya* then.

'Good evening, Milena,' the woman responded in the deep-claret voice of a heavy smoker.

I waited, hoping she would introduce herself, but she was assuming that I knew her.

'How has your holiday been so far?' she asked.

'I am not on holiday. At least not any more,' I said. 'I am working.'

If she reacted, I could not see her expression.

'And yours?' I asked.

'Oh, this has been the worst year of my life,' she said familiarly, but without any audible emotion. 'First Ivan's stroke, and then the accident. You will remember it.'

I had no idea what she was talking about.

'Remember what?' I echoed.

'Well, we were at the Minerva at the same time as you in June. The medical centre, not the spa,' she explained. 'I was with my mother, for her gastric treatment. Gertruda would have mentioned it, I'm sure, but I know you had more important things to worry about. Then Ivan's idiot driver came to collect Mummy and me and, on the way back home, smashed our car. Hit a fallen tree on an open road. Imagine! It wasn't even sudden. I could see it looming so far ahead that I wondered, when the lunatic failed to slow down, if he was drunk or determined to kill us.'

I produced an appropriate gasp.

'He did not stop even when I screamed, and then it was far too late,' she continued. 'If I weren't an atheist, I'd say that only God saved us. In fact it was Soviet car technology. The ambulance took Mummy and me straight back to the spa.'

I guessed she was in her sixties, which made Mummy at least eighty. I wondered if Mummy had the same walrus physique.

I was beginning to recall rumours of the incident she was describing. Her husband, Ivan, was the Minister of Grain Production. I'd seen him, and successfully avoided him, whenever he visited the Institute. He had the body of an average nine-year-old and was reputedly as mean as only small boys can be. His wife could eat him for breakfast, I thought.

'And the driver?' I asked. She stared, surprised that I should mention him.

'Well, whatever – broken, dead, I don't care. He was unconscious when they pulled him out. All I can say is: it's the last bit of driving he will ever do. But what about you?'

She paused, then continued, although I made no effort to respond.

'I understand the father was an Englishman. That very handsome poet who came to the Kovalsky girl's festival, Mummy said. Those Western men are fickle. We've seen enough in their films, and films are supposed to be an idealised image of reality. We were sad to see you having to go through that.'

'Did my bloody—'

'No, of course not, my dear. Gertruda wouldn't.' She saw that I was getting angry, took a longer pause.

It was getting too hot, yet the heat did not seem to trouble her. I was speechless at the extent of her indiscretion, waiting for the first opportunity to leave.

'I guess it's Stanislav's fault,' she finally said.

It was only when she continued that I realised she was blaming my father for my abortion, and not for the rumours.

'This is the twentieth century,' she went on, now sounding indignant. 'It would have been so interesting to keep it, to see what the child looked like. Mummy agreed.'

I could not take the heat any more. I could not take the breathy voice, the inanity, or the idea that this woman – and even this woman's 'Mummy' – knew so much about me. While I imagined myself blissfully alone by the lake, she and the other wives must have allayed their boredom by gossiping about me, mourning my aborted half-English seahorse while slighting its father, someone more attractive than all the men they dreamed of, because they would never find out about the colour of its hair.

Perhaps because she was one of us, inside our private space, I felt more exposed before this woman than I felt when strapped to Petroffsky's parturition table, with my legs splayed. She was a reminder of how claustrophobic our small, insulated world was. From birth onwards, you lived in a kind of enlarged family, all your achievements, failures and transgressions the subject of common knowledge. You could never escape, unless you chose the nuclear option and left altogether. And, in order to leave, you gambled everything you had – your very life.

I stood up and walked out of the *banya* slowly. When the door closed behind me, I grabbed handfuls of snow and, rubbing them against my chest, ran past the plunge pool, out of the conservatory and all the way down to the lake. I reached the edge of a jetty and dived into the water with such propulsion that it took all my strength to draw the air into my lungs when I resurfaced. They rattled, as though deflated on impact, refusing to let the oxygen in.

'Comrade Urbanska? Do you need any help?' the head gardener shouted from the boathouse.

I grasped one of the towels from a snow-white pile that always waited for me on the jetty and buried my head into it, pretending to dry my face while what I wanted most was to scream. I might have enjoyed every indulgence in the world, but I'd never had the luxury of showing raw emotion in public. I was so good at suppressing anger and pain that I often failed to recognise their metallic, humiliating taste. When Misha talked about it to me, I thought him a crybaby. I knew better now. Something had touched the core after all: I realised I was in love.

I took all my meals in my villa from that evening on, finishing *War and Peace*, all three hundred and sixty-one chapters of it, giving the sparsely attended concerts a miss. I did not want to meet that woman again, to have to acknowledge, even tacitly, that our conversation had ever taken place. That dive into the lake was brief, my eyes remaining wide open to see the sand and silky grass at the bottom, but the surfacing was delayed long enough to reach a decision that would change my life.

Chapter Ten

Carried by Dragons

I was carried by dragons
Over countries, bays, and mountains,
By fate, or by what happens.

Oh yes, I wanted to be me.
I toasted mirrors weepily
And learned my own stupidity.

Czesław Miłosz, 'City Without a Name'

I returned to the city resolved to leave it. Whenever I happened to catch sight of myself in any of the mirrors at home, I imagined that the imprint of my decision was as visible as if I had grown a pair of antlers, or coloured my hair bright green. I found it difficult to believe that no one suspected anything, not even Dara, who was usually so alert to my appearance that she spotted missing shirt buttons or stud earrings before I fully entered the room.

I knew I loved Jason. I wanted to be with him if he still loved me, but I suspected that I would have to wait until I left the country to find out. He was worth the risk, I believed. And if I lost everything, but didn't get Jason, I would at least cease to be just Stanislav Urbansky's spoilt daughter. I could never be myself in this country, I thought, without pausing to wonder what 'being myself' actually meant. Silly, stupid me.

The British Council Library was running its annual exhibition of new writing to coincide with our own October Book Fair. I knew better than to expect that the effort would amount to much more than a few reprographic panels. Unlike the Soviets and the Americans, the British rarely splashed out on promoting their literature: we were too unimportant as a country, even if they pretended otherwise, and anyway Britain scarcely sought to rival the superpowers.

I also knew that I would find some trace of Jason in the exhibition. He was the reason I was there. Every British writer who had visited our country without blotting her or his political copybook got a mention in these surveys. The Library was treading a thin line between wishing to celebrate British achievement and champion the cause of Western democracy, and not wanting to be shut down by the authorities. Because so few British writers had visited us over the years, we flattered ourselves by declaring them greater than they were back home. The writers relished the unwonted puffery, and the Council in turn flattered us by pandering to our wilful delusions. It was, after all, in the Council's own interest to pretend that it was bringing over the greats. In that context, Jason was promising enough.

His face, in a considerably enlarged black-and-white photograph, was beaming at me when I entered, standing furthest from me in a procession of photographic portraits displayed on panels in the library lobby. My first thought was that the British writers were, on the whole, a remarkably ugly bunch. My second: but not Jason, definitely not Jason.

The photograph was a couple of years old at least. His hair was sweetly shorn, the curls reduced to a promise, like the fleece of an astrakhan lamb, and his forehead more elongated than I remembered it. His eyes were as shiny as they were when he first towered above me that afternoon before *Jenůfa*. At whom was he looking?

I lowered my gaze. His shirt collar was open and I saw his clavicles, and recognised that shadow where his skin stretched over the bone, then dipped towards his neck. It was like re-entering a valley that you had once visited and never wanted to leave again.

'Hello, hello, Miss Urbanska,' I heard the familiar Welsh vowels and the sing-song intonation. 'So happy you made it, and on the last day. You didn't RSVP to our invitation for the opening night, but I kept my hopes up anyway.'

'Was there a *vernissage*?' I asked.

The invitation certainly wasn't forwarded to Lake Antai and I didn't see what there was to open here. My attendance at any public event organised by a foreign institution would have had to be cleared anyway. I am not sure Father would ever have approved.

'I am sorry, I was away this summer,' I said. 'But thank you for thinking of me.'

'Our wonderful friend here,' Huw said, now standing next to me and looking up towards Jason's portrait. 'He insisted that we include a recent, as-yet-unpublished poem in this showcase of his work. You must read it, Miss Urbanska,' he added, using – unlike most foreigners – the correct feminine form of my surname. 'It is lovely.'

I couldn't see what Huw was talking about. Next to Jason's photograph there was a short biography, which mentioned Lana's poetry festival and quoted a couple of opportunistic lines about the beauty of our capital, which I remembered Jason feeding a local journalist during his visit. Just below the biography there was a sonnet that I recognised from his reading.

'I know this poem,' I said to the Welshman. 'I remember it well.'

'No, not that one,' Huw said. 'The display continues over on the other side. If you come round, on this same panel, you will see.'

We walked behind and there was another procession of writers and Jason's name again, the same photograph, now smaller, and a poem entitled 'The One-Star Hotel'. Before I read anything else, I spotted the last line: 'Still, waiting.'

'How clever of you to use both sides,' I said, trying to maintain an even tone and the regal air of a daughter of the *nomenklatura* displaying a polite interest in something inconsequential. 'It must cut costs.'

'That's a strangely placed comma, isn't it?' Huw said, following my gaze, covering that comma with his thumb, as every atom of my body responded to Jason's words, to his image. The situation was ridiculous – this Welshman, his digit turning red as he pressed it over a punctuation mark, this exhibition, like something in a local middle school, the poetry panel as the most absurd of dead drops – but I had my answer.

If you wanted to travel abroad, the received wisdom was that you were most likely to be granted an exit visa for an organised tour, particularly if the trip involved visiting a friendly socialist republic. I was facing an additional hurdle. No bureaucrat would dare sign off on my travel documents without consulting Father, and Father was harder to convince than the Interior Ministry.

Cuba in late December – Communism's tropical paradise – seemed more plausible than the other options on offer. Havana was a beautiful city, the island promised summer temperatures just as the worst of winter was setting in at home, and the Caribbean Sea looked divine, even in the dated black-and-white photographs that curled in the fly-blown windows of our central tourist office.

I started enthusing about Castro's beaches, while secretly accumulating the paperwork. Mother took it as a sign that I was reverting to whatever, at least in my case, passed for normal behaviour.

'Turn your face to the sun and the shadows fall behind,' she said, never slow to dole out folksy proverbs and banal advice. 'Don't lock yourself away inside your own residence like some ageing spinster. Go for one of those charming little hotels in Varadero that International Workers' Tours take over in high season. You are likely to find yourself sitting next to some promising young man at the communal dining table, or dancing the cha-cha-cha with him under the palms. These hotels have their own beaches too: no vulgar, drunken Westerners.' She flicked imaginary castanets in the air.

I wasn't about to put Mother to rights on Cuban dance or anything else. Package holidays might be run by an organisation called International Workers' Tours, but she knew better than to assume that it ever flew more than an occasional token miner or metal worker across the Atlantic.

*

The most relevant practical detail about Cuba was the fact that there were no direct flights to Havana. Most Cuban itineraries involved a change of planes in Moscow. Vienna was another alternative: more expensive and less readily available, but sufficiently well established to sound plausible. I was hoping that, once I convinced him I needed a winter break even after eleven summer weeks on Antai, Father would see the advantages of the Viennese connection.

He knew how much I relished an *Einspänner* in the airport café, and *Mozartkugeln* in the duty-free. They were not available at Moscow's Sheremetyevo airport. I was hoping that he wouldn't zoom in on the fact that in Vienna I could miss the onward flight by lingering in one of the expensive airport concessions even as my name, blissfully meaningless to most who'd hear it, was repeatedly called on the tannoy system. There was little point in absconding in Moscow, where any connecting flight would wait until I was tracked down and put on it, however long that took, with fraternal socialist consequences to follow.

Ever since I returned from Antai I was brimming with anger, barely managing to hide it. Instead of feeling rested, I shouted or cried at the smallest provocation.

'Molehill meltdowns,' I overheard Mother describing my moods on the phone to a so-called friend of hers. I had picked up the receiver on another extension to phone the Institute and caught her in the middle of one of her interminable heart-to-hearts.

I knew well that the Politburo wives shared confidences about their children – the husbands were out of bounds, too hazardous to touch even inside the inner circle – but the memory of the fat woman in the *banya* was too recent and too raw for me to bear any more of that. I walked to

Mother's room, pulled the cord out of the wall and threw the device through the closed window. She didn't try to stop me and she knew better than to report me to Father. The glass was replaced and a kind of truce prevailed.

I had been through difficult situations in the past and accepted them with cold, and sometimes cruel, detachment, yet my weakness for Jason – if you could call love a weakness – felt new and all too painfully private. I thought I could kill anyone who so much as mentioned his name.

Dara was the only one to utter it.

'I wanted to have a word, Milena …' she said one morning when she found me in our library, 'I know this has been a hard year for you.'

I was holding a dictionary of botanical terms in my lap. I was translating a particularly obscure article on the role of corn silk in the pollination process. She was hugging yet another of those lavishly bound volumes that my father received as gifts, pretending to look for a place on the shelves. I nodded and feigned attentiveness.

'Jason Connor, I mean,' she said. 'The aftermath. Your mother is an emotional soul, and she doesn't let a feeling pass without showing it. I've known you since you were a little baby and realise you are different, more like your father or me, a closed book.'

As she said that, she patted the volume she was holding. She seemed apologetic, perhaps about the cliché she had just used about my father, or about speaking so intimately. Neither of us was accustomed to this kind of personal chat. She too was beginning to irritate me. I think she could sense it, but instead of retreating as Mother would, she caught my glance and held it: Dara was steel to my mother's upholstered silk.

'You may be missing him now. Don't do anything silly and rash. Whatever you are feeling for the Englishman will pass. I promise you, it will.'

I don't know why, but in spite of the fact that she would have been privy to my chatter about tropical beaches, at that moment I assumed that by 'doing anything silly and rash' she meant harming myself. What pushed my irritation over the edge, however, was not that, but her assurance that my feeling for Jason would pass.

'And what do you know?' I answered. 'What do you think you are doing, wasting your life in our house, shelving my father's books? Look at you!'

She didn't dignify me with an answer. She deposited the volume on the top of the rotating stand close to her and walked out of the room.

I felt immediate remorse, of course I did, but I waited a couple of days before I offered an apology. Dara took it with good grace, if not forgiveness, but that was fine. I didn't deserve forgiveness: one can't unsay something when one has expressed it with so evident a sense of belief.

I was too selfish and too preoccupied, first with my own anguish and then with the technicalities of escape, to consider my parents' – or anybody else's – situation. The only thing that mattered to me was the knowledge that Jason was expecting a signal from me, a response to his message. Whenever I visited the British Council Library, and whatever book I came for, Huw continued – unprompted – to recommend *Homecoming* by Jason Connor. I got to know its best stanzas, and the music of Huw's Welsh accent as he quoted them.

'I am planning to take it out soon,' I said one day and his face lit up. 'The New Year holidays are the best time to read poetry.'

In Huw's eagerness to play Cupid, I recognised only his friendship with Jason. I didn't, at that early stage, think of myself as a prize, a potential trophy scalp for Britain, although Britain was one of the chief ogres, perhaps second only to its even more pernicious transatlantic cousin, among that nebulous collection of countries that made up our ideological enemy, the rotten capitalist world. To recognise it would be to acknowledge the possibility that – even in the West – I might remain first and foremost my father's daughter.

I was still talking up the advantages of Vienna to my parents, when Lana Kovalska materialised out of nowhere to play Fate again. I was at the VIP salon of the tourist office, flicking through a Cuban brochure, when she walked in with Agnes, her best friend *du jour* and the only child of our Foreign Minister. They were accompanied by a couple of travel advisers.

'What a joy to see you, Mimi. And all of us going to the same place, it would seem,' she said, glancing at my reading. 'Three friends together are so much better than two.'

I could see that she was already hatching an idea and wondered what exactly she would ask of me. Her friendliness was a giveaway. Lana was a ditz, but an opportunistic ditz. Whenever I called her crazy in the past, her brother smirked. Yes, crazy like a fox, he said.

Lana and I had not been friends before Misha died, and we certainly weren't afterwards. Her festival was a brief exception, but, even then, we were more colleagues than friends. I now stared at her until she changed her expression.

'Three just sounds so much better. Agnes and I won't trouble you in Cuba, Mimi,' she admitted with a sigh. I had started to worry that she was about to propose a triple room. 'My parents will never, ever understand me,' she continued, unbothered by the presence of the advisers who stood, like two pillars, unmoving at her sides. We daughters of the *nomenklatura* tended to divide like that in our public conduct: some carried on as though the underlings weren't there, as Lana did, spilling out indiscretions; others went shtum and surly, like me.

'It's been even more oppressive since Misha died. They think I will change, given the right boyfriend. I won't be able to stand their matchmaking much longer.'

'Tell me about it,' I sighed, trying to put an end to the conversation.

I assumed that she knew about my abortion because everyone else did.

'Agnes and I are flying out via Moscow. She has several artist friends she wants to visit there. You are welcome to join us, but I won't blame you if you don't want to. On the way back, however, we're planning a stopover in London,' Lana said. 'That way, we don't have to lug the shopping to Varadero and back. And I am definitely going to visit several modern art galleries while we're there.'

'Are there any?' I asked, feigning ignorance. 'I thought the English were only good at painting horses.'

Agnes giggled.

'Horses without penises, if I remember our art classes well. Rule Puritannia,' I took my unfunny joke a step further. I didn't want Lana and Agnes to think that I had any plans related to England.

One of the travel advisers sniggered at the mention of penises. I glanced at her and she froze. Lana laughed too, but only half-heartedly and to please me. She was an Anglophile, like her late brother.

'Don't you realise that there are more true Communists in London than in Moscow? And it's proper avant-garde, their new art, not like our provincial daubs. I'll change that soon enough. I am thinking of a biennale, a Venice of the East right here.'

'To rival Leningrad?' I asked. The Soviets were fond of calling their second city the Venice of the North. 'That brewery by the canal is a start.'

Under the aegis of our (relatively) young Culture Minister, an ambitious apparatchik who had studied briefly in Manchester, an arts cooperative had moored a gondola in the murky waters of our city's old industrial waterway. Young couples who would never see Venice took photos of themselves in straw hats and striped shirts against the neo-Gothic arches. It was ironic and painful at the same time.

'Why not come to London with us, Mimi?' Lana said suddenly. She may or may not just have thought of it. 'Why not make a change from boring old Austria? They haven't had anything new to say for themselves since Klimt. My gallery visits are funded: research, you understand. You could make a bit of pocket money, act as my interpreter.'

She was keen to make some unspoken reparation. Her own English was fluent enough. I said nothing, trying to decide on the spot whether this invitation was good news or bad.

'You call yourself an English graduate, but you have never set foot in England so far as I know.' Lana produced her closing argument.

'You are right,' I conceded. 'It makes no sense.'

Lana knew London well, and in her late teens had spent a month in Cambridge, on an English-language course. I had never visited the British Isles. Because of Father's reluctance to let me travel internationally on my own – with good reason, as I was about to prove – I only ever went abroad with Mother, and she was keen on what she described as ancient and cultured European capitals. The rain-stained British metropolis with its haphazard architecture, marooned on its fog-girt island, populated by cultural scavengers feeding off the past glories of the continent's music and art, and enduring the world's worst cuisine, was not one of those. She would have been horrified to hear that her daughter was planning to live there.

Mother had visited London just once, with her opera company, before she was married. The visit could not have been a success. When Father accompanied the President on his state visit to the UK in the 1970s, and the Party decided that both wives should stay at home, she seemed relieved.

In her desire to create a smokescreen for her Caribbean honeymoon with Agnes, Lana talked herself into such peaks of enthusiasm about travelling with me that it was impossible to say no. Of course I would not have wanted to refuse anyway, but for the worry that a sudden diversion to London might arouse suspicion at home. And I would want to go out via London, not spend time with the two numbskulls transiting Moscow.

When I finally turned to them, the travel advisers jumped in, eager to show off their knowledge of the world, however theoretical it must have been. They suggested that changing planes in London was as easy as Vienna – easier in fact. Although the flights to Heathrow from our capital were only bi-weekly, London had a smoother onward connection to Havana. And if I happened to want a stopover, to enjoy an even more restful experience, there was a lovely trade-union hall of residence opposite the British Museum. They flicked through huge flight directories with obvious relish as we spoke: the chance to devise individually tailored itineraries didn't present itself often.

'En suites, of course. And a number of more comfortable units on the top floor: "sky rooms", they call them.' One adviser rushed to explain, in case a trade-union hall suggested bunk beds. 'A four-star hotel effectively, full of that very English charm. But would you need a hotel anyway? The embassy residence is just by Hyde Park.'

'I will let you know,' I said. She batted her ridiculous sapphire-shadowed eyelids all too knowledgeably and too ingratiatingly when she mentioned the location of the residence: it was not common knowledge. And in spite of her servility, I wasn't about to start explaining the technicalities. These were not the sorts of tedious chores I was used to dealing with myself; the unstated reality, which we were all too uncomfortable to admit, was that lesser people had always been grateful to perform them on my family's behalf. The reason I was in the agency in person was not something I could even hint at.

Mother did not seem to mind the mention of London nearly as much as the suggestion of my travelling with Lana and Agnes. Because she was supposed to like Lana, she could not bring herself to explain. She talked about unhealthy friendships as though I could catch an infection from the two of them.

'Never mind,' she said. 'You'll have your own company in Cuba. I hear that Lipski's son is planning the same trip.'

'Now that's a promising young man,' Father butted in. Up to that moment it had seemed as though he wasn't listening to Mother's chatter, but he didn't bother to affect a modicum of surprise at the mention of Lipski's name, in a way that made me wonder if he had ordered the young man to visit Cuba.

'Bound to become our country's top cardiologist. Every family needs one,' he said. 'And not unhandsome,' he added, as if conceding my shallowness. Lipski's father was a high-ranking colleague. Like so many Party stalwarts, he had directed his son towards a more secure career path.

'I was wondering, Dad, if I should fly via London both ways.' I looked at Father, trying to sound hesitant while delivering a prepared speech. 'Leave earlier, take a few days at each end. I studied English after all, and yet I've never been there. Remember how much you loved the Reading Room at the British Museum on your state visit? There are so many sights to see. Then, on the way back, I'll help Lana with her art and her shopping – do some of my own—'

'What, Rome no good any more?' Father interrupted.

He looked uncertain as I began, but his eyes lit up on that last sentence as though he had finally grasped what I was playing at.

Father had spent the best years of his life fighting the Germans alongside some of the bravest women on the planet, but this experience had not altered his conviction that women were more innately consumerist than men. That they needed to be dragged, kicking and screaming, into a bright Communist future without property.

From everyone according to their abilities, to everyone according to their needs: the latter part of the Communist credo, Father thought, would always chafe with the fairer sex. He was suspicious about everything I uttered because doubt was his second nature, yet my talk of shopping fitted his worldview so well that, for a moment, he forgot to distrust my words.

Although creating a cover was my main concern, I later realised that Father probably would not have worried about Jason in the context of my travel plans anyway. Going to the Englishman's feet, throwing myself at him, would have been unthinkable, an abasement too far. If I had dishonoured him once by falling for a dishonourable man – for what other kind would do what Jason had already done to me – surely even I wouldn't dishonour him twice, wouldn't sink so low as to chase after someone so evidently worthless in his eyes?

I had been evasive in the past, but I was now spinning an elaborate invented confection, telling straight lies for the first time. Long afterwards, when I felt guilty about so many things to do with my parents, this particular deception loomed larger than most. Just then I was still convinced I hated them both.

In London, with Jason, I could lead a more truthful, more authentic life, I wanted to believe. Such a life – a life without lies – was worth a sacrifice. If the freedom they boasted about in the West meant anything, surely it was freedom from having to dissemble.

'I am tired of shopping in Italy with Mother,' I seized the moment to consolidate my advantage. 'Not because of you, Mummy, of course, but because everyone here wears the same clothes from the same boutiques in Rome. It's like living in an Italian cultural empire.'

'Fine,' Father said. I heard the sound of destiny's wings flapping. 'Fine. Why not?'

*

Mother seemed to have crossed the same gamut of emotion, but in the opposite direction. Encouraging at first, she became visibly agitated when he said yes to my plan, but she knew that opposing Father once he had spoken would only make him even less likely to change his mind. He was hard-headed enough to realise that trying to keep me imprisoned would be impractical, even counterproductive. Whether it was London or anywhere else was immaterial: the moment I was on the other side of the Iron Curtain I could no longer be directly controlled. Mother's maternal intuition made her fear the consequences of the freedom he had just granted.

'Milena must stay at the embassy residence, Stanislav,' she said. 'Lekovich will accompany her throughout.'

'Oh, Mummy, please. That dreary old man. I'll stay in an English hotel, have some fun. Something like those places you spoke of in Varadero.'

'Yes, I understand, dearest. It's not that I don't have faith in you. But Cuba is different: Cuban people are decent. In England you will be offered spiked drinks or drugs that look like sweets and then—'

Her ideas of what might happen to me on the streets of London were based on crime capers.

'Truda,' Father interrupted. 'Milena's an adult. Let her be. But it shouldn't be just any hotel, I agree. The Workers' Tours will arrange something appropriate.'

I encouraged Father to think that I loved the idea. So long as it did not involve old Lekovich meeting me at Heathrow, I was ready to accept anything, even sleeping on Karl Marx's grave.

A few days later I collected the details of my itinerary: three days in London, in a sky room at the trade-union place, followed by the 'Cuban Culture, Cuban Delights' tour, then a further four days in London with Lana and Agnes, this time in a five-star hotel behind a large department store, each night costing more than one of our workers was paid in a year. Of course Lana wasn't buying the trade-union gaff. Four stars, whatever the charm, just weren't enough.

I half-listened to her reasoning about the location, close to both the galleries and the best shopping in the city. The only part of the itinerary I was planning to honour was the first leg: the first four hours of the first leg, in fact. I knew that eventually Lana would find out. I also knew that she would be too excited to hear about my disappearing act to remain angry with me, but that did not matter, either. I wasn't going to see her ever again.

As soon as Father agreed to my plan, I went to the British Council Library to borrow the *Blue Guide to London* – and *Homecoming*. It was an irony of sorts that the institution Father had admitted into the country, and yet detested, should be a backdrop for, and the unwitting enabler of, his daughter's elopement.

Most Eastern Bloc countries didn't host an official British Council presence – instead its representatives lurked as cultural attachés, without libraries as supporting props. Our enhanced relationship was a product of that brief seventies' thaw, co-engineered by Father and cynically sanctioned by the Kremlin, designed to tell the world that satellites weren't totally in thrall to mother Moscow.

Luckily there were no other readers in the library when I got there. I couldn't have imagined that Huw's placid face could beam enthusiasm that expressively as he emerged from his glazed inner sanctum. I assumed that the place was bugged, but I prayed this meant no cameras, just microphones.

'Finally,' he said, in that overly familiar way of his. Was this my welcome to Welshness? I tried not to leap to conclusions. 'This book will change your life, you'll see.'

'You overestimate the power of verse,' I said flatly. I didn't want him to think I was desperate to leave the country. I didn't need his opinions, either. He was like those women at the tourist office: the moment you availed yourself of their services they started to imagine they could be your friends.

Just a couple of days later, en route to the Workers' Tours offices, my paperwork completed, I returned Jason's collection to the library. I lingered among the stacks for a couple of minutes until I saw Huw, in order to hand him the slim volume personally. The timings of my arrival in London were written on a bookmark tucked inside: 13 45 20 12.

'You are a fast reader,' he said. His smile was wide but his attitude was borderline impertinent again. I needed his assistance, not his opinions. He took the bookmark out, examined it, then handed it back to me.

'This must be yours,' he said.

'Oh, how careless of me,' I said. 'I wonder if you could check for *Orlando*. It seems to be out. I was looking for it back there. I'd like to reserve a copy. Could you please telephone to let me know when it's in?'

The following morning Huw telephoned. Dara handed the receiver over as though it was a wet, snotty handkerchief.

'A very good morning to you, Miss Urbanska. Just calling to let you know that *Orlando* is waiting for you,' he said. 'We chased the copy up.'

We spoke English when we met in person, but, on the phone, Huw used his rudimentary knowledge of my native tongue. His Welsh accent made its wide vowels sound even wider. We used the second person plural, and I feared that the formality, compared to the usual bluntness of Huw's English, would make it sound as though we were speaking in code, although of course we were.

'I love Virginia Woolf,' I said, thinking of those who were listening in on us, knowing I sounded like someone in an overwritten play. 'Something to read on my Cuban holiday. I'll see you when I am next in town.'

I thought it useful to have a reference to Cuba on tape, just in case they sent a transcript to my father.

'It's not really our territory,' Huw said, 'but we do have Our Man in Havana.'

'I am sure you have, but no, thank you,' I answered. I didn't recognise the title, if it were a title. 'Orlando will do.'

Part Two

London

The Stranger's Bread

Wanderer, your path is dark,
Wormwood is the stranger's bread.

> Anna Akhmatova, 'I am not one of
> those who left their land'

Chapter Eleven

The Art of Leaving

December 1984

> All there is to know on the art of leaving
> I've learned in careful pillow-talk at night.
>
> Osip Mandelstam, *Tristia*

My memory of arrival is still fresh. The plane corkscrewed over London for forty-five minutes, in lower and lower loops. A holding pattern, the pilot called it. He used the English phrase. The expression would have been meaningless in my mother tongue. It was unfamiliar, this idea of a rush hour in the sky. The airport we took off from had four flights a day; there was no need to hold anyone in the air.

I completed my landing card, set my watch to UK time and waited, belted, seat upright, spotting landmarks as they emerged from under a grey wing ornamented with a red Communist star. We followed the Thames, moving a few kilometres upstream with each circle. Through wisps of cloud, a bird's-eye view, I ticked off the Tower, St Paul's, Big Ben and what I thought was Hyde Park. I spied a football stadium at one point, then watched ribbons of suburban housing unfurling beneath us, seemingly without end. I tried not to think about Jason making his way to the terminal, or already there, next to some barrier, studying the faces of people coming through, waiting for mine. For one demented split second, I worried that I wouldn't recognise him.

I had studied the map of London for days before this flight. Nothing seemed new except the lack of colour. Nothing had prepared me for that. Three hours and two time zones ago, back home – for home it still was – the crew had welcomed me on board with the solicitousness owed to a socialist aristocrat, and had treated me deferentially throughout the flight. They knew whose daughter Milena Urbanska was – and it wasn't my mother they had in mind. Her haut-bourgeois antecedents might be an amusing titbit for the cognoscenti, but we remained a deeply paternalist society. Everyone knew about my proletarian dad. No one knew, though they would find out soon enough, that Milena was not returning.

Flight: I meant the word in every sense.

The plane had taken off almost empty. I was seated in what I suppose was the business-class area. Although there was no formal division in the national airline fleet, seats were further apart at the front: smoking on one side of the aisle, clean air on the other – allegedly. There was a cluster of middle-aged men in bad suits a couple of rows behind me on the smoking side, red passports poking out of breast pockets like matching squares. They had the focused expressions of hunting dogs scenting trade deals with the capitalist world, off to sell raw materials no doubt, for west of the Iron Curtain no one ever wanted our manufactured goods.

These men smoked a lot and said little, snooping on each other and on me, no doubt looking forward to telling Dad's associates about the paper cup of Albanian cognac that I had nursed as the Ilyushin cut through the air diagonally above Europe at minus fifty-two Celsius. They walked past to get to the lavatory at the front and stared at the copy of *Orlando* sitting unopened on my tray. They might conceivably have interpreted my possession of Virginia Woolf in paperback as an act of dissidence, but it was more likely that they had no idea what it was. The flimsy orange covers made every English novel look like pulp fiction.

Orlando wasn't returning to the British Council Library, either. Huw was unlikely to chase Father for overdue fines.

Whenever one of these apparatchiks came by, I looked away from the aisle and down at the gradually unfolding European scenery: snow-covered fields defined by thin black boundary lines, ancient forests, shards of rock bursting through layers of snow, rolling hills, kilometres and kilometres of lowlands, then just a grey unmoving sea.

Finally another landmass had slipped into the field of vision – an island. I noticed a murky river issuing out of the floodplains. It looked as though the water was flowing upstream, the sea decanting itself into a funnel. It slowly dawned on me that this must be the Thames, that strange tidal river of which I had read, a waterway that could flood the streets through which it passed. We were moving towards its source, into the heart of England.

It was there, in the air above the Thames – and as I apprehended the disjunction between its enormous fame and its slender girth, finding it so much more modest than the vast waterways of my homeland – that it occurred to me that I might never see Mother and Father again.

*

Deeper in the belly of the aeroplane there was a small group of English holidaymakers who had been stupid or poor enough to swallow the promise of winter sun on our miserable coast. I had noticed them in the terminal building before departure. They were spending whatever they had left of our worthless currency on the neon-green bottles of sour Moldovan wine stocked in the newsagent's next to passport check, the only airport concession that accepted local money. They must have consumed their alcohol on the spot because they waddled on board carrying nothing but their own heft.

Their clothing was cut just as badly as the comrades' suits, but it was considerably flimsier and more colourful. The greens and reds and bright yellows did no favours to their northern skin tones, nor did the dozens of words printed on their garments flatter either their figures or the brands that many of the words proclaimed. These people – my soon-to-be compatriots, I suddenly thought, with a degree of disbelief – covered themselves in advertising slogans as though someone was paying them to wear their own clothes.

I knew the type in its proper summer version too. They burned and peeled and drank gallons of cheap lager with equal ease, and they made the locals feel superior to Westerners. Not me. I may have been even more snobbish than the rest, but I also sensed that these people were carefree in ways that my countrymen could never be. The men jostled and laughed and the women shouted across rows of empty seats. You'd be forgiven for assuming that they had chosen to sit far apart only in order to communicate in some special way with their high-pitched cries.

I was surprised when I noticed that they did not relish their return to England. The closer we got to Heathrow, the quieter they became. When the lights were switched off for landing there was silence.

Then the runways appeared below us, a tarmac Star of David with shoals of aeroplanes clustering at each of its points. I grabbed my handbag the moment the engines cut out and rushed headlong off the plane, into the labyrinth of accordion walls leading to the heart of the terminal. Cyclops' camera eyes stared at me from time to time, blunt and unhidden, so unlike those at home. I queued and queued, zigzagging along with dozens of others in elaborate lines, until I finally arrived at this strange island's border.

Why am I visiting the United Kingdom? How long for? What to see? Where am I staying? I had had plenty of time to prepare for this questioning. The immigration officer had a blue turban, a beard in a tidy black net and eyes as luminously dark as crude oil: my first Sikh. He sat at a high desk, on a stool that swivelled slightly left and right as he waited for my answers.

Culture and shopping. Four days en route to Cuba – I took the onward ticket out of my purse, put it on the high desk before me to support my claim – then another four on the way back. The British Museum, I recited, your great National Gallery, Piccadilly, Nelson's Column, London Bridge: I thought it opportune not to perform my routine to perfection.

'And of course,' I said, with the sort of smile I'd heard the English added like a sauce to everything, 'Harrods. Shopping.'

I banked on the probability that the Sikh's view of women might chime with my Father's. It wasn't enough. He looked at my passport again, then, tiresomely, continued with his questions, and I continued answering them.

Yes, first visit. I named the hotel. Why would I want to seek work in the UK? I have a job, a family back home. Translator. Yes, from English. The State Institute for Maize Research.

Parents? Father: an administrator. Mother: an opera singer. Retired.

I wondered if he might recognise my name. I did not want him to.

And still he was not done. I wondered if it was my mother, on all our earlier trips, who had exuded some authority that I was so obviously missing now. Together, we were never questioned like this. The inconvenience was another first, I thought, another low, but I consoled myself that it was for Jason's sake.

The Sikh then asked me to show that I could support myself while I was in the UK, even though I had made an advance payment not just for that sky room I was not planning to use, but also for two unnecessary weeks on Varadero beach.

Would I mind showing him the contents of my wallet? I wasn't sure whether to find this funny or humiliating. I flicked it open. There was more than enough cash, in hundred-Deutschmark notes – the comrades' hard currency of choice – to stay at the Ritz for a few months.

He picked up my passport again and puzzled over its multitude of stamps. The brand of passport I possessed rarely came with so many of those.

Who are you? I could almost hear him thinking. Who are you?

I tried not to show impatience. It was my country he distrusted, I knew, not me, even though I was the liar here. He asked me to wait while he stepped back into a nearby office, divided from the hall by a one-way mirror. I saw myself in it as Jason would see me soon. My face, unmade up, seemed paler than usual. My black wool coat was trimmed with the darkest shade of Ural sable available on the market, originally chosen to match my hair. It was as warm as overcoats can be, its trim as unostentatious as sable gets, a simple cut. 'If you didn't know, you wouldn't guess,' Mother had commented on my choice, disappointed. She preferred people to know.

The mirror didn't faze me in the least. I was used to them.

The Sikh came back some minutes later, without my passport, took his seat and asked me, very politely, to step to one side and wait a minute more.

I felt a twinge of guilt. I was deceiving this man and I had never done that before in order to cross any border. I also knew that I could stay in London if I claimed political asylum there and then. I would not need to show my money, I would not need Jason. I was still the Daughter, after all.

But I remained silent about that. I wanted to live with Jason, to hear him say *Is this all right?* again and again, not to destroy my parents. If you had to have a runaway child, an absconding romantic fool was less harmful than a political fool. And staying in London was not the point. I was abandoning everything for Jason – family, country, a privileged existence. I didn't want London without him. At Heathrow, and in more ways than one, I was finding out what being at someone's mercy meant.

The minutes were beginning to feel too long. Faces behind me came and went as I stared into that mirror. Now I wish he had saved me from myself, just as Father had always done, and put me on the same plane back, that immigration officer, that turbaned man with a beard kept tidy by a black net, looking like an ancient stalwart of the Raj. He was striking, the Sikh, much more handsome than his bland English co-nationals to his left and right. I had a momentary premonition that this story would not end well: not there, not then, but much later. I brushed the thought aside, rationalising it as a consequence of the abrupt way I had uprooted myself.

Finally, a besuited English official with the stocky features of a Vyacheslav Molotov emerged from behind the mirror, carrying my passport. He looked at me, then at my photograph, before asking me if I would mind waiting for another moment, oh so politely, while some minor routine checks were made; nothing to worry about, nothing at all, he said, then disappeared again. It seemed a pointless routine, designed to unnerve me. For the first time in my life I couldn't afford to mind.

I watched the comrades from the plane showing their passports and going through, each one turning to take a good look at me as they moved on towards baggage reclaim. I was in Britain and yet I was not. I saw people clustering outside, waiting for arrivals.

I never found out what was behind that final delay. Molotov came back, a tight little smile on his face, my passport in his hand, just as a Japanese tourist walked by, clutching a ridiculous holdall labelled 'Providence' in large red letters. Destiny's coin landed.

'Welcome to the United Kingdom,' Stalin's Foreign Minister said and handed me my document.

'Have a pleasant stay,' the Sikh officer echoed, as if relieved by the outcome.

Leave to enter for six months. Employment prohibited. I had only asked for eight days.

Jason waited in a gaggle of chauffeurs, taller than any of them, his hair as tousled as I remembered it. A Norse god, I had thought the first time I saw him that snowy spring, when our roles were reversed: he arriving, I waiting. A Norse god, I thought again. Then he beamed and raised a sheet of paper to his chin, my name on it in large letters, as though there was ever any danger that I would not recognise him. His fears might have been more similar to mine than I thought possible, or his sense of humour more childish; but the fact that he could announce my arrival so publicly, even for the few seconds it took to raise the sheet and then lower it as I approached, spoke of our different worlds.

I observed a look of horror on Jason's face as I walked straight past him without giving him so much as a nod of recognition. I didn't expect anyone from the embassy. My parents had, however reluctantly on my mother's part, accepted my argument that the point of travelling to London was to be allowed to explore it alone. The iconic black cabs and red double-decker buses were part of the experience, I insisted, until they promised to let me make my own way around. I knew that Father wouldn't risk breaking his word – and that he realised excessive control would be counterproductive as well as ultimately ineffectual – but I couldn't trust Mother not to go behind his back and ask for a discreet watch to be kept.

I followed the signs for the airbus to central London, without daring to check if Jason was following me. I could hear the sound of footsteps behind me as I approached the bus and I turned just enough to see the Norse god's hideously familiar pair of derbies on the tarmac. It was not until I saw that, driver aside, there was only a small gaggle of conspicuously Western backpackers and no one else near the bus that I turned properly and saw Jason's face right behind and above me, flushed, smiling conspiratorially. 'Welcome to Thatcher's and Reagan's Free World! Farewell to state capitalism!' he whispered finally. He squeezed me against his body, pressing my backpack against a handrail and pushing my face into the grids of that familiar Aran jumper with its smell of lanolin and a summer spent with mothballs.

Free World: he had no idea.

We sat on the top deck above the driver, holding hands all the way from the airport, retracing the path I had just surveyed from the air – two hours of London, only now west to east. The bus was much slower than the Tube but we had all the time in the world.

The upper deck was empty, except for the two of us. My backpack sat on the left, in the front seat next to us, like a fellow sightseer. Christmas lights blinked in the drizzle, becoming more and more assertive as we moved into the city. Sad daisy chains of bulbs zigzagging above suburban roads lined with curry houses and petrol stations gave way to elaborate electric snowflakes and finally to an explosion of illuminations, fireworks frozen in mid-air.

The legroom was inadequate and the bench seats narrow, but Jason had folded himself next to me with a routine movement, knees below his chin, his body filling the space between me and the aisle as if to prevent me from running away. During occasional gridlocks we alternated between kisses and conversation.

'Now, my darling, you must tell me all. No one is listening but me,' he said. He knew that I always played to an invisible audience and I didn't believe him even now. There was a convex mirror in the corner above the window, which projected our image downwards, through a periscope device. If I peeked into it, I could see the top of the driver's head.

I opened my mouth several times, but the joy of Jason's presence, the wonder of the strange new city, the sense that I had escaped minders, perhaps for the first time in my life, and something like jetlag – although the time difference was far from enough to justify the feeling – made it impossible to start. As always, I clammed up. The more words I felt inside me, the fewer I could utter, and besides, using English as a language of intimacy – as opposed to discussing maize-growing techniques – was still unfamiliar territory.

There was too much to say to make speaking easy, and any conversation we started was stilted and awkward, overshadowed by an overwhelming physical longing made more acute by our sudden closeness.

Jason saw that I was struggling. He put his finger on my mouth, as he did that day in my father's walk-in wardrobe.

'I am sorry. I mustn't exhaust you. I am sure we'll have so much to share. You'll tell me all in your own good time,' he said.

Along Oxford Street I surrendered to an exhausted kind of elation as the bus slowed to a crawl. I had been on too many shopping trips in places like Vienna and Milan to be impressed by another row of department stores, but I had never before seen such waves of people of all races, surging ahead in their thousands, storming shop entrances as though they were the Winter Palace. I kept opening my mouth to say something, a silly goldfish behind the front window on the top deck of a bus.

'Disgusting, all of this,' Jason broke the silence. 'I hate Christmas.'

He smuggled me into his hall of residence. I had never stepped inside a student hall before – why would I? Back home, they were for poor kids from the provinces. Here it was single-sex, rooms smaller than ships' cabins, beds the size of a coffin, communal showers, communal lavatories: it was, quite possibly, more spartan than the halls at home.

Jason was keeping up a pretence of working on a PhD because he needed his British Academy grant to carry on writing poetry, just as he might soon have to create the pretence of a job in order to demonstrate that he was able to support me, he said. I realised that he had already studied the letter of the law, thought about our wedding, and that seemed more important than the fact that he had used the word 'pretence', twice.

'But only for a while,' he added. He was sure I would find employment as soon as my papers were sorted out, he explained, and that I would be better than him at maintaining a full-time job.

'You have the experience, and better qualifications,' he said. 'I don't think I could do the nine-to-five and keep writing. I am no Eliot.'

I nodded, only half-listening. It seemed too early for this kind of conversation, too soon for technicalities. I sat on the bed and looked around me. Jason's room had posters of Yeats, Beckett, Joyce and Che Guevara pinned to the walls, like a teenager's den. No Eliot: the suit might have broadcast the wrong aspirations, I guess. The enormity of the move I had made was somehow brought home by the smallness of the room.

'All these Irishmen, Jason,' I said. I loved him and I was determined not to be afraid.

He chuckled, as though he had only just realised. He pressed a finger against my lips again. I bit it, hard.

He fancied himself Irish, I knew that from before. One quarter, on his father's side, like practically half of England, as I was to find out. On that first day in London his Irishness seemed exotic, more exotic even than being English, and not something you adopt and wear like an Aran jumper. I smirked at Che, wondering if Jason knew that Che was part-Irish too.

The halls backed onto the garden of Virginia Woolf's former home. I would have imagined a snob like her living somewhere more obviously grand. I was not yet adept at reading London.

'The heart of Bloomsbury,' I said, nodding towards a wintry little patio with a naked tree. A couple of empty bird feeders dangled from its branches like last year's Christmas baubles.

'Bloomsbury,' Jason sighed as he began to undress me, as though bored even with the sound of the word. 'That bloody woman lived everywhere. Blue plaques like a pox all over the town and beyond.'

We made love for two further London hours before I bothered to start unpacking, before the night fell, before I realised that I had consumed my in-flight mushroom stroganoff somewhere over Austria nine hours earlier, that I was ravenous. Jason was talking about a Hare Krishna Vegan Curry House. It sounded no better than the Communist mushrooms.

His skin was milky in the moonlight, tinged copper in daytime, fitting for a Celt. That first night, after our Krishna dhal, I tried to kiss every freckle, like a mad astronomer mapping a new portion of the sky. I could not know yet that London would be a city of sorrows for me. I think of that moment now and all I see is centuries of sadness rising to meet my lips.

Chapter Twelve

The London Halls

Late the following morning I left Jason in his room, naked, dishevelled and bent over a small desk under the window, like Bartleby the Scrivener, his seemingly permanent erection obscured from view by pages of scribbled verse. I ran a hand down his back, his keyboard of ribs and vertebrae, planted a kiss on his shoulder and buttoned up my coat. I knew from the night before how wrong that garment was for the London winter, its cloth simultaneously too heavy for the mild temperatures and too porous to protect against the wind and the rain. I'd come from a place where winters could be so harsh it was not unusual to see people whose fingers or earlobes had succumbed to frostbite, yet winter days were often brilliantly, if treacherously, sunny. That first morning in London was dark and damp. I couldn't tell if it was actually raining, but I could see that everything was wet.

I was venturing out on my own for the first time. Jason had no telephone in his room and the public line on the ground floor was for emergency calls only. Even if it hadn't been so designated, I would hardly have wanted to speak to my parents from it. I didn't want anyone to hear the conversation I was about to have. By 'anyone' I meant casual eavesdroppers, for it was not in my power to prevent the secret policeman on duty back home. I was, at that stage, not yet alert to the possibility that there might be two of them, a spying duo; that calls between my country and the UK were sufficiently rare for them to be monitored routinely at both ends.

The corridors were empty except for one or two Arab and Asian men who skulked forlornly between rooms with tubs of hot food. The porter was in his cubbyhole, reading a copy of the *Sun*. Displays of Christmas cards on the cork boards next to fire notices and cleaning rotas, and a floppy Father Christmas hat on the man's head, signalled imminent holidays. I dashed past before he could wonder about a woman's presence in the men's halls. He didn't so much as raise his eyes from his newspaper, perhaps deliberately, tolerating a girl for the sake of festive cheer, like a bottle of warm ale smuggled inside under a student overcoat.

I wondered if my face carried, like Jason's, the unmistakable glaze of a sleepless night of lovemaking on a narrow bed. I was not a poetic type, but I understood Jason's impulse to pour himself out on paper this morning. My body still felt so absorbed in the music of our shared movement that it was unnatural to stand upright, unnatural to walk.

'With this body I thee wed,' I had said some hours earlier as the faint first light broke through the ill-matched curtains of Jason's room. I was trying to remember the words of the English marriage vows from films and books. I was holding him tight, gripped by the realisation that those words were not metaphors, but actual – physical – truths. I had given up all I had, crossed the continent, to be with this man. There was no going back, but that seemed fine.

'You got that wrong, my love,' Jason said. 'It's "with my body I thee worship". And I do. I so do. Let me prove it to you one more time.'

Outside, it was drizzling in the half-hearted daylight. The square before me could have appeared in an ancient black-and-white photograph, except for a child's red glove perched on top of the railings, waving hello. Later I would learn that scarves around lamp posts and toys on top of postboxes did not represent strange signals, that the English were kind in that particular way, giving lost objects a better chance to be reunited with their owners.

Somewhere to the right, a few squares below ours, was the British Museum and, close to it, that unused room in the trade-union hall. I instinctively turned away from it, as though there was a danger that a doorman might recognise me as a missing guest, passing in the street. Only a block or two further east from Jason's hall the area became much grimmer, and I knew, from the sandwich bars, the forlorn little shops selling souvenirs and maps, the cheap hotels and the heavily laden groups of pedestrians, that I must be close to an unseen railway station.

I walked for five or ten minutes, trying to memorise landmarks for my route back, instinctively wanting even more privacy than was offered by calling from the phone box nearest to the halls. I found one several streets away, tucked in the corner of yet another waterlogged square, in that iconic shape I had known from photographs since I was a child, its Communist red asking for a golden hammer and sickle on its domed roof. Inside, it was clammy and smelled of urine and wet newspapers. Around the phone itself there were dozens of cards offering a menu of love in variants of broken English: a whole United Nations of prostitutes.

I inserted a dozen unfamiliar coins into the slot and stacked several dozen more into four teetering pillars on top of the machine. Jason had warned me this would be an expensive call and had delved into his small change for me. I dialled the long number. It took a while going through, a sequence of clicks and ticks, and finally the distinctive burr of rings, which now sounded distant and unreal. Someone picked up the phone. The moment the connection was established I heard my coins fall into the belly of the machine. I fed it one more pillar.

I heard Dara's hello, her voice as deep as a man's, and – the moment I inhaled to respond – my mother's yelp from elsewhere in the house.

'Where are you?' she screamed from the other end of Europe. I heard Dara replace her receiver.

'I love London, Mummy. It is so beautiful – so, so beautiful,' I lied, looking out of the kiosk and into a sad little curry house with blood-coloured velvet wallpaper and yellow wall lights. But for a four-armed bronze goddess in the window, the decor would have fitted any of the restaurants back home. I felt a pang in the pit of my stomach.

'Oh, Mimi, I am so relieved to hear you, but where are you, darling?' Mother repeated her question, now sounding even more agitated. 'We rang your hotel last night and they told us you hadn't even checked in. The airline reported that you had disembarked on time. We were foolish not to insist on a car at Heathrow. Never again. We called Lekovich. He did not know where to start. Incompetent fool! I told him that hotels must have registers of foreign guests. How many hotels could there be in London? Even if it's a couple of thousand, so what? Just start dialling, I told the old dunce.'

I tried to interrupt her several times, without success, all the while deciding what to say. I had called planning to pretend that I was where I was supposed to be, in my bloody sky room, planning to rhapsodise about sightseeing. They were even faster and more anxious than I thought they would be, and I had thought they would be both.

'I'm staying with a friend, Mummy. No reason to worry.'

'Friend. What friend?' she gasped. 'You have no friends in London.'

I could hear anxiety draining out of her voice, to be overtaken by realisation, then barely suppressed hatred, which she quickly replaced by something like a fake emollience. It was an impressive performance, being able to squeeze such a range of emotion into nine words. My mother the diva. Another sequence of coins dropped.

'I do have a friend,' I said, unnecessarily now. I inhaled as deeply as I could. 'I am not coming back, Mother. Please don't send Lekovich after me. It will change nothing. I am very …'

I was about to say 'sorry', but I heard the thud of something heavy falling at the other end, then the lighter sound of the receiver bouncing off a surface, a whoosh of fabric dragging and ripping, then silence, followed by two sets of different electronic pips, and finally the clatter of my last three or four coins being returned to me.

She had fainted, I thought. Mother had fainted. I stood in the phone box for a minute or so. I surprised myself by emitting a series of little sobs into the vacuum. The scene – her collapse, my tears – felt fraudulent and operatic, yet there was something deeper and real enough behind it, as though the false note was simply the matter of us not knowing how to stage the exchange. If this is what I really wanted, I thought – this man and this city – why does it hurt so? Then I remembered the night before and the doubt vanished. I didn't know anyone in London, just Jason, but Jason was enough. He would be my home, I thought.

When I returned to the halls, Jason was fully dressed. He ate an apple as he spoke, somehow managing to produce decibels of noise with his crunching.

'Your people,' he said, 'did you tell them? How did they take it?'

I could see that he was anxious, but I also knew he could not imagine the depths of the drama that we had unleashed. My mother. My father. His state. The vice-like grip that families in my homeland were accustomed to exert on their children.

'Not well,' I said. 'Let's leave London today. This after-noon. There'll be enough time for sightseeing later.'

We had planned a day in the museums. His parents weren't expecting him until Christmas Eve. I wasn't sure they knew about me, but I did know that if, with the cold-ness for which the English were notorious, they objected to an extra guest, we had enough money for some country hotel. It was irrational, my wish to get away immediately. I assumed – hoped – that Lekovich couldn't kidnap me, although the deeds of our security services abroad were the subject of some pretty ripe rumours, but I regretted telling Mother who I was with. There were a thousand lies more opportune than the truth.

Chapter Thirteen

Out of London – A Journey to the Heart of Darkness

An hour and a bit out of London we changed trains. The connecting service that chugged into the station was straight out of my mother's beloved *Brief Encounter*, each set of seats with its own door opening onto the platform. No one got off, and only two of us got on. Jason commented that you stepped back ten years in time with each fifty miles' distance from London.

I loved everything about the branch line: the smell of wood and dusty fabric, the alternation between gusts of hot air from the heating and cold draughts from windows ajar further along the carriage, the overhead luggage racks, the dismal black and white images of places to visit so like the travel pictures back home.

Outside, the dark fields stretched wetly like kelp towards an invisible sea, with a weak lunar sheen intermittently reflecting winter water lying on the grass. It was the shortest day of the year, mid-afternoon, and already you could discern only the pale blots of sheep and occasional sets of lit windows in the distance. A file of request halts went by without so much as a ticket kiosk on the platform. People stepped off the train, slammed the doors behind them and walked off into the darkness. I could love this England and its short December days unfolding in the midst of nothingness, I thought.

We got off an hour and some thirty miles later.

'The 1920s?' I asked Jason.

'The 1860s in fact,' he said. 'Venetian Gothic, like all the proper stations on this line. Small but perfectly formed, like you. Look at those arches.'

He had forgotten his own joke about time travel. He thought I was asking about railway architecture.

The building, a survivor from grander times, was unmanned. We went around it, past a row of cycle racks. Waiting for us in the forecourt beside a car was a replica of Jason: some forty years older, several centimetres taller and with a mane of hair that was white rather than blond, as if to emphasise the fact that his wrinkled face had been beaten to cerise by the weather. He was wearing an identical Aran jumper, but with a circular moth hole on the chest, like a bullet wound through the heart. An odd oilcloth cape and a pair of muddy gumboots protected him from the drizzle. I could smell sheep on him from a couple of metres away. Two dogs, a golden Labrador and a very fat toffee-and-white spaniel, stood guard next to him, their tails wagging to a different beat.

'Hey, boy, over here,' the man shouted, waving to draw attention to himself as though he wasn't the only person waiting and the two of us weren't the only arrivals. The Labrador ran to greet us. Jason landed a wet kiss on its muzzle in a way that was both endearing and disgusting.

'Hello, Charlie,' he greeted the spaniel that circled around us more reluctantly, like a shy toddler.

I'd heard about the English and their dogs, that they were a kind of substitute for the closer family relationships we were used to. Like people, dogs could be warm and tactile. They were even furrier. Unlike people, they could be owned. Back home, if people kept dogs at all, they lived, unkissed, in courtyards, tethered on chains, snarling at passers-by.

'How are you, Pater?' Jason finally gave his father a mock punch to the bullet hole. Father as friendly competitor, a sort of big brother: another cultural twist. I tried, unsuccessfully, to imagine doing that to Stanislav.

It was only then that they both turned to me. The older man waited. I saw Jason deciding on the best way to introduce me. He had phoned from Charing Cross to let his parents know he was coming early but, as I had suspected, he had failed to mention he was bringing a guest.

'And who might you be?' the older man said to end the silence, he too trying to work things out. His tone was friendly. He was amused rather than worried by my unexpected presence.

'Milena Urbanska,' I said and offered my hand. 'It would be Urbansky in English, but the feminine version has an "a" in my native tongue.'

He repeated, managing Milena just right, mangling the surname. I should have spared him a lesson in grammar.

'Paddy Connor,' he said.

'How do you do, Mr Connor?'

'Father's actually called Aeson. Would you believe that, Millie? Have you ever met an Aeson before?' Jason butted in, laughing, although I didn't understand the joke, if there was one.

'Ee-son, you said?' I asked, trying to take in the array of names. I assumed it was some odd Irish variant, a Celtic twin of Jason, like Alistair and Alexander, and waited for him to offer a spelling that had next to nothing in common with the way the word was pronounced: Aoiseoinn, or some such. I was already keeping abreast with this family's decorative Irishness, I thought, pleased with myself. I felt better about bothering him with those pesky suffixes.

'A-e-son,' Paddy spelled out the diphthong. 'And I know. I am afraid Jason's grandfather was a classicist. Had a thing about the Golden Fleece. And I got off much more lightly than my brothers. But everyone has called me Paddy since school, and so must you, my dear. No Mr Connors here.'

He moved several pairs of muddy boots and an empty cat basket to one side, shoved our bags into the boot and then opened the doors of his mud-spattered car. The Labrador jumped in the front. Jason lifted Charlie onto his lap in the back. The inside of the car was uniformly dirty. The smell of drying mud and wet dog hit you first, then cat and sheep, like the developing bouquet of some complex wine. Unidentifiable matter crunched under my feet and every surface seemed to be growing hairs. I removed a big plastic bone from under my bottom.

'Shall we take a detour to show your friend our famous Christmas lights, Jay?' the older man said.

He drove through a medieval gate and up a cobbled street without waiting for an answer, then slowed down. Several multicoloured light bulbs dangled above us on a rope suspended between a pub and a tea shop. He slowed down further.

'Ah, OK, you spoilt metropolitans. No reaction, I see. I should have guessed.' He turned towards us, driving on. Charlie wagged his tail.

'Lovely,' I murmured belatedly, when I realised that we had just seen the lights. The rest of the little town seemed abandoned. We zigzagged through a labyrinth of narrow alleyways, then back through another medieval gate and alongside the same railway tracks, out into the open countryside.

'Milena is not a Londoner, Pater. She is my fiancée,' Jason said, as though the former excluded the latter. I was stunned by the suddenness of his declaration.

Paddy Connor looked at me in the rear-view mirror. His car clipped a hedge and he corrected the steering, still looking at me. No one said anything for another two or three minutes. The dog smell increased as their coats dried.

I turned my gaze past Paddy's shoulder and at the dimly lit dials on the dashboard, glowing in the dark as though we were in the cockpit during some night flight. The red petrol one was perilously low.

I realised, accustomed as I was to cars being rare and cherished possessions, that this one was newer and more expensive than I thought. It was battered by misuse and neglect rather than age.

'No, I am most certainly not,' I said, resuming the conversation.

'Not a Londoner or not a fiancée?' Paddy asked, then laughed. I could tell that he was laughing with relief, and wondered why exactly.

'Neither,' I said. 'Your son will need to propose first and then we will see about the engagement bit.'

Jason hit his head against the back of his father's seat as if in exasperation. The Labrador gave a little bark.

The inside of the car got gradually warmer and the windows misted. Paddy said it was about fifty outside, which was either meaningless or absurd. I guessed it was around eight degrees. This chilliness, accompanied by dampness, was becoming familiar. I had been in the country for two days, but I was already thinking of eight as 'the English temperature'.

Finally Paddy turned up a gravel path, without indicating, and, after another hundred of those English yards that Jason kept mentioning, stopped in front of a long, primitive farmhouse, its roof covered in reeds. Several more dogs barked from somewhere inside when we got out of the car.

Jason's mother was almost as tall and as white-haired as her husband, and as thin as Jason. She took my presence so matter-of-factly that I wondered how many previous girlfriends had arrived unannounced in the same way.

'Jay, would you take your guest's luggage to the yellow bedroom? Let me take your coat, my dear. Paddy, would you please fetch a good bottle from the cellar before you go in? The cellar door is jammed again. There's a good boy.'

She said it all in the manner of an army officer, this last while bending down to pat the fat spaniel, and all the while facing me, smiling, lips only. She wore a long tartan skirt, then several layers of woollen clothing topped by a bright-red sleeveless ski jacket, all covered in animal hairs. Her own hair was gathered in an anarchic bun, created as if to expose elaborate diamond drops in her ears. She looked like no woman in my country, where her equivalents sought to embalm their features while pigmenting their hair into auburn helmets. In my mother's world, no woman left her hair untinted before at least her ninth decade, and most not even then. Jason's mother could have been seventeen and seventy at the same time, but, given Jason's age, she was probably in her fifties.

'I am Clarissa. Jay's mother,' she said as a belated afterthought. 'But you've probably guessed that already.'

Chapter Fourteen

Un Repas Anglais

I followed Clarissa inside and she flung my coat onto a staircase just to the left of the entrance. It was as narrow and as steep as a stepladder. Next to it stood an ancient chest freezer covered in dog leashes and mail-order catalogues and, further along the wall, a huge framed black-and-white photograph of several moustachioed men in suits and hats grouped around an ancient mosaic, looking like a conference of carpet-sellers. On the floor under the photo stood a disorderly line of wellington boots with dirty woollen socks tucked inside and, in front of the line, a cast-iron boot jack shaped like a horned beetle and caked in dirt, like a commanding officer leading a dissolute army into some muddy battle.

Clarissa waited for me to take in the photograph – the mosaic represented two deer with interlocking antlers – but made no effort to explain it. She then guided me, through more canine paraphernalia, into the kitchen. The ceiling was low enough to touch by barely raising a hand, and far too low for my hosts. An enormous farm table occupied most of the floor space. It was already set for three.

A couple of cats jumped off the top of a cooking range, which was as out of scale with the room as the table. I had

crossed Europe in order to find myself in a Bruegel painting, I thought. Even the modern household devices – the
range, the fridge, the radio – looked lumpy and old, as
though they were designed in the sixteenth century.

'Would you like to powder your nose before dinner,
dear?' Clarissa asked.

'Milena,' I said. 'Milena Urbanska. Jason calls me Millie, if that's easier.' I had forgotten to introduce myself
properly, and I skipped the gender bit this time. 'And no,
thank you,' I added. I was powderless and it seemed a
strange thing to expect me to do.

'Ah well, then perhaps you'd like to sit here,' she pointed
to the chair on the right, while setting up a fourth place
on the other side of the table. 'I am sorry to hurry everyone so. It would've been nice to have a glass of sherry or a
stiff G&T first, but everything has been sitting in the Aga
for ages, and we don't usually eat this late. And Jason has
sprung quite a little surprise on us. I don't mean you,
Milena, my dear – I mean coming today. We had expected
him on Christmas Eve.'

She gave an uncomfortable laugh. The way she pronounced my name was spot on.

'I am so sorry,' I said. 'It's entirely my fault, Mrs Connor. I was keen to get out of London. And I don't drink
sherry or gin and tonic.' I felt proud that I had recognised
what she meant by a G&T, but realised that Jason's people
were not used to speaking to foreigners. 'A glass of water
would be lovely,' I added, taking extra care to pronounce
my words clearly.

'Oh, please don't worry, my dear. I quite understand
your wish to leave Satanopolis. So dirty, so crowded, particularly at Christmas time,' Clarissa said, without
providing water. 'There's plenty of room in the house and

enough food for twenty. It's the Connor men I worry about, you'll soon learn. I am sure Paddy took you on a tour of the Christmas lights too. But I knew better than to plan soufflés for dinner.'

'Oh, yummy. Clarissa makes the best cheese soufflé in the county.' Paddy stepped into the room with a dusty bottle. The label seemed to have been nibbled at by rodents. 'Only Pauillac, I am afraid,' he said. 'We've had the last of the Pomerol.'

I played with a linen napkin bearing the motif of what looked like a polo player, and listened to Jason stomping around the house above our heads. Appellations meant nothing.

'Dinner, Jay,' Clarissa shouted a couple of times.

Jason's mother and father were completely different from what I expected. Everything in the house was different from what I expected, yet somehow it also explained Jason to me. Compared to his parents, he was an image of tidiness and organisation.

My water never materialised. The wine was some of the best I'd ever tasted, but the food was disgusting. Clarissa produced a series of atrocities from her multiple ovens: a greasy, glistening dumpling, which burst to release a brown concoction with the urine-tinged smell of kidneys; a pile of sulphurous miniature green cabbages; and roast potatoes, which looked as though she had chopped them with an axe, and which were watery on the inside. I was ravenous and yet I had to make an effort to eat in order not to offend my hosts, shunting non-vegetable matter around my plate. Only the carrots, if one forgave occasional spots of unwashed-away mud, were delicious. I didn't know how to ask for more carrots without getting seconds of everything else.

Paddy and Clarissa stared at me as they ate, and described everything my fork touched with the care of silver-service waiters. My English was expanding – 'Brussels' sprouts (a Belgian delicacy of which I had never heard?), and steak-and-kidney pudding with suet, which was apparently some heavy-duty British building material also used for culinary purposes – although I fervently hoped I wasn't going to need these terms ever again. Later I was to realise that true mastery of English involved knowing the several very different meanings of 'pudding'. For now, I thought, if this was what pudding meant, then I'd better forget that word too.

'Could I have some more carrots, please? And a small glass of water,' I burst out finally.

All three laughed, but only Jason hit his forehead with some force.

'Oh, Ma – God! My God, Ma. Millie is vegetarian. I forgot to say.'

His parents looked at me in horror. Clarissa hastily pulled the morass of steak-and-kidney pudding away from me and gave me a clean plate, then piled a dozen roasted carrots onto it. I said no to more sprouts. She explained that the potatoes were roasted in goose fat.

I was saved.

'Why didn't you …' she started, not knowing how to finish the question politely, and looked pointedly at Jason, no doubt knowing that amid his exuberance, consideration for others always evaporated. She seemed dismayed, yet also very amused. I could see that this would become their Christmas anecdote for years to come. She lowered my old plate on the floor, feeding my meaty pudding to the dogs. The portly spaniel got most of it.

'I am used to not making a fuss about vegetarianism in my country – just making do with what is on offer. I did not want to be difficult.'

After dinner, Clarissa declared that she was taking the dogs out, while Paddy did the dishes and Jason dried and I alternately sipped water and wine, all my offers of help refused. I had never done any washing up before but I was sure that the way Paddy was dipping our plates into a pool of grey water, then handing them to his son to dry without rinsing them, would have appalled Dara.

Then Jason and I retired to what he called the library, to roast chestnuts and finish the wine, he said. The long room contained thousands of volumes. Between the shelves there were mottled prints of cathedrals and several canvases of horses. I was in no mood to view the artwork, although Jason offered a guided tour. Beyond the small semicircle of worn seats and pouffes by the fireplace, the room was freezing and smelled of mildew. We sat on the floor while he fed the fire and I held the roasting pan above the flames.

'Isn't this lovely?' he asked. The side of his face closer to the fire was red. He seemed as impervious to cold as I remembered back in March. I managed to feel too hot and too cold at the same time. Back home, people sweltered uncomplaining through our ferocious summers, with fans (and certainly air conditioning) all but unknown in their suffocating, low-ceilinged flats. Now I was learning how the sitting rooms of rural England were designed to turn their inmates into baked Alaskas.

About nine-thirty Clarissa reappeared carrying two hot-water bottles, trailed by four wet and dirty dogs. In addition to the animals I had already met, there was a chocolate dachshund and a plump brindle-coated dog, which looked as though its legs had been bound at birth to create four-centimetre stumps. I had never seen its ugly like before. The size of its muzzle was out of proportion with its body, like an adult male face on a baby. It waddled behind Clarissa like a fat duck.

Clarissa bent down to kiss Jason on the top of his head, handed one of the hot-water bottles to me and wished us goodnight. The four dogs seemed determined to follow her to bed, like a canine posse following their Pied Piper.

'Neville's a corgi,' Jason said. 'The appeaser among the pack; we have to prick his royal pretensions sometimes.' Or at least that's what I thought he said. Too many carrots, too much wine, too little water: I was feeling drunk.

I found out soon enough why I needed that hot-water bottle. My bedroom was in an otherwise uninhabited wing of the house. It contained three ancient electric pillar-heaters, which emitted a pleasant orange glow but no warmth whatsoever. There was no evidence of any alternative heating methods, other than a fireplace that contained a copper pot with a bunch of dusty dried flowers and a peacock feather at its heart. The chimney was surely sucking any surviving fragments of warmth upwards and away from me. The room was so cold that it made the library seem almost pleasant by comparison.

I took a towel from the wooden rack next to one of the two single beds, wrapped it around the hot-water bottle and carried it into the bathroom like a swaddled baby. The only means of heating there, as inefficient as that of the bedroom, was a single electric bar pinned above the door. It bathed the room with an agreeable filament glow, but you had to stand on tiptoe and raise your hand to confirm that it was not just an unusual light.

The bathroom was thickly carpeted and, at first, rather baffling. It did not seem to have a lavatory, until I found it hiding under the lid of one of those French *chaises percées*. The copper bath was magnificent, but it had a couple of pathetic little excuses for a tap. At first, I was not sure how to wash. The water from one of the taps was boiling, the other practically dropped ice cubes. Then I saw a blue rubber contraption hanging on the back of the door and I used it to create a makeshift shower. I kept my ablutions to a minimum. Hygiene was obviously a hurried experience in English houses in winter, and unless one could fill that tub with hot water before suffering the effects of exposure, there was no way of combining washing with comfort.

At least the toothpaste I found was the strongest I've come across. Beetroot-red and thick, it tasted like a concentration of the red stripes from the German brand we used at home, and was impossible to rinse out. I smiled at myself in the mirror, like someone auditioning for a Gothic fantasy.

The narrow bed was a close copy of my father's. I failed to fall asleep for a long while. Although I had expected to share the room with Jason, the solitude was not unwelcome. I dwelled on my confusing encounter with the family. I had been greeted warmly enough by Jason's parents, but where mine would have carried out an interrogation, his exhibited no curiosity about me. We spent more time discussing the difference between puddings and pies than my background or the context of my unexpected visit.

Since they asked no personal questions, I felt I could not pose any in return. Paddy and Clarissa seemed well educated, yet so terribly poor. I had guessed enough from our first encounter in March not to expect Jason to have come from great wealth, but the situation was much worse than I expected. They were unable to afford central heating, duvets, a decent shower. That rubber contraption kept slipping from the taps and I had managed to scald myself. The poorest workers in my homeland had warm homes to go to, even at minus twenty, and here I was freezing at well above zero. Perhaps the fact that the temperature normally stayed at that level meant heating had always been less of an existential need, but right now I understood why people of my parents' type ridiculed notions of high Western living standards – beyond the luxury enjoyed by a small, exploitative elite.

I also wondered what the Connors did for a living. The father seemed old enough to have retired but the mother was too young, yet it was impossible to imagine her commuting anywhere from this place. Marxist theory described alienation through isolation and distance: was this it? I tried not to think how shocked my father and my mother would be if they saw me in a reed-topped farmhouse in the middle of nowhere, hugging a hot-water bottle under several layers of blankets so scratchy that they prickled through the bed linen. I remembered Misha, and I hadn't thought of him in months. He had a foolish belief that everyone in the West was better off than we were, always assuming that the opposite of our fathers' propaganda must be true. What if they were lying only about the life back home, but were spot on about capitalism?

*

In the middle of the night there was a weak knock on the door, then Jason entered the room. He squeezed himself in under the blankets next to me, or rather half on top of me, for the bed didn't allow us to lie side by side. My hot-water bottle emitted a squish. He was wearing just his boxer shorts. His entire body was cold, but his feet were icy, and he was trying to push them between my legs.

I squealed and he covered my mouth.

'Isn't this lovely?' He repeated the question he had asked earlier on, and lifted his hand from my mouth as if to let me speak but then covered it with kisses instead: the same red toothpaste. His eyes shone in the orange glow of the three heaters. He seemed shocked that I'd kept them on – was there some English kamikaze tradition that was eluding me?

He was almost unbearably handsome. I laughed, noise-lessly. We will work, I thought, as his cold hands seized my goosebumped hips. We will both work. We will earn. We won't have to live like this.

I woke up to find him no longer there. The room was as cold as the previous night, but at least now full of sun-shine. From my bed, I could see a flock of sheep moving around a watering trough in the field opposite. I had dreamed I was in some freezing Soviet theatre watching *Swan Lake*. All the ballerinas were wearing sheepskin gilets over their tutus, and the sound of their satin pointe shoes touching the stage was almost as loud as Tchaikov-sky's music. I now understood what must have prompted the dream: the trotting on icy ground, the same muffled beat coming from outside as those feet onstage.

I got up and walked to the window, keeping a blanket wrapped tightly around me. The garden had been lightly touched by frost overnight and it shimmered in the wintry light, proving that eight was just the fixed daytime temperature on this island. It was huge, much bigger than I expected, larger than any private garden I had ever seen, not counting our President's palace grounds. It was divided by hedges and walls of holly into separate chambers, with different patterns of planting in each section. Paddy and Clarissa were both outside, by the conservatory on my right. He was cutting branches of holly, while she gathered them into a basket. She must have sensed herself being watched, for she raised her head, spotted me and waved, her hand in a yellow gardening glove. She pointed towards the other wing of the house, at some sixty degrees from mine, then directed her index finger towards a line of low mullioned windows below the reeds, tilted her head and closed her eyes as if to indicate by sign language that Jason was still asleep, then finally beckoned me down with a gesture of someone sipping a warm drink.

I found an ancient tartan housecoat on the back of the door, threw it over my shoulders and went down into the kitchen. The cats were there, in the same position as the previous night, purring above the hob. Clarissa came in, lowered her basket onto the table and threw the yellow gloves and a pair of secateurs onto the pile of holly. She smelled of lily of the valley: the kind of soapy single-note perfume old women were fond of back home.

'We're going to make some Christmas wreaths later. I waited for Jason to do these,' she said. 'Earl Grey OK? I have two teapots at the ready. Paddy likes strong Indian first thing in the morning.'

'Earl Grey's fine if that's easier,' I said. Although I preferred bergamot in my biscuits and not in my morning cup, I didn't want to be seen as fussy after last night's dinner debacle. 'Honestly, whatever's more convenient.'

Clarissa filled a huge tin kettle with water, shooed the cats away, lifted the lid on one of the hob rings and placed the kettle on the metal surface, then leaned over the Aga and waited for the water to boil. This wasn't going to be fast.

'Did you sleep well?' she asked

'Yes,' I said. 'More than well. Everything is so quiet here.'

'And you were not cold, I hope?'

'No, not at all,' I lied.

'We don't go in for central heating,' she said, 'too expensive, bad for the furniture.'

I didn't know what to say to that. Was the furniture more important than its owners? Or if the heating were cheaper, would it be worth ruining the furniture? If it wasn't bad for the furniture, would its cost still rule it out? The house was so large, and it appeared that normally there were only two of them in it. It seemed strange to indulge only the cats. Most of my compatriots would have slept in the kitchen in the circumstances.

'Do you have central heating in your country?' Clarissa asked. It was the first such question and I had expected many. I wondered what kind of place she was imagining.

'Yes, we do,' I said. 'Our heating works all too well, I believe. Our people keep their windows open even in midwinter.'

'What is it, gas or coal?' she asked. I wondered if she thought this a normal conversation with your son's new girlfriend.

'There are thermal plants that supply the whole city,' I said. 'Early October through to early May. I am afraid I have no idea what they run on. Pipelines from the USSR, I think.'

'Fair enough. Why would you need to know? And what sort of work do you do?' she asked apologetically, as though crossing some invisible boundary.

'I am a translator. English. I work at the State Institute for Maize Research.'

'Oh, how absolutely fascinating,' she said. 'We must tell Paddy about it.'

It was obvious that she could not think of a follow-up question.

'And you?' I asked.

She paused as though no one had thought to ask this before.

'I used to be a schoolteacher,' she said, 'before I had Jay. At a girls' school. I read English at university, as you did, I assume, but I don't think I am as clever as you. Your English is frightfully good.'

'And now?' I asked. I did not thank her for the compliments. I wasn't sure if they were compliments.

It took her a minute to understand my question.

'Oh no, nothing now. Not since I had Jay,' she said. 'Work wasn't the thing for my generation. Young women – women your age – work now. I was happy just to be Jay's mother.'

The phone rang. She apologised and stepped out into the lobby, where I could see an ancient Bakelite contraption resting like a crouching toad, on top of an equally ancient chest next to a pile of post ready for that day's collection.

'Edenholme two-o-three,' Clarissa said, then, after a long pause, 'Yes. I am his mother. I am afraid he is still asleep. But who is this? I see,' she said after another long pause, her voice a touch less sing-song.

She pushed the connecting door fully open with her foot. I saw worry in her face as she pointed at me and then at the receiver, trying to indicate something, then giving up.

'Yes, yes,' she said, 'I understand. Yes, Milena is with us. But I must check if she is actually in the house. I haven't seen her this morning. It is frightfully early to be calling, you know.'

I felt a shiver when I saw her putting the receiver next to the phone and walking towards me.

'It's a man. A foreign man. He says he's your uncle,' she whispered into my ear. 'He wants to speak to you.'

I had no uncle but I had a pretty good idea who this might be.

'Comrade Lekovich,' I said when I picked up the phone, without waiting to hear that it was him. 'To what do I owe this displeasure? And how did you get this number?'

It was already strange to hear myself speak my mother tongue. Clarissa stood in the doorway and listened, glancing anxiously at me. Although I was sure she did not understand a word, the tone was not that of an avuncular conversation.

'A very good morning to you, dear Comrade Milena. It wasn't that hard,' Lekovich said. 'Comrade Gertruda told me that you were staying in London with the poet. I rang his hall of residence.' He pronounced the last three words with audible distaste. 'They said he had left yesterday,' he continued. 'His visa application last spring had not just his home address, but his parents' and his grandparents' names, dates of birth and addresses. We're thorough, as you know. Your hosts are in the phone book.'

'But how can I help you?' I cut in finally. He sounded too pleased with himself.

'Comrade Gertruda wants to speak to you. She wants to know when she can call you. Please don't tell us that she can't, because she will. I offered to call you first only as a courtesy, to agree a mutually convenient time. Not that her own daughter goes out of her way to make anything convenient for anyone.'

The nerve, I thought. Dad will sort you out. Then I remembered that Lekovich was now on Dad's side, and that I wasn't.

'How about two hours from now? Eleven a.m. UK time,' I said and slammed the phone down.

The kettle emitted a long whistle.

Chapter Fifteen

A Foreign Field

'I don't recognise you, Mimi,' Mother whined. 'You are making a huge mistake. That Englishman is not right for you. I've heard about him – not just from Lana Kovalska. And I didn't need to hear anything: it was enough to see his behaviour towards you. He's weak. You need a strong man, a real man – a man like your father – to look after you. Misha was weak too, but we thought you'd grow out of him, and at least here you had all of us to protect you. In England you'll be alone and, far from protecting you, the English will rejoice if you fail, simply because you are one of us.

'That Englishman, you will be looking after him forever, like a child. Or he will let you down, not because he wants to let you down but because he's weak. I don't know which of the two is worse. He's messed your life up already. Don't let him destroy it. Come back.'

'Mother,' I was going to let her finish her speech, but I couldn't take it any more. 'Stop. My mind is made up.'

'But it's not too late to change it. Go back to London, enjoy yourself, spend a couple of nights in a luxury hotel, then take that flight to Cuba exactly as you'd planned, and no one will be any the wiser. Lekovich will fetch you, take you to London in the embassy car and then on to Heathrow, wherever you are. He tells me you are in a village somewhere.'

She uttered the word 'village' with such disgust that I could only emit a half-hearted laugh in response.

'You are laughing at your mother, Mimi. Laughing at your father. He hasn't slept since we knew that you'd absconded. After everything that we've done for you.'

'You mean after you've been controlling me forever.'

'Controlling? Mimi, what are you saying? You've followed your own whims since you knew how to walk. We were only ever involved in picking up the pieces afterwards. Cleaning up your mess. But now you are too far away to be saved by us, silly child. Too far. You must act to save yourself for once.'

She started crying. I could cope with her arguments but not her tears.

'Don't cry, Mummy,' I pleaded. I wanted to promise that I would visit one day soon but that was impossible. If I so much as crossed the border again, they would seize my passport and keep me there. It was not uncommon for defectors to be tried *in absentia*, to get years in prison, sometimes even a death-sentence, although these days it was likely to be commuted. But I didn't need to consider these dreadful scenarios. I was not defecting, I had left the country legally, I was marrying: that was the point.

My plea not to cry had the opposite effect on Mother. She started sobbing so loudly that the lobby I was standing in echoed with the sound.

'Is everything OK?' Jason peered at me from the top of the staircase.

'Is he listening?' Mother must have sensed a change in the atmosphere rather than hearing his whisper. 'I can't believe you let him listen,' she said, her half-sob something she must have learned at the music academy, then changed her tone to steely recitativo. 'You are not my daughter. I curse you both, and a mother's curse—'

'Truda ...' I now heard Father at the other end of the line. Unlike Jason, he had, in fact, been listening all along.

'Mother's curse?' I said. 'What an operatic line, Mother. You are an atheist. Odd that you believe in curses.'

She slammed down the phone. Father remained on the line. I could hear his breathing. We waited, in a stand-off, for each to acknowledge the other's presence.

Finally he spoke, and without preamble.

'You are being silly, Daughter, but young people often are. You have forty-eight hours to change your mind, continue to Cuba and enjoy that holiday, which is already paid for. You'll have had your little excursion and, when you come back, we shall not mention this episode again. Just remember, as you mull over your options in the coming hours, that you'll never find this life, the freedom that you have here with us, anywhere else. England is soaked with the blood and sweat of the millions it enslaved. No one is happy there. No one. Not the poor and not the rich. Even their royal family is miserable. I've met them. Now take a pen and a piece of paper and I'll give you Lekovich's private number.'

I had no desire to argue with him. It was pointless. I pretended to note down the number.

'Goodbye, Milena. I know you'll enjoy Cuba: it's a glorious place, particularly at this time of year. See you in three weeks' time, and suntanned,' Father said, putting the phone down before I could utter my final goodbye. I heard a click, then another a second later, and then the line went dead.

Jason was now standing next to me, my coat and four dog leashes over his arm. He was wearing the same combination of clothes – right down to those stupid black shoes – that I remembered him wearing at the end of the spring festival back in March, but he now also had a well-worn and rather dirty green cotton coat, which seemed to have been rubbed with fat or oil. A stripy beanie hat on his head had ear-flaps and a huge yellow pompom on top, like an item borrowed from a children's TV presenter.

'Time for walkies,' he said. 'Choose your dog, Millie.'

We cut through a coppice behind the house and then climbed up a chalk path rising through the fields. The dogs panted ahead of us. Twenty minutes later we reached the crest of the hill and the landscape opened up for kilometres around. There were villages and church towers and farmhouses strewn like pebbles amid undulating waves of valleys. I saw orchards, an occasional small vineyard and squares of ploughed fields and, although English people might well have disagreed, I found there was something almost atavistically European about the landscape, something erased by collectivisation and the ravages of war from so much of my homeland. Tiny birds dispersed, then gathered into pointillist clouds against the winter sun. An expanse of water sparkled in the distance.

'The sea?' I asked, taken aback. We were closer to it than I had imagined.

'Millie, you promised. I am still waiting.' Jason stopped and turned to me, ignoring my question. 'I told myself that I must wait a day or two, allow you to see that you're beyond their reach, before I ask again. You promised to tell.'

He was a poor guide. I barely knew where we were. I guessed that France was somewhere to the south, London behind our backs, to the north of us.

'Promised to tell what?'

'To tell me about your nine missing months in Hades. What happened after I left in March? Huw told me you'd kept in touch, and that must have been risky for you. Why decide finally to come in December? What changed? Don't misunderstand me – I am happy beyond words. I love the fact that you are here more than anything, but I want to know. If there were any political problems to delay you, then perhaps I also need to know.'

I should have told him about the pregnancy the moment I arrived. On that bus from Heathrow perhaps. The longer I left it, the harder the telling became. I realised that if I didn't speak soon, I would take the secret to my grave. That was easier in some ways, but having secrets meant that I would always face the danger of blackmail, that I would be unfree. I learned that lesson early in life. Too many people knew already, as I had found out by the lake; if that woman knew, surely Lekovich knew. Being in England didn't change anything in that respect.

And I didn't want the two of us to have any secrets from each other anyway. Jason and I would never lie to each other, never pretend. What is the point of a marriage otherwise? The point of love, if not truthfulness?

'C'mon, Millie. We know what I was doing,' he said. 'I told you. Writing and waiting for you to decide to come. Researching Bloomsbury pubs in the evening. Not sure why, but I always knew you would get here eventually. I knew your mind before you did.'

'At the airport, back in March, when I saw you pulled to one side, remember?' I asked.

I was speaking, but still wondering how exactly to phrase this. My accent sounded harder and more foreign in the open air than in the darkness of a shared bed. My Rs were like rock formations.

'I am not sure if that was the border police or customs. They closed the door behind you and I was half-alive until I saw you come out of that room on the other side, into the duty-free. I thought: I'd never see this man again, but at least they let him go home. I was in love with you, I'd known that almost from the beginning, but I now understood that it was perhaps the purest, the least selfish form of love I'd known.'

'Oh, yes,' Jason said. I could see him matching his memory with mine. 'I do remember. They questioned me about exporting local currency. An equivalent of ten pounds, that's all it was apparently, but I was a fool to declare it. They took my money away, produced a receipt, then made a note in my passport, next to my visa, in this hilarious microscopic cursive. For future reference, they said. I could get it back when I was in the country again. You didn't tell me I wasn't supposed to take that money out.'

'I did tell you,' I said. 'I did warn you in the car, a couple of times, to empty your pockets. But you were so obsessed with your mad scheme and you never listened. Anyway, you took that plane and, although I loved you, I thought that love would diminish with your absence, that I would forget you. It didn't, and I didn't. Instead, and soon afterwards, I almost managed to convince myself that I hated you. You were right, I was pregnant.'

His face beamed for a split second and he looked down in the vague direction of my stomach, as though, against reason, something could still be living and developing there, something that had gone unnoticed in the past three days. Then his expression collapsed.

'What happened?' he asked.

'What could have happened?' I asked back.

He understood. He turned on his heel abruptly and started striding away from me. The dogs followed the bouncing pompom. I followed it too. Then he paused and turned to look at me again.

'How could you, Millie? I don't know what to say. I need to think this through.'

'Think what through?' I asked. 'It might be that you have an exaggerated view of abortion. Back home, it is the only available contraceptive method. Would you be angry about the contents of a discarded condom? If not, why didn't you use one? Why aren't you using them now?'

A couple climbing the hill towards us took a sudden turn off the path and into the field.

'If anyone had any reason to feel hurt, it was me ...' I persisted, trailing several paces behind him.

'Yes, it might be that I have an exaggerated view, as you say. But I thought we had no secrets from each other. What's the point otherwise?' He echoed my thoughts.

'I know, and I agree. That is why I am telling you,' I said.

'But only now, when there's sod all I can do. And it's my child too. Surely I—' he broke off.

'A child?' I said. 'How many cells constitute a child? For fuck's sake, Jason. For one single fuck's sake.'

I struggled to keep up and he struggled to escape, downhill acceleration and anger making us both breathless. I understood why he thought me selfish but, in that precise moment, I thought the same of him. There he was, just like my parents, asserting ownership of my body.

Anger gave me sufficient momentum to catch up, even to overtake for a little while, but he strode ahead, faster again.

'Anyway, Jay,' I said, for the first time calling him by the name his parents used, giving up on my efforts to persuade him that I had done the right thing, 'think whatever you like. I bore that pain. At first I was angry with you for inflicting it on me while you took your pleasure without consequences. Then I realised that it was the price of my desire for you. And I paid a further price by giving up everything to come here and offer myself to you. I know I sound pompous. Take me or leave me. Decide. Don't make me wait too long.'

He walked on without turning but I noticed that he was slowing down.

Chapter Sixteen

Moving Home

1985

On New Year's Eve, Jason told Paddy and Clarissa that we were planning to marry as soon as possible. We were toasting the year in after dinner, exchanging a few innocuous little speeches about glorious times ahead, wanting neither to stay up until midnight in a cold house nor to go to our cold beds too early. There was a pause before Paddy said: 'How simply wonderful.' Then an even longer one before Clarissa added: '*Toutes mes félicitations.*'

I misunderstood their delayed reaction as unhappiness, and mistook Clarissa's French for sarcasm. I assumed that she was less than delighted to see her only child marrying a woman from an obscure, far-away Communist country, surely a backward country; that she was hoping we would take our time, give Jason a chance to change his mind. But later that same evening, when I came down to the kitchen to fill my hot-water bottle, she beckoned me closer and whispered, 'Are you sure, darling?'

I was still misunderstanding her gist. I did not know how to respond.

'I do love Jason,' I said.

'I love Jason too,' Clarissa said. 'Everybody loves Jason. He does want to be loved. He's a dear boy, but that's not my point. It's you I worry about. He'll not be able to support you for a very long time, if ever. And I fear he'll prove unreliable, in every possible way. When I married Paddy there was family money. There's precious little now, in spite of everything you see around you.'

'But Jason is talented, a great poet,' I said feebly, while wondering what exactly I was supposed to see around me.

'A poet,' Clarissa said. 'Precisely. I wish he hadn't won that prize: it has only encouraged him. You can't butter bread with poetry in this country, I hope you know that. And it is too early for both of you. You are too young, but Jason is immature, and that's different. He will not grow up until he faces pain and difficulty. Life's too kind to him, but, as his mother, I could hardly wish it otherwise.'

I said nothing more. I assumed, in what I now realise was a frame of mind conditioned by long experience of my own parents' tactics, that she was trying to put me off, that she wanted her son to marry up, to find someone wealthy and from a good English family; that I was falling short. I could never have imagined a mother talking so openly about her son's weaknesses, taking my side. For us the umbilical cord was never truly severed, so it was a form of self-hating that was unimaginable. It must be a ploy to get rid of me, I thought.

The following morning Paddy resumed the conversation over his usual bowl of grainy, salty porridge, supplemented with a large shot of Irish whiskey. I was not eating, just sipping some strong tea from a mug. Jason explained that we were not planning a grand ceremony, that no expense would be involved – merely us and them and a few friends. My parents would not be able to come, I said, without elaborating.

'Sad to hear it,' Paddy said. 'For them, I mean. I expect they are not allowed to travel.'

I was readying myself for further questions but none came. Clarissa was standing, her back to the range, holding one cat against her breast while alternately stroking the other cat and picking up and lowering a mug of tea with the other hand.

'And where are you two lovebirds planning to live after you marry?' Paddy asked, his tone only half-serious, perhaps leaving a way out, should the conversation turn unpleasant. 'It's none of my business, Milena, and I apologise, but I am just checking if Jay knows that banks don't give mortgages on the back of student grants.'

I realised that I was witnessing another reflection of our cultural differences, but could still not quite work out what that difference was. How could a son's accommodation be none of a father's business? Student marriages were common back home. Young couples moved in with one of their sets of parents, indeed often carried on living with them as a matter of course. In fact parents desired that cohabitation more than the couples themselves, competing for the privilege with the rival in-laws. The prize was the companionship of an extended family, and the facilities of a free care home in old age.

I knew enough about the West not to count on any of that when I flew into London but, even so, I was surprised by Paddy and Clarissa's cynicism. Now, I realised, sitting in this low-ceilinged kitchen, at the heart of this uncomfortable old house in the middle of nowhere, that I had assumed things would work out because they had always worked out in the past. Moreover, because I thought they must work out more easily in the West, I had given even less thought to practicalities than Jason. I had studied the map of London, but I knew nothing at all about the English.

You just flew like a goose into fog: my mother's voice came to me, uttering an old saying.

'Pater, I was hoping you would help,' Jason said. 'A small loan to get us started. The moment I get the money from Grandpa's trust, I'll give it back, I promise. There's my grant for one more year, but that's not enough for renting more than a bedsit and we were hoping for a little flat. Millie will find a job as soon as we sort out her documents.'

Clarissa looked at me.

Paddy patted the chest pocket of his jacket as though he was persuaded and was about to pull out a cheque book. He opened his mouth to speak, but Clarissa stepped towards the table and put her mug down with a deliberate loud clink.

Before she said anything, I knew that she was about to refuse her son's request.

'Paddy,' she said. 'We agreed that we would reward our children financially only once they are standing on their own two feet, otherwise they will never learn to look after themselves. I am sure Jay would agree that makes sense. It is in his best interests, marriage plans notwithstanding. And we don't want to have to sell shares just now. It's a very bad moment.'

It seemed odd that she referred to children when they only had one. It was perhaps some agreement reached long ago, before they had Jason – nothing personal. Or, more likely, she wanted to make it sound that way. I sensed that, unlike me and my parents, and especially my father, they were trying to avoid direct confrontation.

'Though we agree that Jason could never find a better wife than you, Milena,' Clarissa said, turning to me. I didn't know whether to take it as a compliment.

'Ah well,' Jason said. 'Never mind. Forget it.'

He put a half-eaten banana on the table opposite the mug and stared at his mother.

'Millie has plenty of money,' he said. It was a surprising, childish thing to say, but the pattern was familiar. I often regressed in the same way when speaking to my parents.

'I am sure she does,' Clarissa said. 'And I cannot stop Milena from spending it unwisely. All I can do is advise her to keep some of it back, for a rainy day.'

Jason gave a long, frustrated sigh, which came out as a whistle.

'Thanks for nothing, Ma and Pa,' he said. 'Good to see a show of trust in me, as usual. I am not sure what I've done to earn it.'

'Precisely nothing,' Clarissa said. 'You are twenty-eight: and what? Four years on the dole after you graduated: writing, you say, and then, when we pressed, you progressed – if that's the word – to three years on Yeats. Four years in a house-share in Brixton, squandering the capital of a reasonable degree. Has he told you, Milena?'

I didn't know what to say. It was clear that the summary was offered for my benefit.

'So, what have you got against Yeats now?' Jason said.

'Yeats is fine. And a PhD is more than fine,' Clarissa said. 'It's just that I don't understand why you are doing it, if you don't want an academic job.'

'One word: grant. You said yourself, when I started, that a grant is better for your CV than the dole.'

'This is silly, Jay,' Clarissa said. 'I am not sure why we're having this conversation again.'

'And do you think Yeats a good idea?' Paddy turned to me. I was so startled by the ridiculousness of the question that a sip of tea went up my nostril.

'She'll have to find out, won't she?' Clarissa responded on my behalf, then turned and looked at the clock above the Aga. 'Is that the time? I'm afraid I can't miss Sue MacGregor.' She took both cats with her, one under each arm, and left the kitchen. I heard her climbing upstairs, then the sound of what she called the wireless.

Jason and I returned to London three days later: three days in which we, all four of us, pretended our announcement had not been made. In the men's case, the jovial façade was so convincing that it was obvious, as they chatted, that there had been a series of similar conflicts in the past. Clarissa kept to herself and her cats and dogs. I wasn't sure whether to be hurt by her refusal of financial help or flattered by her concern for me, wasn't sure which was more deeply felt, so I said nothing. It wasn't difficult to avoid conversation, because she spoke mainly to her animals. I offered a hand when we parted, but she pulled me into a hug.

On 2 January, as we prepared to go back to London, Jason spent several hours on the phone, looking for accommodation while pretending to call his various mates to wish them a happy New Year. These were school friends mostly, he explained: his university and poetry chums were unlikely to deliver the goods. Finally someone came up with an offer of a flat in Minford Gardens, a block away from Shepherd's Bush Green, and that is where we moved on a rainy Sunday, just three weeks after I first arrived in London. It was already feeling like a century.

The bucolic name of the area could have fooled only me, as a London ingénue. The place itself turned out to be a basement that could have been used for fungiculture: dark, low, with grey-beige woodchip wallpaper and grey-beige fitted carpets in each room, including a lavatory so tiny that you had to enter it sideways.

You walked into a dingy, minuscule front garden, really two or three square metres of grubby concrete rather than anything horticultural, then down a flight of stairs and through the front door, straight into a windowless kitchen. Like some absurdist theatre stage, the kitchen had a door on each wall. Apart from the lavatory, there was a strange little shower room, which housed a shelf stuffed with someone's trainers and hiking boots, and a bedroom with a locked fitted wardrobe and the only proper window in the flat. Between them, a vast double bed and a ceiling mirror stretched from wall to wall.

Thus I first got to know Will, the owner, through his priorities in interior decoration. Jason mentioned that he was a banker; his mirror suggested he was another man-child.

We left our luggage in the new flat and went out in search of food. Shepherd's Bush was different from Bloomsbury, more residential, but no less urban. The area had an unkempt air, although the side streets with their family homes looked better cared for. It seemed the opposite of touristy, yet every other house on the main road was a hotel. That sense of transience might have explained the shabbiness. The hotels evoked either the sunnier parts of Europe or the glories of empire, both in name only: the Hellenic Hotel, the Acropolis and the Adriatic lined the main road, alongside the Imperial, the Victoria and the Raj. This was not multiply-starred accommodation; one could only speculate about the kind of people who stayed there.

Dozens of cafés on the main street offered a full English breakfast for next to nothing and this morning meal seemed to be served all day, but almost everywhere was shut – my introduction to the English Sabbath. To Jason's delight, their names displayed the same sense of irony as the hotels: we went past a Ritz, an Astoria and a Savoy. From afar, a fish-and-chip shop opposite a small area of green looked gleamingly white in its strong lighting, like a UFO landed on the rainy grass, but the glare made the food displayed inside look extraterrestrial too: green-and-white things floated in jars – were these some English sci-fi variant on the pickles of home? – and pink sausages rested behind glass, in lurid yellow blankets.

We settled for takeaways from a late-night kebab shop opposite Hammersmith Broadway: Jason for a foul-smelling wrap of shredded meat and cabbage, and I for a cone of deliciously crunchy falafels, which he recommended as the vegetarian option. The orange juice was freshly pressed. I remembered Mother quizzing Dara about the provenance of oranges, so I asked the seller the same question in jest.

'Sunny Anatolia,' the server said and, when I said that I didn't believe him, 'Are you Turkish? You look Turkish.'

Back in our new home, Jason put some music on as we sat down to dine. He told me that his fellow-countrymen called the day Epiphany.

On my first morning – our first Monday – in the flat, I woke up feeling a pair of eyes on me. Jason was fast asleep under a mushroom-coloured duvet. I looked into the ceiling mirror to see a reflection of the two of us, the window at our head and, within it, a fat calico cat staring at us upside down. The angle was so disorienting that I had to sit up and turn my head to see the cat's face through the window grilles and, behind the cat, a walled courtyard dripping with rain, and the bottom sections of six rubbish bins.

I had never experienced poverty before, and this seemed like considerably greater poverty than that of Jason's parents, but I was happy. That we had the place at such short notice and free of charge until the end of February, when its owner was returning from Val d'Isère, seemed joy enough – a sign. Will had his two months off only because he was changing jobs, Jason explained. He'd normally be lucky to get an unbroken fortnight. And his working day was anything between twelve and sixteen hours.

That helped to elucidate why the place looked like a locker room, I thought. Its owner only ever visited at night. It was quite unlike any job back home. It seemed a sad way to live.

'The City devours its children with as much appetite as the revolution has for her own. So many of my school and university friends went there. It's the career of the moment. The pay is so good that it becomes addictive. And so, although you may come to loathe the work, they own you,' Jason said, reading my mind. 'You wouldn't catch me going there.'

Lekovich rang the doorbell ten minutes after Jason had left for the British Library for the first time since the New Year. I was still finishing breakfast, while enjoying the novelty of English radio. There was far too much talk on every station, and a democracy of grumbling – everyone seemed to complain about everything – but that was good for my vocabulary. I didn't recognise the bell immediately: it sounded rarely enough.

My father's comrade must have sat outside in his embassy car, awaiting Jason's departure. I opened the door expecting the postman, then slammed it again in Lekovich's face. In that split-second I registered his revulsion at the sight of the room behind me, but a moment later his voice on the other side of the door assumed its usual emollience.

'I have not come here to change your mind, Comrade Milena, although you know it is still possible to return home without anyone being any the wiser about your movements. I am here to check on your welfare. Your parents have asked me to investigate your circumstances.'

'And you are going to tell them what exactly?' I am not sure why I carried on talking.

'I am not going to worry them. They have had enough grief and anguish already, but we understand. We think that you are suffering delayed trauma, that you will recover. We blame that Kovalsky boy. And please don't think I am disturbed by what I see here. I studied law in Zurich before the war, you know. My digs in Switzerland make Minford Gardens look like Marienbad.'

The comparison was hilarious in its implications. The owner's City salary was high, and Jason told me how lucky Will was to be able to afford this place, and at his age. I was beginning to understand something about London, about there being no easy equivalents.

'So what if it isn't Marienbad?' I said. 'I'm happy here. I couldn't care less about your digs or Switzerland.'

To prove my point, I opened the door wide and exposed the kitchen behind me: the table that served as breakfast bar at one end and Jason's desk at the other, our clothes draped over every chair around it, like some ghostly committee meeting; the sink guarded by ranks of ill-assorted mugs and bowls, waiting for some moment when one of us decided that the trouble of washing up amounted to less than the ugliness of their accumulation. Jason and I were, still, so greedy for each other that everything else seemed like a waste of time.

I wasn't ashamed of the squalor, if it was that. I had nothing to prove to this man and I believed that our circumstances, and the city itself, would soon change. I was already grasping that it took an awful lot simply to exist in a town that was slipping its moorings from being a somewhat decrepit, fog-bound city docked alongside Europe. Will's tiny TV set was switched off most of the time, but I did watch the news once or twice and I heard Margaret Thatcher all but promising her people that it would soon become the *ne plus ultra* of global cities, the financial capital of the world. She had a touch of my father about her, though they were bitter enemies. Will was one of her soldiers and we were lucky to have his digs.

Lekovich stood outside in the rain like a piece of my homeland teleported to W14. His coat and hat, and his thin, clipped moustache, would have suited a member of Neville Chamberlain's entourage on that fateful flight from Munich. His socialist sense of propriety preserved some of those aesthetics as though in a time warp. I experienced a pang of feeling for him – an unexpected stab of homesickness, coupled with sorrow that he was ordered by my father to run this particular errand – but I did not invite him in. Neither did I ask him how he had tracked me down. I had already realised that, whenever he wanted to, he would keep finding me. I also wondered how long it would take his English counterparts to locate me. If they hadn't done so already, I was beginning to suspect that would happen too.

'So?' I asked. I wanted him to go away and never come back.

'So, Comrade Milena. You know where the embassy is. You know I am at your service, for as long as I am there.'

He raised his homburg and I saw a line where it pressed his grey hair in, like a rubber band. He clicked his heels, then turned away and started climbing up the flight of stairs. Just as he was reaching for the front gate and a thin white vertical stripe on his black socks flashed more or less at my eye level, he paused, turned back and looked down on me.

'Look after yourself, Milena,' he said, dropping the Comrade part, forgetting that he was supposed to address me with a formal you. 'English perfidy, never underestimate it. They will stab you in the back, betray you when you least expect it. It's their nature, no point complaining about it: like asking this rain not to fall.'

He closed the gate carefully. I slammed the front door and went back into the kitchen. I sat down at Jason's end of the table, tore a sheet of paper from his notepad and started writing a shopping list: '2 chicken breasts. Garlic. Tarragon.' Both fresh if possible, I thought. Unlikely at Presto's, but Georgiou's would have them. 'Butter, unsalted. 2lb potatoes (= approx. kilo?). Lettuce. White-wine vinegar. Olive oil – or sunflower: price? Wine.'

Jason had a fondness for poets' wines that smelled of petrol and gave you three days of headache. Both our fathers knew better. I must not spend more than three pounds and must not buy Bulgarian or Blue Nun, the student staples of local supermarkets, I thought. I knew already how difficult it would be to find a bottle that matched those criteria.

I had only spent a few days finding my way around the local shops but I enjoyed the novelty of playing an experienced hausfrau. Our evening meals – whatever happened to be on the menu, whether I cooked or Jason did, or whether it was a Chinese takeaway – always had something festive about them. We switched off the lights and lit candles so that the mess of the flat disappeared and only a small circle around us was visible. We put a tape into the cassette player. Jason labelled his compilation tapes 'Music for Study' but the sounds were made for seduction, not for thinking about Yeats. They muffled the footsteps and the car tyres outside and amplified the patter of rain.

Then, eventually, we retired to that enormous bed, where we sometimes made love and sometimes just rested side by side, staring at our own dark outlines in the mirror above until we drifted to sleep. And Jason sometimes sat up suddenly, like a startled hare, switched on the bedside lamp and grabbed a notepad that he kept under the bed and wrote.

'The voyage of the Argonauts,' he said one night when I asked what he was writing and, in the morning, I wondered if I had dreamed it.

Chapter Seventeen

The Wedding Day

They say rain on your wedding day brings good luck. It was fitting that ours was blindingly sunny. It was, I believe, the first cloudless day since I'd arrived in England.

We wed on a Tuesday morning in early February: the earliest the ceremony could be squeezed in, the statutory twenty-nine days after we'd given our notice of intent. The bride was in black as usual, the groom in denim, *sans* Aran for this special occasion. We went to the registry office by bus. It was cheaper than the Tube.

At Jason's request, we neglected to invite Paddy and Clarissa. He was still feeling sore about their lack of support. We had only two guests, doubling up as witnesses and joint best men: Jason's comrades from poetry gigs in London pubs. Glaswegians living somewhere south of the Thames, they had waited for us at the registrar's, tipsy well ahead of the event and amused that they were, by virtue of their signatures, making a marriage happen. They corpsed throughout the short ceremony, and their mood infected the newly-weds. Every promise we made sounded like a joke.

The Town Hall consisted of a series of brutalist boxes that would put Minsk to shame. The office was housed in an offshoot of those boxes, as though love and marriage were an afterthought, with a car park in the forecourt. The few photographs we took – before and after – all looked overexposed, so harsh was the sunlight against the concrete. The best men were a pair of ginger haloes. Jason's blondness made him seem like a ghost. I hung off his arm but blended into the background like ectoplasm poised to disappear: my face white, my hair a dark nimbus, my squinting eyes black dashes.

We took another bus back to Shepherd's Bush. There followed a couple of hours of drinking in our basement: Crémant de Loire for the bride, six-packs of Belhaven ale for the groom and the Scottish party, with plenty of noisy crab-like moves into our tiny lavatory. We ate nothing but crisps all afternoon, tearing open blue bags of these unsatisfying industrialised snacks that would have perturbed my compatriots and grabbing greasy fistfuls to chase the drink down. Salt-and-vinegar: the sour taste more appropriate for an end than a beginning.

I have no regrets about the circumstantial details, only about the central event of the day.

It was a pauper poet's wedding, spectacularly unnuptial. Luckily, no one recited poetry. An attempt at an impromptu limerick competition was spoiled by my failure to understand our best men's accents. The high point of the day was the moment when Jason's lust reasserted itself and he pushed them out of the flat, up the stairs and onto the street, and we retired to our bedroom for the honeymoon.

The following morning the weather reverted to the norm. I opened the door, still semi-awake, when the bell rang, to see a young Indian face covered in raindrops and framed by a blue nylon hood. A cycle was leaning precariously against the fence above, ready to speed away as fast as possible.

'Mrs Connor?' the Indian asked, my name so unexpectedly up to date that I assumed he must be a courier from the registry office.

He proffered a wet sheet of paper attached to a clipboard. Instead of an as-yet-unrehearsed signature, my pen left a squidgy black trail.

It was a shock to see the red embassy crest to the left of the address and then to find, inside the envelope, a thousand-Deutschmark banknote clipped to a flimsy page: a telegram cropped so as to remove any circumstantial details: *hope this helps stop gertruda and stanislav stop.*

I stared at that lower-case string of letters: no congratulations, no love, no best wishes, not even 'Mother' and 'Father'. It was impossible to believe that they knew about my wedding so soon after the event, but I already knew how good Lekovich was at his job. I felt stung, surprised by the depth of my frustration. Sending the money back required more effort than I was willing to invest. And we needed the cash.

I was angry with Jason, properly angry for the first time since I arrived in England, inflamed by his growing insouciance about the practicalities of our existence and his willingness to depend on subventions from my parents in my poor, obscure homeland.

'And if the worst came to the worst, my squat in Brixton is still there,' he'd say, cheerfully, when I dared worry about our future lodgings. 'You'd love it, Millie. The murals are mind-boggling.'

I knew I was marrying a student, of course, but I couldn't have imagined his seemingly boundless trust that the state would provide. The irony was that in capitalist England he could hope to depend on public largesse. I trusted only myself, and the safety net of my family, now forever lost.

Then I remembered that anger with Jason was, probably, the effect my parents would have desired to produce with their gift, so I redirected my ire at them instead.

He walked into the kitchen, pressed his body against my back and slipped his hand under my bathrobe. I looked down and saw his naked feet, his long toes. I did not want to turn, did not want him to see my face.

'Oh, Millie,' he said. 'I do love your parents. I wish mine were more like yours.'

That first winter became a bittersweet cocktail of poverty and bliss. I had known neither before I moved to London.

We ascended three floors, this time as paying tenants, after Will returned from Val d'Isère and reclaimed the basement. There was not much to move, by way of effects. Jason's notes. Lots of Yeats. The posters from his halls, rolled. Jason had barely enough clothes to fill that familiar, well-travelled rucksack. I had been living out of a suitcase.

Meeting a school friend of my husband's was a revelation. Although they represented an exercise in physical contrasts – Will was small, his body compact, his dark hair cropped, his skin tanned after weeks of skiing, but also naturally dark – the two seemed to have been made in the same factory, and the school had applied an identical finish. They spoke, laughed and moved in the same way, and the similarity of bearing had an unexpected effect. The longer you looked at them, the more alike they appeared to be.

Will delivered a bottle of absinthe and a case of champagne as a belated wedding present. His gift arrived in time to celebrate our first Valentine's Day in our attic studio. *Death in the Afternoon*: that's what the two called the cocktail. Will had procured the absinthe from some semi-legal distillery in France, where they were circumventing the law by labelling it as a fennel-and-wormwood liqueur. It sounded disgusting.

I stuck with champagne. It was a familiar brand, one that, my mother claimed, relaxed the vocal cords to the precise degree required for the coloratura. I drank, but did not test her claim. The men experimented until they found the right proportion of spirit and sparkle.

Our new place was marginally less grey than the basement and with better views, although the bar had scarcely been set high. Renting was another of London's firsts for me, as were budgeting and the low-level anxiety that came with it. Every time I exchanged a West German banknote in a smelly little bureau de change on the green, I felt a twinge about my diminishing wad.

The rent was low, Jason said – although it didn't seem low to me – because our bathroom was separated from the rest of the flat, across the landing and two steps up, an arrangement I would never understand and which made even less sense if you looked at the building from the outside. Whoever had carried out the subdivision of that once-sizeable family house into six small flats must have known that the best picture window would have to be frosted in order to fit a bath underneath.

There was a bit of flat roof just below that frosted opening and, later in the year, when the weather improved, we used it as a balcony. We'd step in and out of the bath to get to it, Jason with a bottle of wine, I with two glasses, or three on those occasions when Will joined us. The back gardens of hotels on Shepherd's Bush Road threw occasional surprises at us: a spray of mimosa, the smells of roasting and rosemary, sounds of rebetiko, like coded messages from brighter places.

Although Jason had his poetry circles, Will was the only person we both socialised with. I found him simultaneously silly and fascinating. If Jason never talked about money, Will talked about little else, but he always did so in bizarre, abstract terms. He rambled on about millions and billions, bullion and options and futures, and peppered his speech with names like Warburg and Rothschild and Schroders and Chase. I thought the first was a car manufacturer. Jason pretended to understand. He laughed at Will's jokes, so I laughed too.

'One has to keep making it,' Will would say, with only half self-mocking pomposity. 'Enough is never enough. As our dear Prime Minister put it so wisely: Nobody would remember the Good Samaritan if he only had good intentions. He had money as well.'

They cracked jokes all the time – it was their conversational mode – but the only thing I found genuinely funny was Will's feeling of lust for Margaret Thatcher. He talked endlessly about that dawn the previous autumn when she emerged from the rubble of a Brighton hotel bombed by the IRA, narrowly escaping death, in pearls and with not a hair out of place. Her pluck was admirable, Will's yearning less so. She had a touch of the stern and determined Dara about her, a Dara augmented with pearls and a pussy bow, and she was old enough to be Will's mother or, perhaps more pertinently, his nanny, or a matron at that school he and Jason went to.

Eventually Will would stand up, bid farewell, declare that he was off to some nightclub in the West End, then step back through the window, into the bath and out. We waited until he reappeared in the urban canyon below and waved as he walked in the direction of the taxi rank opposite the Tube station.

In those early days in London, so many things failed to connect: expensive taxis, poverty, champagne, shabbiness. Will's suits were made to measure and silk-lined. How did one square the luxury with the mushroom tunnel that he was living in?

On that first Valentine's Day the three of us took to the landing between our flat and our bathroom for an impromptu party, deciding about the right degree of milkiness in the absinthe cocktails and speaking in stage whispers whenever another tenant appeared on the floors below. The night was clear. I watched the planes move endlessly across the lead grid of the stairwell window – left to right, wing lights flickering.

'This makes such a change from Bulgarian wine,' I said, raising my glass.

'Are you from Bulgaria then?' Will asked.

'Of course she isn't,' Jason laughed. 'I picked up some Bulgarian from the offie a few nights ago, great value, £1.99 a bottle, utterly fabulous wine, and she said, "I can't believe I had to come all the way to London to try Bulgarian wine for the first time."'

'It was good. I'd never have tried it at home,' I rushed to add, lest Will thought me a snob. I am not sure why I bothered. Snobbery was the last thing that would have troubled Will. In fact he thought snobbery commendable because it was a genuine feeling. It was inverted snobbery he couldn't take.

Jason never complained about wine or anything. He was neither a sincere snob nor an inverted one. I knew, by now, that his Marxism was as decorative as his Irishness – it had no practical consequences and called for no commitment to action – but his egalitarianism was honest enough. In Marxist-Leninist parlance, he was a genuine opportunist, in wine as in everything else. He drank whatever was put before him in order to get drunk, like our manual labourers back home, but at least he did not do it all the time. Will, even with his refined palate, seemed perilously close to being an alcoholic.

'Ground Control to Major Tom,' Jason suddenly sang. He had reached that point in his drinking when he found everything funny. His legs dangled between the spindles of the bannister and he raised them into the air every now and then, as though we were, all three of us, on a swing. He wore mustard-yellow knee-length socks under his jeans. Will was sitting with his back against the bannister, his head turned to face the two of us. I kept blinking away a vision of him breaking through the spindles, falling down, his jacket vents flapping.

'My, the only way for you for is up, Jay Connor,' Will said, pointing at the dirty Victorian eaves above our heads. 'This boy has a golden touch. We knew that at school,' he continued, addressing me as if he felt that I needed reassurance about my choice of husband. 'Every teacher adored him. If we wanted someone to sneak out to the village to buy ciggies for the rest of us, we sent out our Jay, knowing that he'd never get caught. We called him Lucky Luck. If he dropped a slice of bread, it never landed on the buttered side.'

'Then I somehow became Lucky Fuck,' Jason said. 'I hated that school.'

'Didn't we all? Anyway, I hope I will be the lucky fuck tonight.' Will stood up, buttoned his jacket, straightened it, pulled his cuffs so that they stayed a centimetre outside his sleeves, then unbuttoned the bottom button again. As he turned and started descending, he tugged Jay's sock off, gave a little wave with it and threw it back over the bannister, where it dangled pungently in front of my nose. I saw that it had Jason's name tag with his initials and surname in a little loop on the rim: twenty-eight and still wearing school socks.

'Too good to throw away,' Jason said, guessing my thoughts. 'I have masses of school kit from my sixth form. Practically indestructible. Remember those plimsolls last year? I hated having to throw them away.'

We listened to Will's footfall, the sound of the front door opening and closing, then the metal sound of the gate outside, the latch falling.

'Lucky Fuck. Don't say you weren't warned,' Jason repeated. 'Happy Valentine's, Millie.'

'I like Will,' I said, just to say something. I neither liked nor disliked the man. 'I've never met a banker before.'

'I wouldn't take Will's banking too seriously,' Jason said. 'He's the same age as me and he has already changed three careers. Commissioned into his father's regiment, left quicker than you could say "Hong Kong", then joined MI6. Intelligence didn't pay, he said. One wonders.

Promptly left that for the City, where he's now changed jobs again.'

I failed to understand much of what Jason said there. I knew of MI6, though I was too drunk to ask whether they were the internal or the external secret police, or both. My father knew that sort of stuff. I was amazed that Jason and Will could speak about intelligence work so publicly.

'Will doesn't seem cut out for spying,' I said. 'You'd have thought he'd be more curious about me. I don't think he knows what part of the world I am from. We've had so many drinking sessions together and he barely even knows my name.'

'Fair cop,' Jason said, as though he had just realised. 'I'd have made a better spy than Will. Or you, in particular, Mata Hari. They'd love you, I am sure.'

Chapter Eighteen

Clarissa's Visit

In early March, Clarissa announced a visit to London. Jason found her card, a reproduction of *The Death of Chatterton*, in his pigeonhole at the university. So far as I knew, she and Paddy were not aware that our wedding had actually taken place, and had only a vague idea that we were staying at a friend's place somewhere in West London. It made Lekovich's success in tracking us down all the more impressive.

If Jason's parents had our number, and I am not sure they did, they never called. I'd known from my stay in the country that, unlike back home where it was practically free, in England the phone was considered terribly expensive and hence was barely used, with Jason's parents waiting religiously for the times when the rates were cheaper to make even brief social calls. The Royal Mail, on the other hand, was affordable and seemed a miracle of efficiency. Our post was delivered twice a day and a letter rarely took more than twenty-four hours to arrive.

I had prompted Jason to write to his parents a few times, then gave up, assuming that he was still nursing his hurt. I realised, from his reaction to Clarissa's card, that he was not as angry as I had thought. Criticism and rejection were always water off Lucky Luck's back. When he finally remembered to mention it, he seemed pleased his mother had written.

I couldn't quite grasp their relationship, the inconsistencies of warmth and distance, just as I couldn't guess if Clarissa's choice of card was an accident or a joke.

'Darling boy,' she wrote. 'I hope this finds you – and Milena (?) – well. You have fallen off the edge of the Earth even more than usual this year. I am coming to London on 8 March. Staying with Louise in Camden. There is a suffrage commemoration on Friday, then, on the Saturday, an all-female performance of *The Taming of the Shrew*. Lou designed the costumes. It's all a bit *de trop* for your father, so I am coming up alone. I wonder if you (two?) would like to join me for lunch on Sunday at L'Escargot. One p.m.? You can walk me to Charing Cross afterwards. Do let me know and I'll book. Love, Ma.'

The card sat on top of its carelessly ripped envelope, among Jason's papers on the table, for three or four days. I didn't want him to think that I cared about the lunch one way or another, so I didn't ask about it. I hadn't been aware even that his mother had a sister in London until later, when he explained who Louise was. Clarissa's question marks showed that he was no more forthcoming with information for her.

'Oh, I knew that, Millie. I had already told Mater,' he said, when I gave up waiting for him to mention the card and suggested I wouldn't mind seeing his mother. 'Why would anyone object to a free lunch?'

I had expected to meet both sisters at L'Escargot, but it was Clarissa alone, striking in lilac and green against the red plush of the banquettes. She stood up when she saw us,

walked forward to kiss first me, then Jason. It was her march-
ing outfit, she said, when she noticed me admiring her dress.
She touched the green trim on its sailor collar. Her white
hair, like one of those English clouds, piled as carelessly as
ever on top of her head, made her almost as tall as Jason.

I hadn't experienced the interior of a proper London
restaurant before that lunch, and this was an opulent
start. The food was as rich as the decor. Jason ate a dozen
snails flambéed in some aniseed liqueur, using the best
part of a baguette to mop up the buttery puddles around
them, then ordered a huge plateful of cassoulet.

'Simple peasant food,' Clarissa said, watching the
waiter fillet her fish. She surprised me with her obvious
relish for her son's appetite and her delight in hearing
that I loved my salad of chanterelles and salsify. It was the
first time anything in England reminded me of home
cooking. Where I came from, we didn't go to restaurants
for our best food, I told her, and she laughed.

Mother and son chatted as though their spat on New
Year's Day hadn't happened. Jason managed to discuss his
forthcoming reading on the sixth floor of the Royal Festival Hall before he remembered to tell Clarissa that we
were married. I was so used to secrecy with my parents
that I assumed his omission was deliberate, but the way
he hit his forehead with his palm when he remembered to
impart the news suggested otherwise. If there was a gesture that captured my husband, that was it.

'Congratulations, my dear,' Clarissa said, turning to
me without missing a beat. 'My son is a very lucky man.'

'It was a small event. We had to, for my papers, as you'll
remember,' I said, feeling guilty and not quite knowing
why, then realising how wrong this sounded.

'Nice to feel so loved,' Jason said. 'Thank you, Mills.'

'This calls for a toast. I can't wait to tell Paddy,' Clarissa interrupted.

I was sure that she liked me, that she wanted to do the right thing, but she seemed a touch too joyful. She had a brief consultation with the sommelier and ordered a bottle of champagne. It was no wonder they were so poor. She was exactly like Will. Just that bottle must have represented the equivalent of our weekly food bill, I thought, then realised how hemmed in I was by such concerns in our new life. I would never have had a thought like that in the past.

Whenever I mentioned money, Jason changed the subject.

'Shush, Millie, don't spoil the moment,' he would say, although the moment I was spoiling might have been something as prosaic as taking the bedding out of the washing machine.

I washed our sheets every other day: not every morning, as Dara would have preferred, but near enough. We had just one set and we lived in them.

'Consider the birds of the air,' Jason said when I dared suggest that we might run out of cash.

'What do you mean?' I asked. 'Leave metaphors for poetry. Be serious, for once.'

'Things will sort themselves out,' he said. 'No need to worry. They always do.'

My husband trusted his luck. For a while, I was that luck. I did not begrudge the fact, yet I can't now explain why I hid the thousand-Deutschmark note my parents had sent, even while we were still living off those many hundreds I brought with me to London. Although he was in the bizarre position of being sustained by hard currency from my soft-currency homeland, Jason had no idea exactly how much we had left. He never asked because he didn't want to know.

And for an even longer while – interruptions by Will aside – we were sufficient for each other. Jason went out in the morning – took the Central Line to the British Museum or to Senate House – and came back at wildly different times, sometimes bringing an early lunch of baguettes and pâté, or a block of Cheddar and pale, cold Dutch tomatoes, which tasted only of water and refrigeration; sometimes at teatime depositing, with a heavy sigh, pages of handwritten notes at that end of our all-purpose table that was his desk, as if to say: Look, I do work. He called his doctorate a sham, a ploy to ensure he kept getting his student grant in order to write poetry, but he took it seriously enough.

While he studied, and when I wasn't filling and emptying the washer-dryer, I explored the city on my own, not yet a Londoner, no longer a tourist. I trailed French and Italian teenagers on school visits to the National Gallery, listening to and half-understanding their guides explain the basics of Impressionism. I visited those modern art galleries that Lana had had on her list, guessing that she was among a handful of people who already knew exactly what I had done, but wondering if she understood. Wondering if she too would have chosen love over luxury.

'How was your day?' I would ask Jason, or he would ask me in the evening, and we told each other long, detailed stories about trivial events. We got drunk on cheap wine or on each other, then watched late-night films on a TV we had acquired from an electrician on Shepherd's Bush Road who sold reconditioned sets on the side. You can call it happiness, if you like.

We went out to readings regularly enough for me to get used to the fact that what passed for the poetry scene in Britain had little in common with its equivalent back home. I sat in darkened pub cellars, where I watched small gatherings of enthusiasts reading, but not always listening, to each other, trading their willingness to be bored for their right to bore, amid an atmosphere of confected enthusiasm orchestrated by the poetry scene's own impresarios. I felt the sadness of an outsider, alleviated only by the regular recurrence of that miraculous transformation I witnessed the first time I saw Jason onstage – the sight of a dolphin taking to the open sea. He felt more real somehow while performing, even to me, his wife.

And he was different from the others: he had a quality I could, even in our cynical times, and even now, after everything that's happened, call genius. I understood something about the nature of his gift from the beginning, but I couldn't be sure how much he – and probably, more, how much I – could depend on it. Or how much sacrifice we owed it. In my country, things would have been simpler for him; he'd have been feted or imprisoned, but all he would ever have to do for his living was write verse.

Chapter Nineteen

Leave to Remain

The day it arrived, I sent a copy of our wedding certificate to the Home Office along with my passport. Jason said it would take ages to get them back. I didn't need the passport, because we had no money to travel. The more urgent issue was that I had no right of employment until my leave to remain was confirmed. I both needed and wanted to work. It was money, but not just money. I was bored with sightseeing in the rain, with having Will as my only London acquaintance. I hoped it wouldn't be ages. I trusted British efficiency.

Four days later, the telephone rang. The man gave his name and job title, said that he had my papers before him, that he was looking forward to processing them promptly. He asked a few brief questions about my arrival in the UK and the history of my acquaintanceship with Jason. He said *yes*, or *yes, of course*, to everything, as though he just needed to hear what he could already see before him. Then he asked for my father's full name.

'Stanislav Urbansky,' I said. 'It's in the form, too. And in my wedding certificate.'

'*The* Stanislav Urbansky?' he asked, making it obvious with that oh-so-English hypocrisy that he was feigning ignorance. I must have been bleeping on their radar screen at least since Heathrow, if not earlier.

'Are there others?' I asked back. Names came from a smaller palette in my part of the world. There were lots of Urbanskys, and since Stanislav was a common first name, surely the combination was not unprecedented, but there was no point in obfuscating.

His voice livened up, as though the conversation up to that point was simply an exchange of social courtesies and I had, by confirming the name of my father, given him permission to change tack. Although I now expected questioning, none came. British 'due process' was more baffling than the predictable cruelties of our bureaucracy.

'This procedure normally takes many months,' the man said, 'but it can be speeded up in cases such as yours.'

'That's good to hear,' I said, suspecting but not quite knowing what he meant by 'cases such as yours'.

'I am afraid we'll have to set up a formal interview. We'd be very happy to visit you in your own home if that is convenient.'

'If that is the usual procedure, then yes, of course,' I said. I couldn't imagine it was.

'Normally you'd be expected to apply from outside the country, submitting all the paperwork in advance,' the man said, avoiding a straight answer, 'though we understand that would have been wholly impractical from your country, and in your position. We have your arrival records.'

He had the courtesy not to suggest that I had misrepresented my intentions at Heathrow, but we both knew that, just as we both knew that I was in his hands.

'We do visit later on to establish that the marriage credentials are bona fide,' he continued. 'I am sure it will be a formality in this case—'

'You mean to establish that it isn't a sham marriage?' I interrupted.

'Yes, I suppose so, although that's putting it more bluntly than we would,' he said. 'You'd be surprised by the number of cases in which one of the parties is paid to marry the other. But we're not for a moment assuming that yours is one ... or that someone like you would ever need anything like that. All a formality, as I said.'

He sounded almost too reassuring for comfort. I knew that adherence to form was only part of the truth, that my marriage was secondary anyway. I knew that even now, even here, in London, I was the Daughter first. I didn't need a husband to stay in Britain.

The man confirmed that much implicitly when I asked if Jason needed to be present at this interview.

'No, not really,' he said. 'But he would be very welcome, of course. Whatever you prefer, Mrs Connor.'

This was not about my marriage. It was about Father. Unless they feared that I was a spy already, I suspected they would love to recruit me as one.

After we made an appointment, I left the house, distracted. I had been planning to go to the British Museum – perhaps surprise Jason at the Reading Room and offer to take him out for lunch at a cheap Italian place I had discovered on Sicilian Avenue – but I realised that I had overshot the station only when the train pulled out of St Paul's. At Bank, I walked up to street level and found myself among men in pinstripe suits, carrying rolled umbrellas. One, an anachronism among anachronisms, was even wearing the sort of bowler hat I thought people wore only in *The Avengers*. It was among the first – and last – TV series bought from Britain after my father's visit: a harbinger of a thaw that proved to be anything but. Instead, it was followed by an even colder war.

'We thought they were opening up to us, admitting their weakness,' I remembered Father saying as Mother and I watched the actors playing the parts of well-fed men who looked like his worst capitalist nightmare, 'but we soon saw that it was a plot, all the better to defeat us. We aim to liberate the proletariat, and they to keep the workers in chains, and these two visions will never coexist.'

I had forgotten my A–Z. I wanted to return to Bloomsbury and I thought I was walking west. The City was bewildering – quirky alleyways still arranged as though they represented the imprints of a jumbled medieval town, and main roads with forbidding walls, heavy doors and nothing much else at eye level, like the Praesidium District back home – and my sense of direction was poor at the best of times.

After about one of those English miles that I was forever trying to get my head around, I found myself in the middle of a cluster which looked so much like the world I grew up in that I wondered, as I took to the walkways in the sky, who would actually volunteer to live somewhere like this. I assumed that it must be state housing. There was a lot of it in London, boxes of dwellings often built, just like at home, in those places where German bombs had pockmarked the cityscape.

And, exactly like large state housing schemes back home, it had an Art Palace in the centre. The parallel went further than I expected when I saw that it was staging an exhibition of contemporary art from the German Democratic Republic. I was surprised to find that one had to pay, since I knew that much better art was freely available elsewhere in London, but I paid, then wandered through the empty rooms. The whole day seemed to be acquiring a meaning, albeit one that was somewhere just out of my reach.

As I examined familiar objects and prints, I heard other footsteps and then, for the first time since I arrived in London, the sound of strangers speaking my language. I spotted a couple in their late sixties. Their rustling rain-coats and their sensible shoes in unsensible colours could only have been purchased in England, so I assumed they were émigrés and yet I worried they would recognise me. My fear was irrational. My father notwithstanding, I didn't have a famous face: we didn't go in for celebrity families at home. I slowed down and waited for them to move on.

And, for the rest of that day, I had an impression that someone was following me, a familiar feeling, but one I had not felt before in Britain. I kept identifying likely suspects, young men dressed so conservatively that I could not decide if they were sent by Lekovich or by the British. I wondered how free I was, how free I could ever be, anywhere. I felt lonely. If Jason wasn't taking his PhD seriously, as he claimed, why was he leaving me on my own so often?

Yet, when the day of the interview came, I nudged Jason out of the house so as to have the conversation alone. I assumed the talk would be largely about my father. I didn't think I knew anything relevant about him that the British intelligence service or the Home Office, or who-ever these people really were, did not already know, and I hadn't anything to hide, but there was a possibility that they were about to offer me a deal of some kind and I wanted to hear it without Jason. I didn't feel disloyal about urging him to spend the day in the library; I thought I was merely evading the traps presented by what I already knew as Jason's poet's enthusiasm for freebies. It never occurred to me that he could ever find himself in a position to confront different traps on his own. I thought him as transparent as a glass of water.

Chapter Twenty

Interview

The man they sent was as young as Jason, thirty at the most. I pressed the buzzer to let him in, then watched him climb up two steps at a time and finally offer his hand for a vigorous handshake. Rather than making him look older, his grey suit and his striped tie with its diagonal white lines, reminiscent of an English school uniform, had the opposite effect. It was, perhaps, also the energetic way he climbed those stairs – unthinkable for an official in my homeland. He spoke my language perfectly.

'I am impressed,' I said. 'How big is the Immigration Office, to have such linguistic specialisms?'

He ignored the irony and followed me inside. His pace was as firm as his handshake. He took the seat I offered, very conspicuously not looking around, then produced some notes from a black satchel-like briefcase and flicked through them as I made two mugs of instant coffee.

For the next fifteen minutes we repeated the conversation I'd already had on the phone with his colleague: my job back home, my flight to Britain, my arrival at Heathrow, my activities in London. The questions were less probing than I expected, almost – but for his precision and note-taking – like the enquiries of an accidental companion on a train journey, whiling away the time. I kept expecting him to ask me about my favourite museum.

I saw the faintest shadow of a smirk as he noted down that Jason was a full-time student at UCL. He knew Jason's age.

'This might be a problem,' he said, 'the fact that your husband is supporting himself on a standard doctoral student grant and so – clearly – is not able to support you. You are not supposed to have to rely on public funds.'

I already knew enough to realise the silliness of mentioning that Jason was a poet, but I mentioned it nonetheless. The man showed no awareness of Jason's publisher, not a flicker of recognition when I referred to the Shelley Prize. He apologised, assuming it was more important to me than it was. He was a historian by training, he said, as though it provided an explanation for his ignorance. He read Larkin occasionally, he added, but even that not very often. Neither of us had any will to pursue that conversational tributary further.

His tone changed slightly as he asked about my first impressions of London. I looked at the piles of Jason's papers on the table, lowered my now half-empty mug, declared the city charming, mentioned a few museums I had visited. He asked me how it compared to other cities I knew, how it compared to back home. He scribbled some notes. I didn't think they had anything to do with my tourist trail.

'You say that you have no friends of your own nationality in this country, no one in the Friendship Society, for example,' he said after we chatted some more. 'You say that you have no desire to change that, but you have only been in London since December. Your compatriots in the Society are very helpful to newcomers from your country, and there are vanishingly few newcomers. Meeting you would be like gold dust to them. It's not at all political. There are lectures on your architectural heritage, folklore, that sort of thing. Wouldn't you like that? Like to be involved, I mean. It could be a first step in finding your feet here.'

'I am impressed. You're surprisingly well informed for someone who deals with residence issues,' I interrupted.

The briefest of smiles crossed his face.

'I have only been here for four months,' I continued, 'but I wouldn't have thought it a good idea for someone like me to approach the Society. Those people came to Britain with our deposed king, forming a government in exile whose aim was – still is, for all I know – to overturn the revolution my father helped to lead.'

I paused, realising that I was, after all, the first to mention Father that day.

'Still helps to lead,' I corrected myself, now feeling liberated by the fact that I had brought Dad out into the open, to the table, as it were. 'Father assumes the revolution to be permanent. He and the Friendship Society would be mortal enemies, although they would agree on the beauties of our folklore.'

'Your father, yes, but not you. I assume that your views are not identical. You're your own woman and you chose to come here, after all. They would love you,' he said. 'And it might be interesting for you – interesting for us – if you established contacts there. We are impartial, we don't prefer them to your father.'

'I am sure you are,' I said. I didn't ask who *we* were.

'And I am sure, more than anything else, they would love to hear about life in your country at first hand. Between you and me, they're old and out of touch,' he continued, his boyish face warming to an idea he was about to propose, as though it had only just occurred to him. 'I could see you becoming a public lecturer even beyond the Friendship Society. I think you'd be in great demand. Nothing that you're not comfortable with, of course, merely stories of life back home. Your education, your holidays, your birthday parties even. The things you've seen. You don't even need to mention your father's name.

'I don't know if you recognise the extent of interest here. There are bodies that foster public knowledge about your country in Britain, there are magazines. I am talking of work, you understand, of growing your own job, a fellowship tailored to your experience. I imagine you'd prefer not to have to wait months for the work permit, not to have to wait five years for a British passport. Everyone would love to hear your impressions of home while they are still fresh. The fresher, the better.'

'I am not in a rush to get a British passport,' I said. 'Not ahead of the queue. I need indefinite leave to remain, a work permit. And whether I mention my father's name or not is irrelevant, as everyone will know. Such difficulties as I had – and I didn't have many – were all private and personal, not ideological. I am not a political person. I had a reasonably happy life back home.'

'Of course you had. Happy. I wouldn't expect you to say otherwise. And I know you aren't political,' he said. 'But ... I've been there a few times. It seems such a grey, miserable place compared to London, as I am sure you would agree. And frozen, not just literally, but in time. Even Russia will overtake it soon. This new leader in Moscow, Gorbachev. It's only been a month, but already there are signs of a different world.'

He looked out of the window and across the rooflines of Shepherd's Bush. I wasn't going to say anything. To deny the beauties of London seemed disloyal to Jason, although the view from our flat displayed the city to disadvantage; to agree with the greyness of home would not only be disingenuous but disloyal to my parents. I had already been disloyal enough.

And I knew nothing about Gorbachev. I saw him on television, but I wasn't impressed. His strange birthmark, his broad southern accent and, yes, his comparative youth: he looked like one of those agricultural engineers who used to visit the Maize Institute. He was just a placeholder, I thought. The Soviets would get rid of him soon enough. I expected the next leader to continue the revolution.

'There's so much more suffering than you can imagine,' the man went on. 'Hunger even, in spite of the richness of what God and nature threw at your country. And it is strange, isn't it, that even the children of high-ranking Party members have such a high incidence of suicide and defection; they who should be the happiest.'

'Misha was a fool,' I said, not bothering to explain who Misha was, for there was clearly no need, and angry now that this man was telling such blatant lies about my country. I knew better than to enquire what he was doing there, a lowly Home Office official. He reminded me of that awful woman in the Antai baths, pretending that she was my friend, that she wished me well. I wanted him out of the house.

'And I am not sure that is of any relevance today. I haven't defected,' I said. I put both my hands on the table, fingers splayed, like that artist Lana took Misha and me to see years ago. He read my mood better than I expected. I liked him when he arrived, liked him a lot even, but we were no longer on the same side. Or, rather, I finally understood I was on nobody's side. I wasn't even sure what the sides were any more, yet they were there, committed to clash until one or the other ceased to exist. Jason was an ornamental Marxist: he could belong anywhere. I belonged nowhere, only to him. The man smiled, and the smile seemed sincere enough, attractive even, but I had a vision of a snail drawing in its horns.

'How right you are,' he said, lowering his notepad down onto the table, straightening it carefully so that everything, in theory, was out in the open and spread on the surface, like my hands. 'Is there anything you'd like to ask me?' he added, not looking down at his notes. 'I am here to help you, at your disposal.'

'Thank you so much, but no,' I said, gathering my fingers in, lowering the fists onto my knees, staring at a faint broken ring on the table where his coffee mug had rested. 'I'll just wait for my papers to come through. The due process, as you say.'

Only two or three hours later Lekovich rang, as though he was in cahoots with whatever tentacles of Her Majesty's Government were reaching out to me. I admit, by then I had had a couple of large glasses of Bulgarian Sauvignon and, against every principle I had held since I was thirteen, a Danish salami sandwich. The lurid red of the salami left trails on the artificial whiteness of the British bread with every bite. I promised myself I would not let Jason do the shopping ever again. Even plain lard, with a sprinkling of salt, must taste better than this. And any ordinary peasant bread. No one in my country, not even social parasites or dissidents, had to endure this kind of salami, I thought, this kind of rubber bread. And that man talks to me about hunger.

I felt ravenous after he left, and there was nothing else but that plastic packet of sliced salami in the fridge, yet it was anger that made me betray my vegetarian principles; anger and self-disgust. I didn't need Lekovich to compound it. I kept feeling I was about to throw up.

'I am very sorry to disturb you, Comrade Milena. Just checking how you are. You know I am here to help you.' I was surprised to hear from him. I half-expected that British man, Lekovich's counterpart, again.

'Everyone says that today. I am so lucky,' I said.

'Don't believe them, Comrade Milena. Be careful. Be very careful,' Lekovich said. 'You know us. You know who we are and where we are.'

'I certainly do,' I said and then, regretting the harshness of my tone, like a swing that goes too far in the opposite direction, I swung back, echoed his sentiment. 'Thank you, Comrade. I do know you care. I know that I can turn to you for any help I may need.'

He gave an embarrassed little chuckle.

Chapter Twenty-One

Job Search

My passport came back faster than I expected, in spite, or because, of that interview. Perhaps the man wasn't lying after all, perhaps I misinterpreted our conversation, perhaps the British and their processes really were unbiased.

Free to look for work, I leafed through job supplements in the public library, copying addresses and details of requirements, and then, back home, typed endless covering letters and variants of my CV. I sent applications out for any graduate job that I was remotely qualified for. The man at the local sub-post office had booklets of second-class stamps ready whenever I entered his store, and I got to know the names of the young assistants in the photo-copying kiosk, but I felt more and more at sea as the weeks passed. This was not remotely like starting a career at home, where state planning and job allocation made things simpler for everyone, but especially for people like me whose quest was lubricated by powerful connections. Nor was Jason of any use – he never seemed to have applied for any kind of work in his own country.

Even without the obvious strangeness of my qualifications, too many of the ads described as desirable qualities that I did not feel I possessed: a positive attitude, team spirit, a sense of humour. In my homeland people didn't have to pretend they loved their work and their colleagues, and a negative attitude was, paradoxically, what kept up their spirits. At the same time, a sense of humour was likely to be unsettling in a foreigner while, with its potential for cynicism and disrespect, it was also, in my mind, incompatible with a positive attitude. I thought the English, of all people, would not feel obliged to pretend otherwise. In an attempt to show my sense of humour, I sprayed one or two envelopes from my ever-diminishing stack with the last squirts of an expensive French scent I had brought from home but had never used in England.

Rejections – and they were all sent unscented – came with spurious apologies. So sorry, your application was impressive, but the field was very strong and you were unlucky on this occasion, potential employers would say; or, so sorry, we are no longer hiring. So sorry: is there a phrase more English than that?

I imagined office juniors sifting through CVs, adding mine to a pile of others destined to get the same polite note of refusal, second-class, pp-ed. I couldn't know if my feeble attempt at passing as a native – I called myself Millie Connor, like some minor character from Joyce – was commendable or counterproductive. The name would have been exposed as a sham by every factual detail of the attached CV, right down to the absence of referees, for who, back home, would dare recommend me for anything, even if they were contactable at all? I didn't want to imagine how my reincarnation as Millie would have depressed Mother and Father.

I proved to be the opposite of Jason: determined to get a job as fast as I could, where he saw no rush; apprehensive about my foreignness and insecure about my English, where he was at ease with the world around him and, without much effort, articulate and endlessly charming. My compatriots called me striking or beautiful, but never charming. I seemed to lack some essential sweetness even among my own, where I knew everyone. Here, in Britain, I knew no one but Jason and his family and, with each word I spoke, I declared my unbelonging.

My self-confidence, boundless at home, took a knock each day. I wondered how many days it could withstand. Jason insisted that I spoke English more correctly than most native speakers. I feared that grammar was only a small part of what I communicated the moment I opened my mouth.

When, by some chance, I happened to be shortlisted for interview, I became so petrified that I scripted and rehearsed even the phone call to confirm attendance. I sat opposite selection panels gulping for air, blushing, sweating, giving monosyllabic responses. It was as though all the gumption that brought me to England had suddenly evaporated and been replaced by anxiety, measure for measure.

I began to wonder if the idea of socialising with émigrés in the Friendship Society might not have been so bad after all. How difficult could it be to talk about the life back home and, while trying to stay out of politics, be reported as having done so, or to file occasional reports on that sad small circle, to whosoever wanted that here in Britain? Would I have to exaggerate the importance of the information I was supplying in order to keep the job going, as, I suspected, my father's researchers always did? Could I even send the same reports in two directions for double the money, for what is a double agent but someone with two jobs? I wished I could share that last as a joke with Jason.

I gradually realised that my official visitor's suggestion was craftier than I had given him credit for. Back home, you knew that, in politics, words meant their exact opposite: the stuff of a thousand jokes. In Britain, everything seemed like a double bluff.

Public lecturing was a periphrasis, I understood. What could I possibly lecture about but myself? The Friendship Society wasn't so much about seeing as being seen, about switching sides and being seen to do so. I would be expected to repudiate my father, in deeds if not in words. My very appearance at the lectern at one of the Society's events would be a kind of denunciation. The more heartfelt that denunciation, the better I would do. And I wouldn't be able to denounce Father just once. I would have to do it again and again, until every choice I ever made – including my marriage to Jason – started to look like a part of my betrayal of him.

'You chose freedom,' the young man had said, at the precise moment when I realised that I could never be free. 'It was the right choice.'

'It was silly of you to close that door,' Jason said when I finally gave him a full account of my interview. 'There is no sweeter word in English than *fellowship*.'

I started looking for basic admin jobs. My sights were lowered, but my performance anxiety was not.

'Are you planning to stay in England permanently?' the Head of Institutional Sales at a language textbook publisher asked while interviewing me for a minor office position. His expression was matter-of-fact, revealing neither benevolence nor malice. He sat opposite me, across a wide conference table, wedged between two women. I studied a line of shelves behind them with its parade of language textbooks and cassettes, while a poster on the wall asserted 'We understand the world'.

I had had what passed for a training session with Jason, but once inside that interview room, I realised that my preparation had been a waste of time, and not just because my husband had even less idea about possible questions than I had. There was a glass of water in front of me, but I did not dare touch it for fear of revealing the trembling hands with which I was shredding a paper tissue under the table. I observed a tiny insect flying above the water, landing on the surface, trying to get a purchase, failing.

'Yes,' I finally answered. 'Very much so. I married an Englishman in February.'

'Well, I suppose that's one way of getting a passport, but it does not necessarily imply permanence,' the man said, and the merest shadow of a sneer crossed his face. 'And what attracts you to this line of work?'

Milena Urbanska might have walked out at that point, but not Millie Connor. I stared at him, drying sweaty hands on my thighs under the table. I hated skirts and I hated tights. I lowered my eyes and my calves seemed unfamiliar, ridiculous in their compressed, hosieried shape, like legs of ham.

He was an insolent little bastard. I should have put him in his place. I should have acknowledged that nothing whatsoever attracted me to that line of work and told him that my reasons for marrying were none of his business. And that he was right about permanence. Marriage did not imply permanence.

Instead I said nothing. My throat felt parched.

'Are you planning on having children soon, given that you are newly married?' he continued. The women did not seem troubled; perhaps this line of questioning was normal in Britain. The one on the left, who had introduced herself as working in personnel, was taking notes, evading my glances. The one on the right was smiling, but showed no intention of interrupting.

I might have informed them that I was about to book a visit to a family planning clinic, having discovered, somewhat belatedly, that, in England, 'family planning' was a euphemism for contraception.

'No, I am not planning to have children,' I said instead.

The woman taking notes looked up and nodded.

My interview was nearing its end. No one asked about my languages. The man took a gulp of water from his glass, his hand perfectly steady.

'And do you have any questions for us?' the smiling woman said, and dabbed her upper lip with a tiny linen handkerchief embroidered with an even tinier violet in cross-stitch.

I had no questions.

Two days later this same woman phoned to congratulate me. She did not bother to ask if I wanted the job. She was already in the middle of explaining something about subsidised meals in the staff canteen and fortnightly menus, when I surprised myself and shocked her by turning the offer down.

'Oh,' she said after a beat, 'I am so sorry to hear that. And I championed your case so strongly. You came across as a bright young woman who really needed this work. This may not be relevant, but my mother is from Brno,' she continued when I said nothing, because I didn't know whether to thank her for the compliment or be offended by her perception of my desperation, which was genuine enough. 'I represent Eastern European languages. I know a bit about the world you come from,' she said.

'I do need the job,' I finally answered, 'but I can't ... I am sorry. I am very grateful to you.'

I sounded as though I was about to cry. I emitted a little snotty gurgle. I don't know why but I saw Misha's face, staring at me, the moment before his gun went off. He was not in the habit of haunting me.

'I am so sorry, dear,' the woman said, and the tone of her voice implied that she was embarrassed by the exchange and was now stepping back. 'I can see that there is a problem, but I am afraid I am not in a position ... You do know that in this country we have counselling services if there is anything you'd like to talk to someone about. Things you perhaps can't talk to your family about.'

She sounded uncomfortable, a bit scared perhaps, certainly keen to end the conversation.

'So sorry,' I said. 'It's nothing. I am just so overwhelmed by the news. Flattered too. But no thanks.'

'Of course you are. I understand, perhaps better than you think. Anyway, the best of luck,' she said chirpily and all too quickly, the awkward moment retrieved by my apology. I did not think I would ever hear from her again.

A week or so later the phone rang.

'Hello, am I speaking to Millie Connor?' It was a male voice this time. 'Peter Hubbard, Royal Entomological Society.'

'Yes, it's Milena Connor,' I said. I was done with the Millie business. 'How may I help you?'

I made an effort to sound serious, wondering what he was after, and trying not to think about the beetle jokes I would come up with when I reported this latest phone call to Jason.

'Dorothy Blake gave me your number. Her husband William is an esteemed colleague. She spoke very highly of you. And your languages.'

It took me some time to realise that Dorothy was the woman who had offered me the job, that she had effectively become my first British referee. When it came to nomenclature, her husband's parents clearly had that elusive sense of humour I was lacking.

'Dorothy suggested you might be able to help. We have some pamphlets here, in Russian, that need translating into English as soon as is feasible for an ongoing research project, and no suitable translator. The beetles of Central Asia, I am afraid. Do you think you ...'

'Yes, of course,' I jumped in, without asking how much they were paying, without worrying that my Russian was not up to the specialist task. Back home, everyone studied it between the ages of seven and eighteen, although my friends and I had tried hard to forget it. It was another Slavonic language, so was automatically far more similar to my mother tongue than monoglot English speakers could imagine. Our Orthodox heritage meant that we shared an alphabet – plus and minus a few characters – and, for centuries, a liturgical language had bound us together. I'd managed maize. I'll manage beetles. Thank you, Dorothy. Thank you, William Blake.

It was well timed. Jason's grant had three months left to run. We spent my money thriftily, but the dwindling supply would last five, six months at best.

It wasn't a living, but it was the beginning of one.

Chapter Twenty-Two

Family Planning

I had noticed it before: the same kind of late-Victorian building as ours but more deeply darkened by the grime of the main road, the sign by the door bearing the names of the practitioners, three Indian and one South African, or that is what their medical degrees suggested. And only women coming and going, as though family planning, at least for its clients or recipients, was not a man's business. When I first spotted it, I misunderstood the implication of family planning, assuming that Britain was the sort of puritanical place where you had to map out your children's future before actually having them.

The longer I went without becoming pregnant, the more I was convinced that I had become infertile after Dr Petroffsky's intervention: he had warned me that it was a possibility. That spring I had conceived instantly. Now Jason and I had made love for months – and nothing happened. We didn't speak about it. I wasn't sure I wanted children, and I assumed Jason was content to leave things to another kind of Russian roulette.

'I was thinking, Millie.' He broke this particular silence in our coupledom one Sunday afternoon, while we were circling the pond in Kensington Gardens, watching ducks waddle and defecate around its rim, and adult men play with miniature, remotely controlled sailing boats. To me this typified Englishmen: either they were the ruthless capitalists of my father's worst nightmares or overgrown children playing with toy boats and sonnets.

It was a windy day. The surface of the water rippled, and the sails leaned perilously close to the waves.

'Yes, congratulations. Go on,' I said, because I sensed that he was waiting for my acknowledgement in order to proceed.

'Ha-ha. Very witty,' Jason said. 'I was thinking about children. Or, rather, about us having or not having them … I don't know what you … but I don't think I am ready. I don't think I'll ever be ready. I am not sure I even want children. I am not cut out to be a father.'

'But you were so upset when I told you about …' I said. I could not finish the sentence.

'Yes, I admit I was, but I've come round to thinking you were right. You didn't need to consult me. You knew me better than I knew myself.'

Dr Patel searched my insides, asked questions, offered options. He was as formal as Dr Petroffsky, but diffident, scared almost. There was no parturition table in his office, no cherubs on the ceiling, just a narrow examination bed covered by a sheet of paper, in the corner of a tiny, crowded room. I stared at a statue of an elephant god on top of his filing cabinet, avoiding his eyes as I answered questions, and as he listed my contraceptive options.

We agreed on what seemed like the least invasive, the most easily reversible choice. He took measurements of my cervix and a week later I collected a pearlescent plastic box with a diaphragm, after a practice session on its insertion with a Chinese nurse who looked too young to be doing that sort of work. I found the episode awkward and embarrassing: squatting, squeezing, pressing the neck of my womb with my index finger to make sure that it was covered properly. The Dutch cap, the nurse called it – much less of an obstacle to marital pleasure than the French letter. We both chuckled, mortified.

In terms of laughter and mortification, things were not much better at home. If I inserted the cap early in the day, I became angered by the state of readiness it implied. I was becoming a geisha, I thought. If I interrupted love-making in order to protect myself from pregnancy, the interruption felt as arousing as getting up to eat a slice of cheese. Assertive women talked about equality on day-time radio, but the news had yet to translate into this aspect of medical research.

'Make it part of your foreplay,' Dr Patel suggested, sounding unconvinced and vaguely uncomfortable that passing on this kind of advice was in his job description. I am sure Dr Petroffsky would have found the idea of a medical doctor being forced to utter such words as 'fore-play' inconceivable.

Jason did not seem bothered with either the geisha or the cheese-eater approach. His readiness to combine sex and humour continued to baffle me. I wondered if that too was an English thing. Laughter and lovemaking occu-pied separate chambers in my mind. Where one began the other ended, perhaps because, if you paused to laugh, the whole sexual enterprise became hilarious.

Since I adhered to Dr Patel's recommendations despite believing I didn't need to, it was perhaps doubly surpris-ing when some months later I woke up one morning feeling queasy and with an unmistakable hardness in my nipples. I knew these signs from the spring before last, but I also knew that things would end differently this time. This child is mine, I thought, and the thought seemed neither startling nor entirely logical. Mine, it implied, and not Jason's.

'All I know is I'm not having another abortion,' I told Jason some twelve weeks later, at the end of my second winter in London, thirteen months into our stay in the Minford Gardens attic, a month after our first wedding anniversary.

My wad of parental money had thinned to nothing, and Jason's grant was about to cease. The steady dribble of my translation fees, now spreading into other branches of zoology, kept us afloat, but only just: thirty-five pounds per thousand words, three or four hundred pounds a month when I was lucky. Jason talked enthusiastically about us translating verse together; but there was no more money in poetry translation than there was in poetry itself. When I suggested working together on other kinds of books, something more commercial perhaps, he changed the subject. My English wasn't idiomatic enough to risk doing it alone, and I had no idea where I would start. I kept applying for jobs, and Jason kept promising that he would too, once his grant ran out.

'Something will come along,' he kept saying. How right he was.

I thought of my parents in their huge echoing house, not knowing. Of Jason's parents in their chilly farmhouse, in their big, frosty garden, not knowing, either.

'All I know is I'm not having another abortion,' I repeated, then put my hands on top of my stomach as though there was something to see, or as though someone was about to attack me. I was just past that date when the dangers of a miscarriage begin to recede.

Down the road, at the clinic, Dr Patel and his nurse already knew about the failure of his family planning device, but it was only now that I told Jason about his impending fatherhood. Dr Petroffsky had warned me that abortion greatly increased the chances of subsequent miscarriage. I didn't want to talk about my pregnancy until I knew it was for real, for fear that I could somehow jinx it, although, I admit it, my silence might well have amounted to an act of selfishness.

Jason told me that much as soon as he took in what I was saying.

'Not again,' he said at first, shaking his head in disbelief. I wondered if he meant pregnancy or silence. I waited to find out which before I mounted my defence, irritated that I needed to defend myself. Whichever it was, the world was harder on me, as it was, generally, harder on women.

His face fell. He arrested it in its fall, but then his expression gradually changed. He was warming to the idea of fatherhood. It was not in his nature to worry about how to bring up a child in a rented attic flat with a bathroom across the shared landing. My mother had sung an unmemorable Mimi in *La Bohème*; I was living the part.

'When is she due? Do you know?' Jason asked, now beaming, lifting me up so high that I felt I might throw up over his shoulder. I had no idea why he assumed it would be a girl.

'September the ninth,' I said. 'To be confirmed by the dating scan, in two days' time, but Dr Patel and I are fairly sure. And please let me down.'

That was the only occasion I had to ask.

Again his face fell as he computed how long I had withheld the information for, then beamed again.

'My publication date,' he almost shouted. 'We'd better postpone the launch by a week. My daughter will attend it. It will be her first. I'll write a speech around that. I'll write to Tristan now.'

'The launch?' I asked. I had no idea. He had his own silences too.

'Yes, at the Poetry Society. I wanted to surprise you, throw a big party: this book is dedicated to you, after all. Tristan is driving up from Brighton with the entire print run in his car boot,' he said, as though we were talking about thousands of thick tomes and not a couple of hundred slim volumes. 'We think it will be the Poetry Society Autumn Choice.'

This was the Jason I knew, seeking to fix the date of his launch party before anything else, assuming that it mattered to others as much as it mattered to him. And, in Minford Gardens at least, he was right. I forgot about my pregnancy for a moment and discussed venue capacities instead. When his international success finally came, I knew that it had taken not just his talent and his drive, but this particular form of self-centredness.

'And can we call her Livia?' he said when we tired of rehearsing what he would say about the child in his speech. 'Livia Plurabelle Connor.'

I was lying on the sofa, my head in his lap, my hands on my stomach, defending the potential Plurabelle. I could feel the faint chemical approximation to the smell of strawberry in the air above me. Jason had, absentmindedly, grabbed the wrong kind of shampoo in the supermarket and we were too poor to throw it away.

'Over my dead body,' I said and laughed. 'I have other ideas.'

'Oh no. Not Gertruda ...' He laughed too. 'Gertruda Montserrat Caballé Connor: you can't saddle an Irish colleen with that.'

'We don't have this multiple-name tradition,' I said, ignoring his point about Irishness for perhaps the millionth time. 'Just the one. And that one won't be Gertruda, I assure you.'

'Clarissa Stanislava then, a compromise? Wedding your father to my mother?' Jason said, ignoring, in his turn, my point about a single name. He liked the sound of that. 'Or Stanislava Joyce Connor?'

'Urgh, yuck – stop, Jason.'

If I laughed at the idea of Plurabelle, the mention of Gertruda and Stanislav hurt. Of course I wasn't going to have my daughter named after my mother. And a feminine version of my father's name was as unthinkable. But I felt guilty carrying this child, their blood, without my parents knowing. I hoped against hope that they did know, for once wanting Lekovich to have his informants in the family planning clinic, since he seemed to have them in the Home Office and everywhere else.

Jason came with me to the ultrasound scan. I was lying on my back feeling the cold gel on my skin, the probe pressing on my stomach. Then the black-and-white image flickered into being, the rhythmic whoosh of my blood flow following it like the sound of a deep ocean, and, somewhere behind the waves, a double heartbeat. We would need two names after all.

*

I alone worried about feeding those babies. After he sub-
mitted his thesis, while waiting for his viva and while my
stomach grew, Jason spoke about 'signing on', about 'the
dole'. I associated the word with dolorousness, with
depression. I could not believe that anyone could ever
progress from the dole to a good job.

'So what?' he said. 'I don't want a job anyway. I expect
great things from *The Argonauts*.'

His second poetry collection was now in the final stages
of production with Polaris, his publisher. The much
spoken-about Tristan, the owner-editor, was a tweedy
man based in Brighton who produced stylish-looking
books, and who sometimes sat at the back of readings
manning a sales desk.

Polaris was ensuring that the small fortune inherited
from its proprietor's novelist grandmother became ever
smaller. It was the opposite of commercial, the opposite
of trade. Jason never tired of pointing out the irony of
Edwardian pulp fiction funding today's high art. While
the Polaris print runs usually amounted to two hundred
copies, cumulative sales of twenty or thirty per title were
not uncommon. Jason was the imprint's star. His first
collection had won him a poetry prize that, in turn, led
him to me, his red princess, he liked to point out. It also
resulted in high three-figure sales.

'And that is how many discerning people you have in
the UK,' Tristan said when Jason suggested a small ad in
a literary review, 'no point trying for more.'

The new collection, *The Argonauts*, was a sequence of four
sonnet coronas that Jason had already been working on
when we first met: fifty-six sonnets, interconnected, written at a rate of roughly two sonnets a month. I remember

small notepads in his trouser pockets, scribbled in ant-sized hieroglyphics. He called that a high level of productivity; I am unable to judge. The formal discipline was at odds with the lack of it in Jason's life.

'And before you call me fusty, Millie, remember how experimental these sonnets are,' he said.

I wasn't about to call him fusty. I had read and loved the poems and, although I was no critic, I knew that the book was going to be every bit as good as its predecessor, better actually.

A week or so after our wedding day, Jason and I had walked to a cinema on King Street to see a film about Mozart directed by Miloš Forman, a Czech man who had defected to the US in the seventies. All his films were banned back home, but Misha had managed to get hold of *One Flew Over the Cuckoo's Nest* and *Hair* and we had watched them together in his home cinema. It was strange, and poignant, to see this new one in my new country. The drabness of the auditorium was lessened by the joy of Mozart's music and by Jason's company. My husband was, I thought, both proud and feckless, not unlike young Amadeus. And I still loved him: you couldn't not love Jason, I thought.

I loved Jason's poetry too, but I expected nothing material from *The Argonauts*.

Jason spotted a large card with Father's picture in a Communist bookshop in Covent Garden and decided to send it to Huw. The address of the British Council Library was stamped in my copy of *Orlando*.

He called this a postmodern joke; I wondered what the censors back home would make of it.

'Hello, Comrade. Greetings from Blighty,' Jason read what he wrote out loud to amuse me. 'Hope all's well with you. I have another book in the works. Out in September. M is expecting. The babies are out in September too. You read that right: she is carrying twins. I have now taken my formal education as far as it could go on government money, only the blasted viva remains. Talk about all-round productivity! Do get in touch when you're over here, Boyo. We won't be visiting you, unless you get a new posting this side of the Curtain. I know you want it and am hoping that this card will help effect the move. A sealed envelope has never stood in the way of M's compatriots. The image is bound to please my father-in-law.'

I wished Jason had announced my pregnancy less facetiously, but I wasn't going to play his censor. I felt certain that the news would now reach my father, if it hadn't already, but the card was returned to us three or four weeks later. It was still in its envelope with Jason's initials and our address on the back, but now in a transparent wrapping from Royal Mail, with a handwritten note indicating insufficient postage. It looked as though it had never left England. One of the larger stamps was missing from it, although I was sure it was there when I posted the card. I would once have laughed at the idea of the Brits steaming off stamps in sorting offices, but I was no longer sure about anything. Jason called me paranoid. Why would anyone want to stop his card? I had no answer to that question.

I know it couldn't have been like that, but I later imagined Jason's card on the mail train to Dover, then sitting in some sorting office in the shadow of the white cliffs, and being returned to us just as that nuclear reactor exploded and sent its poison into the atmosphere. I had never even heard of Chernobyl before, but I had nightmares through, and after, that summer, worrying about the effect of its toxic rain on my children, wondering what was more telling: British hysteria or Soviet silence. It took Gorbachev two weeks to speak.

The card sat in its plastic pouch, looking itself like some irradiated object. I threw the envelope away and put my father's image on the mantelpiece in our bedroom. It was a familiar three-quarter view.

'And this is the world you created,' I wanted to say, as though he had built the nuclear plant with his bare hands. 'The world you believe in.'

He looked past me, and past my living quarters, with his usual lack of expression. I was out of date. I no longer knew who Father's enemies were.

There was a short biography on the back of the card, mentioning neither Mother nor me. The note reminded me that my babies could very easily share Father's birthday: they were due less than a week earlier. There were public celebrations to mark the occasion back home, not as big as those accorded to the President but grand enough nonetheless: a Pioneer march past, an athletic event, a concert in the Philharmonic Centre.

Father normally watched these events alone, from his box, like the Great Gatsby, but I sometimes scrubbed up and joined him, though you wouldn't have known it from the official photographs. They bore captions with his name alone even when, very rarely, my blurry image appeared next to him. Mother hated seeing up-to-date images of herself in the newspapers, and she was not expected to appear in public anyway. I wondered if these occasions had become more modest since I left.

I leaned out of the window, feeling a movement in my stomach and a pang of hunger. That whole summer I often had the impression that I was eating for six, not for three. Minford Gardens was empty, but there was a cluster of red buses stuck in a traffic jam on Shepherd's Bush Road. On their sides, ads were announcing the forthcoming premiere of *Aliens: This Time It's War*. People clustered on the lower decks, jumped off as their buses came to a standstill and walked on. It was faster on foot. I might well have been on another planet.

My moodiness may have been hormonal and pregnancy-related, but the thought of Father would not leave me. I went to Bloomsbury, to the School of Slavonic and East European Studies Library in Senate House, where I found copies of our main newspaper, several weeks old, sitting in a sad line on a long rack next to copies of *Pravda*, *Rudé Právo*, *Rabotnichesko Delo* and the *Berliner Zeitung*.

These broadsheets were not meant to disseminate news. Instead, they delivered seemingly immutable interpretations of events: hundreds of words and no images other than black-and-white photographs of stern-looking men and, very occasionally, women in sombre suits. I could have checked their pages weeks and months ago, but I was held back by imagining informants lurking among the bookshelves and, perhaps less consciously, by my own need to affect indifference about the world I had left.

My father was there all right, going about his usual business week after week. It was a world without Chernobyl, without Gorbachev almost. I flicked through the old issues, travelling back in time. On a photograph big enough to cover most of the front page, published about a month after my departure for England, I saw Father on a rostrum, his index finger pointed sideways towards some unseen apparatchik, like God's finger in Michelangelo's *Creation*, and medallions with profiles of Marx, Engels, Lenin and our President looming above him on the building's wall. I examined the photograph closely to confirm that it was not an archival shot.

If he was there, I thought, if Stanislav was on that rostrum wagging his finger four weeks after I left, when the circumstances of my departure were known by all who needed to know, then everything must have been all right in the aftermath of my departure, is still all right now and will continue to be all right. He and Gertruda will still be in our house on the hill.

I looked at a further pile of back issues below the shelf, but I did not think it was worth flicking through. However far back I went, even the day after my departure, I knew there would be no mention of my defection. To the very limited degree that I was ever part of it, I was erased from official history.

I had feared that I would prove a liability but I was nothing.

'Are you still looking at those?' an old man said in my mother tongue, reaching towards the pile of newspapers. He had crept up without my noticing.

The library in the North Block of Senate House was full of shadows like him, nearly always men, shabby but respectably so, and of a certain age, flicking through old newspapers, copying things into notebooks, preparing articles for émigré newsletters.

I was startled at the sound of my own language, thinking that the man must have recognised me, but then I realised that my reading made it obvious I spoke it.

'No, I am done,' I said and pushed the pile towards him.

'Thank you so much,' he said, picking the newspapers up, lingering, considering another question. 'Are you researching a thesis?' he asked, paused, noting my stomach. 'What is your name? Whose child are you?'

It was an odd question, but I saw almost instantly that he assumed he knew my parents, for the few local students who bothered to look at these newspapers usually came from the same small émigré circle. If only he knew the truth. I gave a little chuckle, but it sounded too loud in that quiet space. Several pairs of elderly eyes rose from yellowing newspapers.

'I am not researching anything,' I said in English. 'And I am nobody's child.'

Chapter Twenty-Three

Labour

September 1986

My third trimester passed in a daze. The summer was far from scorching. There was not a single day between May and September that you could call truly hot. The temperatures lingered in the low twenties, yet I sweated with exertion even when I moved slowly, like an enormous container vessel on a placid sea. We slept naked, without covers, windows open to the London streets.

'You are pure form, Milena,' Jason said to me in bed, gazing at my taut body, at my growing breasts, at my stomach, which often swayed of its own volition. 'And pure form is the closest we get to beauty on this Earth.'

'Is that why you're writing sonnets? You have a form-fetish?' I teased him for his unaccustomed pomposity.

I had little idea what he was talking about, but I knew that he had never loved me as much as that summer.

September arrived, and Dr Patel had the due date wrong. It was not the ninth but the fourteenth, an early Sunday afternoon so quiet that I could hear the sounds of jukebox music through the open doors of the pubs as my womb contracted at ever-shorter intervals and the cab glided down Goldhawk Road towards the maternity hospital.

When we were taken inside, Jason constituted such a charming example of anxious impending fatherhood that the midwives looked after him as well as they looked after me. He nearly fainted when the labour was over and one of the midwives produced a needle and a spool of surgical thread.

'We'll make Mum as good as new,' she said, her Antipodean accent as sweet as her heart-shaped face.

And before I was made as good as new, I had neither Livia Plurabelle nor Gertruda, but a boy. Then, four minutes later, another boy. When I heard them cry, first one and then the other, when I saw them covered in my blood and mucus, something pushed me into an even deeper silence.

'Here, Mum.' The midwife gave them to me, just as the consultant stepped in to congratulate Jason. I did not know how to hold two at once. They felt so fragile, so tiny, so mine.

Although I chose not to have the babies' sex revealed ahead of that September day – which happened, astoundingly, to be my father's birthday after all – I had intuited that I was carrying sons very early on and with a certainty I could not explain.

When I was alone in the flat, I sometimes studied my ever-growing shape in the mirror, the dark line down the middle of my stomach, the navel, like some ugly little mushroom pushed out by the heft of the two bodies I was carrying, and I'd see images of two boys nurtured by a she-wolf, like something that belonged both to some mythical past and to my own future. Loneliness can make you psychic even when you don't believe in psychic powers. My father had taught me to believe in historical inevitabilities. I had known my own destiny all along, it turns out. Jason was a Western man, he believed in free will.

The births were recorded as uneventful, although that adjective encompassed waves of unspeakable pain. I do mean unspeakable. I could not find even the most basic of English words. I kept opening my mouth only to produce a rattle, the scraping of a dry tongue against the parched palate.

A memory, a split-second thing, crossed my mind between two contractions, while the pain still circled around me, retreating then closing in. Father was just back from Egypt, and Dara had made sure that the house had already been cleaned of every last trace of Misha's violent death. I walked into a room without knocking, to find him just off the phone to someone, still in his overcoat, pressing the receiver down with his gloved hand as though he was trying to flatten it against the surface of the desk.

'I want you to stop snivelling now,' he said without looking up, and I was sure that he thought he was speaking to Mother, for, whatever else I did, I certainly never snivelled. Then he saw me and his expression didn't change. He took his gloves off, paused. I knew that he wasn't going to acknowledge his error, if error it had been.

'Not a sound, you understand. Be a man from now on,' he said.

Nothing had ever hurt as much as that delivery. I would like to claim that I surprised myself in the cab, and later on the ward, by being unable to produce a sound beyond a rasp. The midwives kept wiping the sweat of my brow, encouraging me to let go, to pant or to scream as much as I wanted, but I could not. It wasn't the loss of language, but something deeper, I realised: the years of home drilling and some anchoring in a trauma that was both specifically mine – the only daughter of a National Hero – and also bigger than me. My father's mother must have laboured exactly like me, in her draughty mountain home, on a wooden floor warmed by the breath of animals sheltering below, and without a sound. I wondered if the maintenance of silence had been passed down through my father like that odd hazel-green of our eyes, and I also wondered, for the first time, now that I had two boys, if he ever regretted not having a son.

'My God, Millie,' Jason said. 'You were so unbelievably brave. The midwives had never seen anyone like you. I knew you were tough, but I had no idea how tough.'

'Just because I didn't scream,' I said, 'it doesn't mean that I am tough. I thought perhaps the pain was greater because it was trapped.'

The choice of names was limited: we had agreed to restrict ourselves to those that sounded the same in both our languages, and we needed two. Jason wanted flamboyance, something fitting for the artists he thought our boys would inevitably become. He might have been writing verse about the Argonauts, but he disliked his own Argonaut name with a passion, had always wondered what possessed his parents to honour the family's classical tradition by choosing the most humdrum item on the menu. Yet he went through his list of famous twins only to tease me. Neither Romulus and Remus, nor Castor and

Pollux, was ever a possibility. I insisted on names with which to travel unnoticed. We called the twins Nicholas and Philip.

Everything in the English maternity ward seemed make-shift, happy-go-lucky. There were stricter hygiene rules in a boys' gym back home. There, mothers were separated from babies after delivery. Here, Nicholas and Philip were allowed to snuggle in my armpits, tiny and creased from the pressure of the womb, like two loaves of warm brioche.

There were six new mothers on the ward, each of a different ethnicity. Large family parties visited with picnics of hot food first thing in the morning and last thing at night. Jason's permanent perch on a stool by the window was inconspicuous by comparison. He feasted on my pale hospital sandwiches, munching and talking about father-hood while I received my first lessons in breastfeeding.

'Poets make appalling fathers, and few become fathers knowingly,' he opined both to entertain me and to show off to anyone who happened to be in our proximity. 'Not Auden, not Eliot. Pound gave his away to be looked after by some Italian peasant. Oh, OK, yes, Yeats, but at almost twice my age. Ted Hughes too.'

'Let's not take Hughes as your yardstick,' I said. Ted Hughes had become Poet Laureate six days after I landed at Heathrow. I had never heard of him, but the press coverage suggested that his love life was more exciting than his verse. His was a story fit for a Greek tragedy and not for a maternity ward. Jason and Clarissa had had a furious row over some article in *The Observer* at the kit-chen table: the son speaking out for Ted Hughes, the mother defending Sylvia Plath, a considerate Paddy quietly explaining who everyone was. And the mistress killed herself and her child while the wife killed only herself, he said. The former was not Russian, in spite of her and her daughter's Russian names, he added, answering my unspoken question.

I knew nothing of any of this before I came to England. Our university syllabus ended with the Great Depression, and although I tried to stay informed about developments in fiction, I was insufficiently interested in English poetry to bother getting more up-to-date at the British Council Library. It is hilarious, in retrospect, that I married a poet.

'Shouldn't you look at your own contemporaries? Ravi Kumar or Sean whatshisname? Or even Tim Koff?' I indulged Jason, pleased that I remembered his closest rival, whom I'd heard reading alongside Jason at the Stag's Head in Bromley. 'He has a three-year-old daughter.'

'I forgive you, Millie, for you are foreign.' Jason pretended to be insulted. 'The whole of London, including *Dummkopf* himself, knows that *Dummkopf*'s daughter is in fact Sean whatshisname's, as you so nicely put it.'

He spoke fast, clipping his syllables, imitating me. I did that often when I tried to outwit him: spoke as quickly as I could, with a skill gained in my interpreting days.

He lifted Nicholas out of his cot, kissed his fontanelles. The sight of his shaggy blond hair next to the baby's silky black Mohawk frond – a small head carefully held in a father's hand like a large peach – suggested that Jason, in spite of what he was saying, would know how to be a good parent. He looked more mature, more responsible, more masculine somehow in his new-found gentleness. Philip was lying in his separate plastic basin, but he must have sensed that his brother was no longer near and emitted a kitten cry. I held him and, in that moment, we were happy, a perfect little family group.

I spent the evening of Jason's book launch still on the ward with the boys. The following morning, when he arrived to help us leave the hospital, he declared the event a stunning success. There would be a small but perfect review in the *TLS*, he said. The reviewer attended the launch, told him that he loved *The Argonauts*.

'The best week of my life, Millie, just the best,' he kept repeating.

We took the boys home to Minford Gardens and it felt good to be back there, among familiar things in a now-familiar place. I was still too sore to sit but not too sore to attempt translating a study of the moths of Dagestan, in those all-too-brief moments when both Philip and Nicholas slept. Jason sat next to me on the bed, notebook on his knees, and wrote.

'Just something about these two munchkins – impressions, nothing formal yet,' he said, looking at the Moses baskets on the floor by our bed. 'I have never felt so contented in my life. So contained.'

I had never felt less contained. I bled and my breasts leaked. The room smelled of milk and meconium. The boys' faeces, dark green and oily little slugs at first, gradually turned runny and mustard-yellow, and started arriving in unpredictable explosions, which escaped their nappies and stained their Babygros. When you lifted them to soothe them, they posseted milk, as uncontainable as their mother.

I learned a hundred new words during each session with the health visitor, and those words were only ever useful for a week or two.

'It's normal,' she would say about whatever it was that she was explaining to me. 'It's normal. Don't worry. It will pass.'

The first weekend after we were discharged from hospital, Clarissa and Paddy arrived with a picnic basket from Fortnum & Mason. There were cold pies, ripe cheeses, tubs of coronation chicken, biscuits, apples and grapes, a fruitcake. I was startled to realise it was their first visit to Minford Gardens, but also that in England presents and treats were a rather easy substitute for real, practical help. Since that lunch in Soho, we had met Clarissa rarely and always in central London, in places where distraction reduced the need for conversation: an exhibition, a matinee at the theatre, an afternoon concert. Whatever it was, my mother-in-law always booked our tickets. She seemed to be a member of every arts organisation in England. As far as we knew, until that visit to see his grandsons, Paddy had always stayed out in the country.

Clarissa asked to wash her hands before she held the babies, and started when Jason told her where the lavatory was. It was a split-second reaction but I saw the flat afresh through her eyes, its flimsy rental furniture, badly hung curtains, scatterings of baby things, my dictionaries, Jason's books everywhere, our papers, and six of us in it.

'How perfect they are,' Clarissa said about the boys. 'I never thought I'd become a grandmother so early.'

I looked for barbed meanings in every sentence she uttered, then instantly thought myself too prickly and defensive. I nibbled at fruit and biscuits and sipped elderflower champagne. It was thoughtful of them to remember I could not drink alcohol. Paddy sat at the edge of the bed and drank red wine from a mug. There were champagne flutes in the hamper, for Jason, Clarissa and me, but Paddy didn't like fizz, and all our wine glasses were sitting, unwashed, in the sink.

At one point, when Clarissa and Jason were arranging food, their backs turned to us, Paddy leaned over and squeezed my hand.

'You will master this,' he said. 'It will get easier. You are a strong girl, Milena. Your father's daughter. At your age he was in prison, wasn't he?'

I was so taken aback by this very precise reference to my father that I had no idea how to respond. I knew Father was eminently researchable – any public library would furnish the goods – but I had no idea Paddy would bother. Clarissa turned towards us and smiled. She might have heard.

'Their hair, so black and smooth. A first for the Connor tribe,' Paddy added, now looking at the boys.

'Uncle Edward was just as dark. It runs in our family too. Anyway, babies' hair colour changes quickly – don't you remember anything at all?' Clarissa said. She seemed almost too keen to forestall some hurt that no one had felt, too quick to say that darkness did not arrive with me.

I smiled and said little. Ever since I had felt betrayed by it while in labour, I found my English much slower and more halting than before. It was fine for writing and for translating, but it was as though spoken words were slowly deserting me. I'd heard of my compatriots abroad losing their knowledge of their mother tongue, sometimes without achieving true mastery of another language, because it failed to offer the omnipresent embrace that the English language did. It was a terrible fate, being literally lost for words. I spoke to the boys in my mother tongue all the time, and that was strange and new, the words flooding back after so many months of using them only in my thoughts. Sometimes, particularly when Jason was out, the rooms filled with my voice.

Jason was right about his year of miracles. Everything speeded up all of a sudden. His viva took place while I was still too shell-shocked by labour to take much notice and, although he said he'd sailed through it, he also said there was nothing to celebrate. He did not like to talk about his academic work. It conferred a sense of obligation he'd rather not shoulder.

On the other hand, he seemed transformed when *The Argonauts* set sail.

At first it was just a ripple: that short review in the *TLS*, a handful of letters forwarded by Clarissa, a phone call or two. Then a famous actor chose this 'amazing new collection' as his *Desert Island* book alongside Shakespeare and the Bible. Michael Parkinson, the interviewer, surprised us by saying that he'd read it too. Jason was invited to record a sequence for Radio 3, where it ran, in fifteen-minute instalments, for five nights. We listened every evening. Even the boys were alert, like clever puppies, sensing that their father's voice was coming at them from two places.

'We're huge,' Jason said and danced with them in his arms when a rockstar was photographed reading *The Argonauts* on a beach in Mustique.

The first run of two hundred sold out. Tristan invested in another.

'I am pushing the boat out here,' he told Jason. 'We might risk a little advertisement somewhere too. I remember you asking for it last time. Let no one say I don't spoil my stars.'

Even Will, our neighbour from downstairs, realised that Jason had a book out.

'I bought *The Astronauts*,' he said, while helping me carry my double pram up several flights, having spotted me at the gate from his basement window. 'Although I read only thrillers these days, and even those less and less. Mainly on planes. Do tell your man that I am impressed.'

In mid-October *The Argonauts* won a poetry prize named after a Welsh poet I had never heard of: a thousand pounds, to be awarded at a festival in the Black Mountains, in a writing retreat that had once been the poet's ancestral farmhouse. Two collections, two awards: the prizes came easily to Jason and I couldn't be happier about that.

For four days, while he travelled to receive the cheque and give his celebratory readings, the boys and I slept and ate and went out to take the cold air on the rainy little greens and forlorn shopping parades that dotted the neighbourhood. The babies squinted at the clouds and I wondered how much of the world they could already see. When I offered my hand, they held my fingers with an ever-stronger grip. They would be handsome men, our boys, I could already see; as handsome as their father, and more. Their faces filled out later on and their hair slowly lightened: eventually they had silky curls of Connor blond. The midnight blue of their newborn eyes finally turned to my hazel-green. Urbansky green.

I pushed the double pram through Shepherd's Bush Market and piled vegetables into the tray. I was learning to cook with exotic stuff I had never come across before: plantains, yams, bitter gourds, sour pawpaws. The stall-holders knew me by sight, gave generous advice, nodded in sympathy when I looked frazzled, which was most of the time, smiled when I made the effort to rim my eyes with kohl, as in the old days. Markets like that, a warren of railway arches and rainbow-coloured awnings, were the only places where fruit and vegetables were both cheap and ripe. In the shops you had to choose one or the other: sweetness or quantity.

London was vibrant and welcoming on the surface, but feral underneath. You felt that everything you owned could be snatched if you stopped paying attention for a moment. Perhaps that feeling came because, for the first time, I possessed so little, yet had so much to protect. I wanted Jason to find a job, to move out of Minford Gardens, to stop renting, but I also wanted him to be able to live for his talent, and these two desires were not compatible, not in London, not in Britain, not anywhere in the West perhaps.

I spotted a small stack of copies of *The Argonauts* in the window of our local bookshop. 'Signed by the author,' a sticker said. I went in, squeezed the enormous pram between the book tables, then opened a copy to see Jason's signature.

'It's a local author, you know,' a plump girl at the till said. 'And a really handsome and charming man. He was in here the other day. I can't recommend the book enough.'

Jason had never mentioned this local initiative. There was no reason he should have. Despite its shabbiness, Shepherd's Bush was BBC land, so boosting the book locally was an astute move. The collection was priced at £4.99, twice as expensive as the novel next to it, but I knew no one was making any money out of the enterprise. On impulse, I bought a copy, told the girl it was a gift and waited as she wrapped it and tied a silky green ribbon around it.

Jason had been away for just four days and yet I missed him already, when he telephoned to say that he was extending his stay by a couple more nights, for a gig in Hereford. At the cathedral, he said, excited, and I tried to share his joy, although my mind was too hazy with sleeplessness to take it in properly. Cathedrals meant little to me; I didn't realise people read poetry in them. I found Hereford on a map: there, next to Wales, on his way back to me.

In the evening, when the babies slept, I opened my parcel with slow deliberation as though it were truly a gift. My husband's handsome face beamed from the back cover, sharing the joke of the purchase with me. Inside, his familiar signature was scribbled under the printed dedication. 'To Milena Urbanska,' it read.

I had seen the dedication both in manuscript and in proof, because Jason had asked me to proofread the book for him, but I had not bothered to check the final version. I had been Millie for months and, at proof stage, that's what the dedication was: 'To Millie'.

I suggested that 'To M' would be more than enough. A printed dedication seemed too much, my official enthronement as the poet's muse, but I couldn't say so to Jason without sounding ungrateful. He could be flippant about everything else but he was always dead serious about his poetry. I liked M, the mystery of it. He never said he changed that. I now stared at my maiden name on the page and felt foreign, visible, exposed.

Chapter Twenty-Four

Betrayal

Since you walked out on me
I'm getting lovelier by the hour.
I glow like a corpse in the dark.
                    Nina Cassian, 'Lady of Miracles'

It was sudden, but betrayal so often is. Its revelation usually spills out unprompted and unplanned. Jason returned from Wales and what he called the Welsh Marches, and for some days afterwards our life seemed normal, indeed better than normal. I should have noticed that he was contrite. He had never been contrite before.

He talked, at long last, about finding a teaching job. He read advertisements in *The Times Higher Education Supplement* and he applied to universities, polytechnics and colleges of higher education for every literature lectureship on offer that autumn, however unlikely. He spoke about crammers. There were several in Holland Park, less than a mile from us but a different world, he said. I had wanted him to look for work for many months but, now that he seemed eager, I felt guilty. I wished he would be more fastidious. I didn't want him to end up in some dreadful establishment that would crush his spirit.

'We can manage a little longer, Jason,' I said. 'We've managed for two years. Don't rush for my sake.'

He shopped. He cooked. He ironed. He took the babies out for long walks in their double pram. We had always shared both the chores and childcare, but he now bore the brunt. He knew how much I had sacrificed by coming to England, he said. He had at least glimpsed my previous way of life. He wanted me to relax, to put my feet up. He wanted me to read. He wanted to read to me. He wanted me to be happy.

And he made love to me more often and with even greater passion. I had never felt as attractive as I did after the twins were born. Never mind the British magazine chatter about maternity and its aftermath. It didn't apply to me. There was a brief period when the raw wounds of labour were still healing, but, after that, motherhood made me feel powerful. It still does.

I can't, even now, begin to believe that Jason's lust was not genuine without at the same time starting to feel murderous rage. Even at my most cynical, I attributed our heightened feelings to the aphrodisiac of nascent fame arousing him – and me, for that matter – rather than to his duplicity or feelings of guilt.

Yet I did notice that he was also going out more, that autumn after he returned from the west. After he'd per-formed the duties that had once fallen to me, he would put on his Aran jumper and his cagoule and head out alone, to walk. He needed silence and space to compose, he said. He'd come back talking of the riverine tides, of schoolchildren rowing on the Thames. What kind of wife would I have to have been to say: 'Show me the verse'?

He went to poetry readings in fringe theatres and pubs I'd never heard of, at the other end of London, unlisted in

Time Out. I thought nothing of it. He was a rising star; it was to be expected that he would get many more gigs. Since the boys' birth I had stopped accompanying him. It wasn't just that babysitters were expensive and that I wasn't a literary person at heart. I had studied English literature but I had no aspirations to become part of it. I loved being alone with the boys. I remembered songs from my childhood and I sang to them. I was the daughter of an opera singer, but I had never sung before. I had a voice, it turned out.

Then the English Christmas started its slow approach and Jason seemed restless, but even the prospect of enforced winter holidays does that to people.

Women are betrayed all the time. Most forgive: some because they have to, others because they want to. In the end, I neither wanted nor had to. I don't feel stupid about any of this, except perhaps about responding to my husband's lust with an equal measure of my own.

'Good morning. So sorry to bother you. May I speak to Jason Connor?' The voice was smooth, confident, female and not young, I thought.

'I am afraid he has stepped out,' I said. 'Could I take a message?'

'To whom am I speaking?' the woman said, sounding, in her pedantic starchiness, like one of the antiquated English tape recordings we listened to in the language lab at university. Philip emitted a squeal from his Moses basket, like a kitten, pushing at its straw sides with his feet, then Nicholas imitated him, as he always did. I saw a hole on Nicholas's Babygro, through which his big toe peeked. They were already growing out of those flimsy baskets, out of their Babygros ... surely out of our minuscule flat as well.

'His wife,' I said. There was a longish pause, another squeal, now from Nicholas, another wobble of the straw wall.

'Oh, I see,' the woman responded, in that assured way I have come to associate with a certain type of Englishness. 'Yes, of course. Please tell him Artemis Rutherford called, from the BBC. It's about that recording we discussed last week. I'll call again. When's the best time? I don't want to disturb you or your child.'

'Children,' I said.

'Of course,' she said. 'Your children.'

When Jason came back from the Black Mountains, for a day or two he amused me with silly anecdotes about the sorts of people he had met, including his white-haired audience at Hereford Cathedral. He always did that, after his events. He was good with accents and voices, good at capturing the essence of any personality, and he enjoyed making me laugh. I always felt I had been with him. I always felt I'd met everyone.

Yet he had failed to mention this woman. I'd have remembered the name.

To discuss a recording for the BBC and forget about it, not tell his spouse: Ted Hughes maybe, not Jason Connor. I felt alone, trapped in my own fear of appearing to over-react. I was new to this kind of suspicion.

'Artemis Rutherford called,' I said when he stepped back into the flat, pulling his cagoule over his head, a stupid green cagoule without a front fastening, so that his face, his wet face, was hidden from me for a couple of seconds.

In Britain people discuss their marriages on television. I could never imagine stooping as low as that. Let's just say that I still find it difficult to explain the contradictions of that particular moment. It wasn't denial on my part, so much as intentional ignorance as defined by law. I didn't want to know, partly because I wanted no one else to know that I knew.

And Jason was happy to indulge me. As it emerged from the cagoule, the only emotion that his poetry-performer's face displayed was casual curiosity.

'Oh, what about?' he said. 'Did she leave a message?'

The flatness of his voice betrayed him. Jason was someone who became animated even when speaking to the person who came round to read the electricity meter. I sensed something definite now. Perhaps my instincts were sharpened by coming from a society where so much was suppressed, rather as the blind are sometimes said to have a keener sense of hearing. I had spent most of my formative years on high alert. Britain, and Jason, had put me at deceptive ease.

That was over now. My heart beat faster than I thought possible. I felt its drumming in my ears and my temples. I could appear hysterical if I say anything more, I thought. It's a call, just a phone call, a working relationship – maybe flirtatious but maybe still innocent, although he seemed to have some guilty feelings. Hysteria: women are locked into silence by the fear of it. I put my fists in my pockets and repeated exactly what Artemis Rutherford had said.

'About that recording you discussed last week. She said she would ring again.' My voice was flatter than Jason's.

'Did she say when?' Jason asked. 'Did she leave a number?'

Later the same day, when he went out to Presto's to buy nappies, I moved a book he was reading, in order to put my typewriter on the table. I had a piece of translation to deliver the following week.

It fell from the book, fluttering to the floor: a thin sheet of cigarette paper, and on it, in blue ink, bleeding slightly, a number. And then an A. A narrow, sharp, pointy A, like an arrow, with a hook down on the right, revealing an amount of pressure that had been just enough to pierce the paper and, next to it, a blue heart. It could have belonged to any number of people. This was surely the number that Artemis Rutherford did leave after all. With its telltale heart.

I remembered how Jason used to draw a shamrock next to his signature, as he had that evening when he was bestowing his autographs at the Youth Palace, three months short of four years ago. That was the sort of frivolous thing people from carefree countries did, I thought then, because they never had to grow up. I now wished Lana Kovalska had hired a different interpreter.

Yet I still tried to explain every suspicion away: he was careless, Jason was, misplacing bits of paper all the time.

I put the note back inside the book, and the book to one side. I wasn't sure it was the right page, but I was sure Jason wouldn't notice the placing. In the space of the thirty minutes before he returned with two multipacks of nappies under his arms, our marriage changed. Not in a way he'd have noticed when he came back, for our evening progressed much as it had been destined to progress, except now not one, but both of us, acted.

I breastfed the boys, we supped on pasta and salad, both of which Jason prepared while I sat with my feet up, watching him. After supper, he washed and I dried the dishes and he told me that he had some excellent news to impart. He had known it since that morning but was holding back because he wanted to choose the moment, and also because he wasn't sure how to respond to the news himself, although the news was good – great even.

'I am surprised how you can hold things back like that,' I said, drying a plate and examining it from both sides. 'That you can choose your moment. I thought you were an open book.'

He paused, looked at me, his hands deep in suds, hunting for a knife or a fork underwater. He must have wondered what I was getting at.

'Particularly when the news is good,' I said and smiled, a big, beaming smile. I could see his shoulders relaxing.

Jason had been shortlisted for a post at University College London, a postdoctoral fellowship, part of a research project about Yeats, a natural next step, one could say, conferring the luxury of eight thousand pounds a year. He had a letter and the date for his interview, at the very end of term, although his own start date could be more flexible if he got the offer. Yet he was wondering if this – the run of luck with *The Argonauts*, he explained – had not already made him bigger than a postdoc placement. A bigger name, you could say.

'What do you think, Millie?' he asked.

'Whatever you think best,' I said. 'I don't want to influence your decision.'

He was unsettled by my response. He must have prepared his arguments for and against, expected me to urge him to seize the opportunity, or offer him reassurance if he chose not to. That I didn't do so was confusing, maybe even upsetting for someone as self-centred as, I was now beginning to realise, Jason was.

Nor did I use the moment to quiz him about Artemis Rutherford, as I could plausibly have done, if only to enquire about the recording. I asked no questions, because I still didn't know what I would do with the answers I received, and yet my husband hanged himself, step by step, wrong letter by wrong letter, like that stick-man in the children's game.

'It's a small world,' he said.

We were in bed. It was almost midnight; the boys were asleep in their baskets. Jason was reading the book I had seen earlier – a novel called *Oranges Are Not the Only Fruit* – and I was listening to the sound of rain on the roof.

'What makes you say that?' I asked, feigning drowsiness.

'Just thinking about Artemis,' he said. 'Artemis Rutherford.'

I still said nothing. It was for him to tie his rope into a noose.

'My grandfather was her father's tutor at Oxford,' he continued. 'We met at Grandpa's seventieth birthday party when we were five or six, and then not again until now. Her father is Jocelyn, the Earl of Clay.'

I am not sure it was Clay, but I didn't want to ask him to repeat it.

'I thought you didn't believe in titles,' I said, knowing Jason's circles well enough by now to realise that their public egalitarianism often concealed not a little snobbery and a fascination with wealth and power. 'I thought she worked for the BBC.'

'Yes, to both,' he said. 'A producer.'

'That's a nice combination,' I said. 'A countess and a producer.'

'A very junior producer,' he said, mistaking the target of my irony. 'And she's not a countess. I know those titles are confusing. But there's no nepotism at the BBC. You've got to be bloody good.'

'I'm sure she's bloody good,' I said. Then, not wanting to overdo it, 'She sounded so nice on the phone.'

'Yes, she is. Really nice. A lovely person,' Jason said. 'However, and more importantly for me – for us, Millie – her father funds a five-year poetry fellowship at Oxford. To honour her ancestor, the first Earl, who also happens to have been an Oxford man who dabbled in poetry centuries ago ... Jocelyn's on board, adores *The Argonauts* and has a lot of sway.

'A poetry fellowship is a much more exciting proposition than working a seam in UCL's Bloomsbury mines. It's a residence really. No obligations for five years. Pays as well as UCL too, but sounds so much more distinguished. I am flattered even to be considered. My nearest rivals are all old farts, and Artemis has been telling her dad that it is high time to appoint someone students can relate to, for a change. It would be a novelty to have an Irishman and not just another Brit. I think I can swing this one, Millie. It might take another push perhaps. You wait ages for a bus, as the cliché goes, and then two come along at once.'

'Let's talk about the Earl of Clay tomorrow morning,' I said.

I didn't want to hear the details of the Oxford job description and I certainly didn't want to know about the two buses. If I didn't like the idea of Jason the casual philanderer, I liked Jason the calculating, opportunistic philanderer even less. I could already see that Artemis and I had something in common: we were both princesses.

Except my father's kingdom was far away, and I had renounced my inheritance.

'How old is this Artemis Rutherford?' I asked, in an effort to stop torturing myself. It was a mistake, that question. I wanted to sleep, forget about my anger.

'Twenty-six, -seven perhaps. Like you, give or take a year,' he said. Paused. 'What is it? Why are you asking?'

'Her voice sounded much older,' I said.

In the light of his bedside lamp, I saw him blush. That was something, I thought. He is not yet utterly shameless. He switched the light off, reached out to touch me. I took his hand and then, gently, put it back down on his chest, like the hand of a dead man. I had never before refused to make love. I sensed him lying in the dark, and felt not so much guilty as worried that he would know something was afoot. So I changed my mind.

I could do this, I realised. I could be deceitful too. I moved closer, put my hand on his lower stomach, made things OK, trying to put out of my mind where he might have been and what he might have done. Then he slept; orgasms – at least his own ones – usually sent Jason to sleep. At our feet the boys were sleeping too. I couldn't. I waited in the dark while the world moved by half a turn and the morning came.

Our flat was full of sunshine the following day. To judge by the light, it could have been June outside, not December. Jason suggested that I might like to have some time to myself.

'I feel your tension,' he said, 'I felt it last night. And I know how tiring it can all be. The boys, the work. I have my hopes and plans, but you are the only breadwinner now, and at a time when most new mothers would be on maternity leave. Treat yourself, have a massage, a facial, a manicure, or all three – whatever it is that you girls do to pamper yourselves ... You deserve it, Millie. I will look after the boys.'

I accepted his offer and resisted the temptation to be sarcastic about girls and pampering. I needed time to reflect, to think things through on my own, for, very soon, there might be no going back.

I left the twins with Jason and walked out into the cold light. The massage parlours around Shepherd's Bush Green seemed too dubious to enter. As I weaved my way through the back streets, I spotted a small, clean hair salon, tucked away near Olympia. I hadn't had a haircut in months. That Juliette Gréco bob was a distant memory. I had worn my hair in a messy ponytail throughout my pregnancy, cutting it myself with kitchen scissors.

The salon was empty. The hairdresser assumed I was her compatriot when I stepped in, for she addressed me in Italian. I mentioned the name of my country. She had no idea where it was and, conveniently, no desire to find out.

It was the first time in England that I had had my hair washed by someone else. I found the pressure of the woman's fingers on my skull, her chatter about inconsequential things, so soothing that I felt on the verge of tears as I relaxed. She must have sensed something of my mood, and I was grateful that she didn't enquire. She put on some light music, wrapped my head in a warm towel, guided me towards the chair, then handed me a small pile of glossy magazines and offered a cup of coffee.

'How do you take it?' she asked.

'Strong and bitter,' I said. 'No sugar. Stronger than they usually make it in England.'

'If you give me a minute,' she said, 'I'll make you a perfect cup, just the way you take it. To remind you of home. We're in no hurry. My first booking is not for another hour and a half.'

She disappeared into the little kitchenette at the back. I sat in front of the mirror, looking at the magazines she gave me. Fashion held little interest, gossip about unknown people even less. I opened a publication with a funny name: *Country Life*. 'Christmas Double Issue. Advent Calendar. Tips for Your Festive Season,' it promised. The cover image was a picture of a fat black turkey in a snowy field somewhere very flat, its snood and wattle obscenely red.

I flicked through pages of photographs of country homes for sale. Some estate agents tempted buyers with images of lavish drawing rooms dominated by decorated Christmas trees, boxes of gifts at their foot, and roaring fires in fireplaces. In front of one house several cows stared into the camera.

Then, twenty pages or so into the magazine, just as I began to wonder if I would ever reach the contents page of this strange periodical with its bizarre celebration of a habitat and way of life that my fellow urbanites back home would have wished at all costs to avoid, and as my hairdresser returned with a cup of coffee, I saw a full-page portrait photograph of a smiling young woman in a flat tweed cap and a tweed jacket. She was pressing her cheek against the cheek of a horse.

'Lady Artemis Rutherford,' the caption read. Then, in the line below: 'Artie (27), elder daughter of Jocelyn, the Earl of Cleigh, and his wife Sophia, the three-times Badminton champion who featured on this same page thirty years ago. Having taken a degree in English at Exeter, Artie travelled the world for two years, writing and searching for rare honeys for Bee Yourself, her mother's honey boutique in Chelsea, before embarking on a successful career as a producer at the BBC. A poetry lover and a keen horsewoman, Artie is pictured here with Nemesis, her favourite.'

I put the magazine down. I didn't need its tips for the festive season. I wish I could say that Artie – this *poetry lover* – looked stupid or that she resembled Nemesis. Instead she had a beautiful, warm face, with long silky chestnut hair and brown eyes, and she faced the camera with all the trust of someone who had never known any obstacles in her path. And it was not only her path – she was merely the latest traveller on a trail that had been travelled by her forebears for generations. I realised, staring at her smile, that I could wield the same power as Artemis, or much, much more, that I had done so in the past, but that I had never had – and would never have – the same trust in the world I lived in.

In fact Jason was the only person I had ever fully trusted. I trusted my parents, of course, but their vision of my happiness was not the same as mine. And I trusted Misha, but always suspected that I needed to protect him from too much reality. Jason and I were allies, I thought, comrades in arms. In the world I came from, the betrayal of trust was literally a matter of life and death, more important than any sexual transgression.

I now wondered if my instincts had failed, if I had thought Jason incapable of lying simply because I had never been so close to his faithless kind before. Our native opportunism – and there was no shortage of it in my father's social and political penumbra – came with the more obvious telltale signs. What if I had chosen my comrade wrongly?

I got my severe black bob back from the Italian, exactly as it used to be. I liked the look. My head felt lighter without the tail. It felt familiar, as though I had just erased my London years.

Chapter Twenty-Five

The Golden Age

Clarissa laughed when I told her that the worst thing about the holiday season in London was hearing the same jingles in every shop one entered. I could swear that even the babies were beginning to recognise the sound of Wham!'s 'Last Christmas'. She offered to take me out somewhere 'quiet and civilised'. It had been three months since her visit with Paddy.

She suggested a lunch away from the ubiquitous office Christmas parties and, before that, an exhibition of eighteenth-century Scottish painting at the Tate. It was billed as 'The Golden Age', she said, and reeled off a list of unfamiliar names. I knew nothing about Scottish painting, but, given the period, I anticipated a lot of powdered wigs and I didn't expect to be entertained.

'Not my glass of G&T, either,' Clarissa admitted, 'but our other obvious alternative is some Impressionist show that is likely to bring charabanc loads of ghastly types from the Home Counties, for their pre-Christmas cluck over the water lilies.' She didn't seem to suspect that she might be seen as one of those cluckers herself. Anyway it was just an excuse to spend some time with her lovely daughter-in-law again, she said. 'We could both do with a ladies' day out,' she explained. 'Have a good chinwag.'

I relished the idea of her company, although I was not planning to wag my chin too much.

Jason seemed delighted to give Ramsay and Raeburn a miss. He would be happy to spend a day looking after the boys on his own, he said.

I was pleased to find that Clarissa didn't seem angry with me. Soon after that conversation with Artemis, I had written to cancel our family Christmas visit. I offered heartfelt apologies but no reason. Doing this required as much steel as I could muster.

To Jason, I had offered the flimsy excuse of translation deadlines. He protested but demurred, out of what I assumed was a new-found guilt, either for being financially supported by his wife or for betraying her, or a combination of both. In any case the Christmas period in London was potentially better suited to his adulterous designs than spending the festive period in the sticks. I didn't know and I didn't care any more.

But Clarissa didn't deserve to be lied to. When she phoned to propose this pre-Christmas outing, I felt both relieved and anxious. I hoped she wasn't going to ask me to explain, for I had no excuse other than not wanting to be there with Jason, not having to pretend in front of his parents as I had to pretend in front of him. If I had to be in England, I would rather be in London, planning what exactly to do. It was sad, depriving the boys' English grandparents of their company, but it couldn't be helped. At least the boys were too young to know.

'Ah well ... we must make up for it in the New Year,' Clarissa said, sounding disappointed, but not pressing, and I was grateful for it. 'The boys will be sleeping better then, I am sure.' She furnished a generous pretence of an excuse.

'Yes, they will. They say that the colic phase ends at four months,' I agreed, taking care not to say anything I would regret later, even as I felt my heart breaking.

She couldn't know that Christmas might be her last chance to see her grandchildren. If that turned out to be the case, she would find out soon enough, I thought, just as she would find out it was their father's, not their mother's, fault.

Clarissa waited for me in the Tate's large portico. When I spotted her, I thought, as I thought each time I set eyes on her, that she looked like a time traveller, the bohemian mistress of some double-initialled writer from the past, like H. G. Wells, J. B. Priestley or G. K. Chesterton. She surprised me by opening her arms and pulling me tight against her soft paisley shawl. We walked inside, through the grand sculpture gallery, and she started quizzing me almost immediately: this was most unlike her. I looked so pale, she said. How was I coping with two babies? God knows, one was hard enough. Was I getting enough rest? Was Jason helping? Was he really helping? Was I happy? I tried to reassure her while not elaborating on happiness.

The exhibition meant little. I pretended to scrutinise canvases but I was too distracted by my situation to take anything in. In every bewigged beau and in every curvaceous female I saw Jason and Artemis. And over each landscape and each interior hovered the admonishing face of my father, as if to say: 'I told you so.'

*

Afterwards we walked eastwards along the Thames, towards the French bistro where we were going to share a light lunch before I saw Clarissa off at Charing Cross Station. We paused in front of the Houses of Parliament. She surprised me by producing a camera out of her bag and asking my permission to take a photograph of me. A crocodile of boys in long red robes, like tiny priests, were processing on the other side of the road. I turned towards them when she clicked.

She was pleased: she managed to catch me and Oliver Cromwell on his plinth behind me in the same profile angle, she said. She looked apologetic when I said there was no need to explain who he was, perhaps thinking that she had patronised me somehow. I mused over the fact that, amid all the strange statuary, I at least knew of him as the leader of England's bourgeois revolution of the seventeenth century – a necessary, progressive precursor for the socialist paradise. Although in our British history lessons we always skated over his behaviour in Ireland, something that might present different problems to me as the bride of a self-identifying Irishman.

'Strange to build a statue to the one who destroyed so many,' I said, and she laughed. 'They should have left the plinth empty in Oliver's honour.'

'You are so witty, Milena,' she said. Her rolling, crystalline laugh made me snap out of my unhappiness for a moment. 'And you deliver your lines so deadpan, which makes them even funnier. My son is the luckiest man.'

As she returned her camera to her seemingly bottomless bag, I realised I had no London photos except for a handful of bad wedding ones. A random passer-by had been co-opted on the day to take some snaps on a camera produced by one of our best men. Then, many months later, Clarissa took some photos of me and Jason with the twins when she visited with Paddy.

We had passed both the Abbey and then the church beside it, which looked like its calf, before walking past Big Ben, one of the few images of London that existed in my mind long before I met Jason. Clarissa pointed out places of interest, explaining things briefly, just as she had done at the Tate. She prefaced everything with 'You will remember that' or 'As you probably know', as if fearing that she could offend by stating the obvious. I enjoyed this belated tourism. I had done a lot of sightseeing on my own or with Jason, but Jason talked and talked, and never explained anything.

I reminded Clarissa about the photos she had taken. She had never delivered the prints.

'Oh, of course,' she said. 'How silly of me to forget.' She raised the palm of her hand in its soft green glove as if about to hit her forehead, in a gesture exactly like her son's. We were now moving away from picture-postcard London and into an area that looked much more like my father's world: large stone-built ministries, impersonal administrative offices and monuments to Britain's infinite capacity for conflict. Ahead of us, Nelson's bicorn loomed high above the roofs.

'You know, Milena, I must say something,' she said. 'I was going to confess something to you over lunch, but, now that we speak of photographs, I can't wait any longer. It was one of the reasons why I wanted Jason out of the way today. It is difficult to know how to start.'

We paused between the Cenotaph and the Ministry of Defence. The crowds had thinned and a couple of men in uniform overtook us. Their heels had been falling on the pavement behind us with a steady metallic beat for a while and, until that moment, I had the impression that they were following us. Whitehall was more intimate than home, but not dissimilar.

'Please don't worry about what I am going to disclose,' Clarissa said. 'But I have to say I was as surprised as anyone when she rang.'

I stared at her, my insides clenching.

'She sounded so distinguished, so refined, one of us, as my mother would have said,' Clarissa said and paused.

'I know,' I said. 'I suppose it makes sense, given her background.'

I thought I understood why Clarissa didn't press me about Christmas.

I wanted Whitehall to open up and swallow me. Instead it was about to disgorge us as we reached the top of the street, our walk still punctuated by a seemingly endless supply of martial effigies.

'And so very cold at first, but then, as she explained the situation and the reason for her approach in more detail, you could see that there was a very different side to her, and I suppose I warmed to her. A lot, even. Forgive me, Milena. Perhaps I shouldn't have spoken to her at all. Should have put the phone down the first time.'

'But how could you do that?' I said. 'Jason is your son.'

'And it turns out she went to school with my first cousin,' she said.

'I am sure she did,' I said. 'This cousin of yours, she must be very young.'

I can see now how I was unable to reverse my particular train of thought, although it was beginning to dawn on me that we were not both talking about Artie Rutherford.

'You do have a peculiar sense of humour, Milena,' Clarissa said and paused to look at me. 'Cousin Christabel is a bit older than me, in fact. She remembers your Aunt Dara very well. A strange girl, she said. Dara was a Communist, but that was not too unusual in itself. Other girls fancied themselves to be Communist in the thirties. There were more Communists than foreigners at the school in those days.'

'Strange, you say? Strange how?' I gulped with relief, trying to pretend that I was talking about Dara all along. It was easier than knowing what to say about Artemis bloody Rutherford. 'What do you mean?'

'She spoke all these languages no one had even heard of before. She had an odd haircut, a strange name. And she was corresponding with a young man who was in prison in her country. She feared that her father would disown her if he found out, for this man was a terrorist of some kind. On Sunday afternoons, when the girls wrote letters to their families, she wrote letters to him and sent them via someone in Switzerland, another Communist, who forwarded them. The oddest thing was, all the girls thought she was obsessed, yet they weren't love letters. Christabel asked, and Dara just laughed at the idea. The school would have put an end to that anyway if they could have decoded the language. They were philosophical discussions, Dara told Christabel, as though romantic love was beneath her. He was a dear comrade, an important revolutionary, a comrade she would give her life for, not give her life to. No one knew what to make of it.'

Clarissa chuckled, visibly taken by the strangeness of it all, but not nearly as taken as I was. A dozen feral pigeons took off into the air as we crossed towards the fountains and the large spruce standing in the middle of the square.

'Anyway I didn't mean to gossip,' she said. 'You have a very eccentric aunt. She took our number from your uncle, of course, but I kept wondering how much she was risking to call us like that. And all because she was so concerned with your well-being. She said she had met Jason, so I can well understand her. We will talk more in the restaurant. You know the crucial details, but I have so much more to tell. Let me explain about the Christmas tree and the fountain now.'

The day dissolved into a blur after that, presided over by Nelson, the huge Norwegian spruce, the bronze mermaids floating out of the fountains, the lions, the buskers, people protesting about apartheid in front of the South African Embassy, endless zebra crossings and finally the dark little restaurant off St Martin's Lane, with its midafternoon candles and its garlands of plastic grapes. Permeating it all were Clarissa's voice and Clarissa's face, and Dara's unbelievable story, which made me forget my anguish over Jason for a while.

Major William Howard became a Communist in the late 1930s, at Oxford. William was a close friend of Iris Murdoch, Clarissa said. His brother later became an eminent historian, an Oxford don and a colleague of Paddy's father. The English world was as small as ours, it seemed.

'You know of Iris Murdoch, of course?' she asked. 'The famous novelist and a Communist herself.'

Our salads were sitting in front of us on the table, uneaten. I sipped my wine from time to time. Clarissa kept digressing from her narration to give further context, to explain. You could see she was a natural teacher, had been during those two or three years she called her career. I tried to nod by way of speeding her along, just as I nodded to get rid of the solicitous waiter who kept interrupting in dubious French, worried that we were not enjoying our *frisée au chèvre chaud*.

I cared little about England in the 1930s. I knew nothing of Iris Murdoch, and I cared even less than I cared about that salad. I was getting impatient. These quintessentially English cultural name-dropping digressions around supposedly famous figures reminded me of dogs sniffing, then urinating to mark their territories. I wanted to know what this Major Howard had to do with Dara.

'William joined the British army in 1939, even before the Communists said the war was legitimate. He became part of the Special Operations Executive,' she moved on finally, but again explaining at unbearable length what this 'executive' was. 'And in 1942, along with two other SOE commandos, he was parachuted into your country to serve as a liaison officer between the British and your partisans. He spoke Russian and Arabic, and he had picked up some of your language, but far from enough. The partisans gave him an interpreter, herself an intrepid fighter who had gone to an English girls' boarding school. To translate and to report, I imagine, for who can blame your people for that? The British might have been your allies, but no one ever trusts the British. I am sure even William didn't trust them fully himself.'

Clarissa gave a wry laugh.

'Anyway, it seems that far from – or in addition to – spying on each other (no one ever really knows the detail of such things!), William and his interpreter fell in love. He was now fighting alongside your partisans in the mountains, you understand. In 1943 he was wounded and taken prisoner by local quislings. There was a show trial, then he was executed by firing squad. One of the other SOE officers reported that the interpreter escaped unwounded and went on to fight for two more years, that she in fact became suicidal in her courage: Germans or quislings, no other woman killed as many.'

'And you are saying that woman was Dara?' I asked. I didn't believe this story. And Dara's tragic love wasn't its least believable aspect. This Major Howard would have been a National Hero in my country, avenues and schools would have been named after him if this were true.

'Yes. I am saying that was your aunt,' Clarissa said. 'Paddy and I knew nothing about any of it when we received her first call. We were intrigued by her, of course. Her English was just too good; it made me curious and so, as we spoke, I asked where she had learned it. We mentioned her name to Christabel, and the school story came out. Then Paddy started digging around. You know how he is, at a loose end, always after a project. There are boxes of his father's papers in the attic, some letters from Major Howard's brother. The brother also wrote two books, detailed accounts, which we had never read until now. Why would we? It's not our sort of stuff exactly, either British communism or the SOE. Your aunt isn't named in either of these books and it took a little while to join the dots, but it was hardly Bletchley Park stuff.'

'I can't begin to believe it. Had my aunt had an English lover, I would have known.' I found it easier to go on calling Dara my aunt than to delay the revelations further. 'I would have known about it, long before I came to this country.'

'And look at you, Jason's interpreter,' Clarissa said, pursuing her own train of thought. 'Isn't that a strange parallel? History repeats itself, first time as a tragedy, then ...'

She stopped, gave an embarrassed laugh.

'A romantic comedy,' she completed her own sentence. 'A happy ending, I mean. But the reason you wouldn't have known about any of this, apparently – at least that's what Paddy has found – is that a year or two after the war, your country's relationship with Britain soured. There had been a monument to Major William Howard in your capital, but your people removed it in 1949, just as they removed every last trace of British assistance.

'Howard's brother observed that the interpreter and lover must have suffered too when the tide turned, but, knowing your aunt now and the way she has been able to contact us, Paddy and I are pretty sure that someone high up in the system must have vouched for her, protected her. We think it most likely that your father took Dara under his wing, not simply because she was family, but because she was so dedicated to the cause. He had the authority then; he still has it. Christabel thought the same when we discussed the story. Please, darling, don't fear that any of this will leak out in any way. Paddy and I have only your interests at heart and Christabel's husband is a retired diplomat – she knows how to keep shtum.'

Stanislav, I thought. Dara's prisoner comrade. It took a real effort of imagination to grasp the stark earnestness of the 1930s and '40s in my country – a time of fervent belief, devotion, imprisonment and even execution, set against a backdrop of poverty, unrest and warfare. Yet, once grasped, that seriousness put into bathetic context Jason's trajectory, a career path lubricated by risk-free, fashion-chasing attitudinising.

I wondered if Mother knew any of this. She didn't meet Father until 1960. That year the opera season opened with *La Traviata* and my mother's nicely maturing soprano. I could more or less date their first meeting by working back from my own birthday the following year.

So I was beginning to piece the story together at long last. Dara had rung Clarissa a few times, an English-woman to an Englishwoman, Clarissa said, though that made no sense. She did it to find out how I was, to check if I needed help, to keep an eye on me. She asked Clarissa for a photo of me, a photo of the babies, and Clarissa had supplied them in September, after her visit. Dara swore my mother-in-law to secrecy. It wouldn't be helpful for me to know any of it, and indeed it would be extremely danger-ous for her if anyone got to know. This was enough to convince Clarissa to remain silent: she couldn't have been aware that her silence made no difference. The calls would have been recorded anyway.

Unlike her son, Clarissa was not by nature the kind who reneges on a promise, but she began to question the need to keep things away from me, began to worry that she was betraying my confidence. After all, her first duty was to me, not Dara.

'You sent my aunt photographs? You wrote to her?' I asked, disbelieving. 'To what address?'

'Just a very brief note to explain the photos,' Clarissa said. 'They were lovely photos of you and the boys, noth-ing else, and you looked so very happy in them, beatific almost. Your aunt gave me the name of her club. Nothing else was required to mail the letter. Not even the street name. Simply her name and the club.'

Dara's club? What club? But for the risk of making Clarissa feel stupid, I could have laughed. Dara must have had Father's permission to solicit the photos, encourage-ment even. She had always seemed to me, in her nun-like existence, to be his bodyguard, his Cerberus. I now knew that the devotion was mutual.

The short winter's day meant that it was already dark when Clarissa and I reached Charing Cross Station. There was a group of carol singers in the big hall. Two white-haired women in front of them rattled their collection boxes, and office workers staggered tipsily onto their commuter trains.

Something was shifting in my mind. I was very fond of my mother-in-law. I could have learned to love this England, I thought, but it might well be too late. I hugged Clarissa tightly because I wondered if we were seeing each other for the last time. I was not sure yet, but I felt guilty all the same. She responded in kind and we held each other briefly as the tannoys announced final destinations and whistles blew. I caught again that simple sweet scent she was so fond of, and which I now knew was stephanotis. Having seen what was under that strange English shell, I now also knew she was a good and strong woman. Sadly, her son had neither quality.

Chapter Twenty-Six

Jason's Kiss

Wrench yourself out! try to fly
with the pin piercing your heart.
The space confronting you is boundless.
Freedom has the salty taste of sea and solitude.

> Blaga Dimitrova, 'Butterfly on a Pin'

'Hello, good morning. Artemis Rutherford here,' she said. Her manner was the same polished, finishing-school act I remembered from the last time she called. She inhaled and I butted in, just as I had learned to do in my interpreting days.

'I am afraid Jason's out this morning.' I didn't offer to take a message this time.

'I know, and I apologise for intruding,' she said, 'but it is you I wanted to speak to, Milena. I hope it's a good moment. I hope I can call you that. We're the same age.'

She called me My-leena, but I didn't correct her.

'Jason is here with us, at Broadcasting House, as you probably know,' she said. 'Though not with me at the moment. There is an editing session this morning and then we have a planning meeting at midday.'

'Thank you for letting me know,' I said.

'But that's not it … I have taken the liberty of calling you without his knowledge. I know that, by betraying a secret, I might be risking his anger, but I am sure you'll understand when you hear me out. This is potentially huge.'

She might be about to offer a timeshare in Jason, I suddenly thought. I had read an article about the way British people shared holiday apartments in Spain. I was ready for anything, but – particularly after my conversation with Clarissa – I didn't want another farcical misunderstanding. I proceeded cautiously.

'Go on,' I said. I knew I sounded rude, but people like Artemis were taught to be kind to foreigners, just as they were to their horses and dogs.

'Jason and I were talking about different programme ideas we could pitch in today's meeting. Jason has a real future in broadcasting, you know. Wonderful voice and delivery, original thinking, charisma: we're looking for people like that all the time. In Wales he and I already discussed several possible stories and one of them – the most promising one – was a programme about life behind the Iron Curtain.'

I didn't like Artemis and I didn't like the sound of this – I thought of saying that maybe any programme involving her should be called *Tales of the Cold Whore* – but I wasn't interrupting.

'He told me some of your life story, My-leena. Stunning material, if I may say so. And then the way British people think that you all live in shoeboxes over there. We're shamefully ignorant. Let's counter those prejudices together, you and I and Jason. We wouldn't gloss over the truth. The detail about the friend of yours, for example, the boy who killed himself because he was a vegetarian and they force-fed him in the army: that's just horrible. But your privacy is as safe with me as it is with Jason, don't worry, My-leena. We wouldn't use your name, or even the name of your country, if you are uncomfortable with that. We could move it all to Prague. English people know about Prague. Or, even better, East Berlin. Berlin has this added *noir* aspect—'

'*Noir*, you said?' I finally interrupted.

'Yes, I'll explain what I mean when we get to production. Background music, sound effects, that sort of thing. It's merely cosmetic.' Her natural haughtiness was now diluted with a little forced politeness. 'The thing is, Jason didn't think you'd like the idea. Yet it's pure gold, and I thought I ought to give it a try – try to persuade you, woman-to-woman … It could be the making of the three of us. I know I am taking huge liberties here, betraying his confidence. It's just that now's such a good moment, the year not just of Chernobyl but of glasnost, perestroika and all that. By the time the next round of planning comes along, God knows what will happen. Gorbachev himself might be old news.'

She took a deep breath. The effort to pronounce the strange Russian words appeared to have been more taxing for her than the ethics of her proposal.

'You know what, Artie?' I said, pausing while trying to sound as calm and composed as if I was English, a countess myself.

'Yes?' she said expectantly, perhaps taken aback by my sudden familiarity.

'Fuck off.'

Misha used to have a print depiction of Dante's *Inferno* on the wall of his studio. It was a Venetian woodcut from the early sixteenth century, in theory out of place in his minimalist architectural heaven, but in practice its black-and-white circles suited the simple geometries of the space he had created. He would put on a record, something long, repetitious and infuriating for whoever from our security services was on listening duty – it could just as easily have been *The Dark Side of the Moon* or Stockhausen – and he would make love to me, long and slow, on his Barcelona chaise. We never made a sound, Misha and I, at least nothing that you could hear over the music, not until his very end.

Without even realising it, I managed to learn hell's layout by heart, and it all came back to me. Adulterers were in the second circle. Traitors in the ninth: not only those who betrayed their country but those who betrayed their cities, their families, those who betrayed their friends with a kiss. This distinction made no sense then – for what was adultery, if not treachery? – but it did now.

I am not going to flatter Jason, or me, by exaggerating the significance of his betrayal. I wasn't going to be taken to some English gulag or put against a wall of sandbags and executed, just because my husband had spilled the beans about my past to his lady producer. I am simply saying that I grasped the difference. His infidelity didn't seem half as cruel as his casual disloyalty. I would now teach him what cruelty means.

If Artemis told Jason about our conversation, and whatever his reaction to it might have been, he never mentioned anything to me. Slowly I began to think that she didn't say anything at all, that she left it to me to decide how to proceed. And I was angry but still uncertain. To leave him seemed unthinkable; to continue, impossible; to forgive, unbearable.

He and I carried on as usual, with a few more silences perhaps, but he didn't seem to notice. It was as though we were walking around an unexploded bomb, each wondering what the other knew, and each affecting to know nothing. He would look up from his manuscript, look at me and the boys, smile at us and I would smile back, lighting up his Peter Pan face by doing so, yet all the while contemplating the exact calibrations of his betrayal.

How quaintly exotic we must have seemed to Artemis, poor old Misha and I, and how pathetic our efforts to deny our barbaric world, with our flimsy Potemkin villages of Ray-Ban spectacles and Saint Laurent jerkins. And what else was coming my way? Had my husband told this woman that he had had me in the Vice President's bed before an evening of Communist opera?

I wish I could say I was better prepared for the next blow, when it came. It was barely a week or so after Artemis called, yet I felt that the Christmas season had already lasted forever, that the year was never going to end.

Jason was in the bedroom, bent over Philip and Nicholas, who were lying side by side on our bed, on their backs and naked on their nappy mats. He was tickling their tummies, one and then the other, and their chubby legs moved in the air in an apparently coordinated wave. All three loved the routine.

I didn't recognise the man's voice when I answered the buzzer. He said the item he had was sign on delivery, for me personally. I ran downstairs and I knew him the moment I opened the door and he handed over the letter. It was the same courier who came the day after the wedding, the same young Indian man, the same bicycle even.

He had a piece of silver tinsel tied around his neck this time, one end dangling, the other tied so that it looked like a noose after a failed execution.

The embossed crest of my homeland shone on heavy watermarked paper with the intensity of fresh blood. I felt it as though it was a blister under my fingers. In my native language, the envelope proclaimed it was private and confidential. I opened it on the first landing, going back up to the attic, only to find another, smaller and thinner, sealed envelope inside, with an unfamiliar reference number, a mid-November date and a repeated confidentiality statement. The number was handwritten, the date stamped. I didn't think it was more money from my parents. It looked like a summons of some kind, except that it was no longer in their power to summon me.

I leant against the mezzanine wall and opened the smaller envelope. It contained two photographs and a note. The first photo showed an unfamiliar street in what looked like London, the frontage of a pub called the Saracen's Head, with clusters of people standing in front, speaking or smoking, or both. Some were holding pints, some wine glasses. It was a common enough London scene: no one stood and drank like that where I came from. On the right, where the iron bollards ended, there were two vehicles, parked alongside the kerb.

The second photo showed one of the vehicles, a black Golf, much closer up. Then I saw it wasn't the vehicle, or its make, that mattered, but the two people behind it. I had been focusing on the wrong details in the first image, because these two were in it too. It was the same picture, the detail now hugely enlarged. Leaning against the car on the pavement side, so that I could only see her back, was a woman with long chestnut hair, wearing a green jacket. A man was kissing her. His copper-blond hair was only partly tamed by a stripy beanie hat.

His head was tilted and – where it wasn't obscured by hers – I could see, although I didn't need to see, a section of his face. He was bending down towards her. The car made it impossible to tell if the woman was standing on her toes. She was, it seems, some twenty centimetres shorter than the man. I could see their embrace well enough. His arms were wrapped around her back at waist level, hers clasped him higher up. It seemed that her right hand was holding his chin, the left resting on the back of his head, as though the man's head was a honeydew melon. It could not be described, by any stretch of the imagination, as a friendly kiss, or one of greeting or parting. It was a lovers' kiss.

The man's part in it seemed more passionate than the woman's, although I may have been reading too much into the image. A woman who has lost her head doesn't hold the man's with such rehearsed poise.

On the other hand, I knew the man well enough to be aware that he was a top-class act.

And, still, I didn't scream.

'You know we're here to help you,' said the note, unsigned. The writing was Lekovich's, of that there was little doubt. It was not immediately obvious how he thought he could help me, although it was perfectly clear how this photograph could help him. Even I could see how many points Lekovich would score with my father by sending someone to keep an eye on Jason, either under orders or, much more likely, given what I now knew of Dara's calls, on his own initiative. I realised how much he stood to gain by proving so clearly something that my father had already suspected – that Jason was indeed a worthless individual – and, finally, if it all worked to plan, by despatching me back where I belonged, not as a kidnap victim but of my own free will, a chastened returnee.

And there on that landing I finally admitted two things to myself: that I could never trust Jason again, someone who was now embarrassing me with public displays of his opportunistic libido; and that, whatever the distance, I could never escape my country. Since I could not escape it, I would use its might, however rusty, to punish my husband.

I heard Jason calling my name from the top of the stairs, asking if everything was OK. I stuffed the photos into my bra and walked up, envelope in hand.

'What was that all about?' he asked when I stepped in. He had brought the Moses baskets into the kitchen-study-dining room and was beginning to lay the table for lunch.

I showed him the two envelopes, the note saying, 'You know we're here to help you.' I translated the words into English, then shrugged.

'Your guess is as good as mine', I said.

'And nothing else?' he asked.

'Nothing else,' I said.

'They are seriously weird, your people,' he said. 'Just weird. But nice that they are offering to help, I guess.'

The boys were lying on their backs, still moving their limbs in the air like a couple of synchronised swimmers. I was so lucky with them. They were good babies, placid, acting like each other's toy and, unlike their mother and father, contented inside their little bubble of two.

Jason was chomping on a celery stick, loudly, taking an occasional bite, while dressing some lettuce leaves in a big wooden bowl. He had long proclaimed himself the master of the perfectly balanced salad dressing. A couple of huge jacket potatoes sat in the middle of the table, an unopened pot of cottage cheese next to them. Beside the sink there was a plastic tub of trifle.

I stood there, watching him and all the food, holding that envelope, feeling the photographs under my bra, their old-fashioned serrated edges (just where had Lekovich had them developed?) threatening my breast with paper cuts.

I couldn't bear to be in the same space with Jason any more.

'Actually, Jason, I have no appetite. My stomach aches terribly all of a sudden. I'd rather take a warm bath, have a nap. You carry on,' I said.

He looked up from the lettuce bowl, puzzled. I was already half-inside the bedroom. I took the bathrobe off its hook on the door, and our little transistor radio from my bedside, and walked out of the flat and across the landing into the bathroom. I didn't slam any doors, although I wanted to. I was aching, indeed, but the pain wasn't radiating from my gut.

I locked the bathroom door, ran the hot-water tap and switched on the radio. I found a commercial station, chirping its advertising for Christmas offers against the sound of pop music. I didn't want to risk the BBC or anything produced by Artemis Rutherford.

The bath was full, the bathroom mirror misted. I undressed, leaving my clothes on the floor, climbed in and sank into the water. I remembered Antai, the beginnings of my now-failed escape. As my breasts lifted towards the surface, I saw the perfect serrated imprint on the left one, a thin line, barely red, just under the curl left by the scalloped edge of my bra.

I would like to imagine that the bomb Jason and I had been tiptoeing around for some weeks had finally exploded in that miserable attic bathroom, blowing open the roof of Minford Gardens as the IRA had torn asunder the Grand Hotel in Brighton. It was the first and only moment during my humiliating London fiasco that I could not hold myself together. I think I screamed. I had never screamed before. I would like to say that I heard myself, but I didn't. Nor did I hear Jason running across the landing. I heard him, clearly enough, banging at the door.

'Are you OK, Millie?' There was genuine panic in his voice. I could sense his fear, even against the Christmas cheer of local radio.

'I am very well, thank you very much,' I said stupidly, sounding like Will's imitation of the Iron Lady emerging from the seafront rubble.

'Are you sure?' he asked.

'Something fell. I slipped,' I said, already composed. 'Go back to the kids, Jason. I want to finish my bath. I am fine.'

Two days later he went for his job interview at UCL, just in case.

'No harm in trying for it,' he'd said. 'I can always change my mind if I get that Oxford offer.'

I watched him from the window and, the moment he turned the street corner, I got the boys ready and telephoned for the black cab to take us to the embassy in

Bayswater. It was a short journey. I resented the cab fare, but I didn't feel like wrestling my way onto the Tube or a bus with the twins, and I did not want to be seen and recognised until I was at the embassy doorstep. The driver helped get the twins into the car. They now rested at my feet in the carrycots I had detached from the pram, at first too bewildered to cry, poor kittens, but the movement soothed them. They were asleep before we passed Holland Park.

I had no appointment. I was sure Lekovich would see me without one.

I observed the apprehension in the face of the secret policeman-qua-concierge who opened the massive black embassy door when he saw the cab driver carrying the two cots up a short flight of stairs. His trepidation mounted visibly when I gave my name.

The same alarm flickered across the face of the secretary who emerged into the lobby from somewhere deeper inside the building, then pretended to take my name before she disappeared into Lekovich's office for several long minutes.

I waited in the lobby, sitting on what seemed, incongruously, like a piano stool, examining huge framed tourist posters of my native country on the wall: the lakes, the mountains, the monasteries, the coast, happy peasants in embroidered shirts, even the white wedding cake of that spa hospital where I aborted my first child.

'Return rejuvenated,' the caption read.

Lekovich stood up from his enormous empty desk and walked round it to shake my hand, briefly glancing at the babies. The merest shadow of some emotion crossed his face. I would like to be able to say it was the same alarm that had infected his subordinates, but I am not sure.

'Comrade Milena, what an unexpected treat. How can I help you?'

He was so tight-lipped that his moustache barely moved as he spoke. At the mention of helping me, he attempted a smile. He must have guessed why I had come, but not what exactly I was after. I was, I guessed, already famously capricious.

It was like watching an anaconda grin. I savoured the stand-off.

Lekovich was a slightly younger member of my father's generation; he had barely graduated when he killed a German colonel. It was one of the first acts of resistance in the whole of Europe, and Lekovich, just back in his small town after four years of studying in Switzerland, acted alone. He shot the man from a crowded pavement and, although recognised, managed to escape, not to be seen in town again for the next four years. He returned at twenty-seven, on a white horse, a colonel himself and a liberator. The Germans executed a whole year's intake at Lekovich's old school in retribution, every last eighteen-year-old boy in the small town, to ensure that no one attempted anything similar again. And here the assassin was, forty-odd years later, an eternal survivor, an impetuous youth transmogrified into this more cautious version of his earlier self, delighted at having to mop up the consequences of Jason Connor's decadence.

The boys were quiet through it all. Nicholas opened his eyes when he heard Lekovich's voice, spotted me, then closed them again. Philip's sweet little face remained calm throughout, his eyes wide open. Those were their natures – the older one a bit more alert, more nervous, the younger more sanguine, more like his father – but only I knew that. Jason wasn't always sure he could tell them apart. That didn't matter any more. He wouldn't need to be able to tell them apart ever again.

'It's OK,' I said, both to the boys and to Lekovich. 'They don't cry.'

'They take after their mother,' Lekovich said. I thought I detected malice in his voice. 'And how may I help you, Comrade Milena?' he repeated.

'I received your note,' I said, 'and I thank you for it.'

'My pleasure. And your reaction to it is … ?' He did not sound tense any more.

I was at a disadvantage after all. I had come to meet him on his territory. Nonetheless, I didn't want him to overestimate his own strength. I was not about to discuss Jason's behaviour with him, any more than I had discussed it with Jason.

'We both know my father well. I believe, if he knew what I was about to ask, he would want you to assist me as promptly as you can,' I said.

'Of course,' Lekovich said. 'I am at your disposal. Please say what you have in mind.'

'I would like these two boys – my sons – listed in my passport, as fast as that can possibly be done.'

I took my passport and the boys' birth certificates out of my bag and put the documents down on his desk as if to say: I am in your hands. The passport was wine-coloured; its golden coat of arms glistened. The morocco binding was real leather. Strange how my country, not known for luxuries, produced such expensive-looking documents, much more expensive than Jason's British blue, perhaps because it had to produce so few.

I remembered Jason boasting that his passport took him anywhere. He was about to find out that wasn't true.

'Oh,' Lekovich said, grasping everything in a moment. He was quick, as sharp-witted in his late sixties as he was at twenty-two.

'I want to take the boys to their motherland,' I said. 'As simple as that.'

I looked at the oil portrait above him, heavy in its massive frame: our President in a grey suit and a red tie, with a red five-pointed star in his lapel. His familiar face was usually stern, yet now, in the play of light on the brushstrokes, he was almost smiling at me and the babies at my feet, like a reassuring, benign father of his nation. I assumed there was a camera hidden in the ornate carvings of the frame, and anyone watching through that camera might well have been smiling too.

Next to the presidential portrait was a framed photograph of the monument to international brotherhood, two massive concrete fists in a clearing in our highlands, and an inscription that read, in Russian: 'There is no defeat while Moscow is behind us.' A few centimetres below these, just to the right, was that image of the President with my father, two young and handsome guerrilla fighters, their eyes fixed on the Communist future.

I took a deep breath. There was a split-second in which to change my mind, but I did not seize the opportunity.

Rather, I remembered the Saracen's Head.

'I've had enough of this country,' I said. 'There's nothing here for me. I want to go home. As soon as possible. With the boys.'

'And without …' Lekovich paused. There was no need to ask, but he wanted to savour his moment of triumph.

I nodded.

He returned to the other side of his desk, took a box of cigarettes out of a drawer, then lit one with a heavy jade tabletop lighter. He put the box next to the matching jade ashtray, with a couple of cigarettes sticking out, as though uncertain whether to offer me one or not. I used to be a smoker; he was right to hesitate. *White Sea Spirit*: the sight of the familiar sail and the black outline of a swift on the carton made my innards lurch.

The secretary who had seemed so diffident when I arrived now stepped into the room after the most cursory of knocks. She stood just inside the door, confused by the sight of Lekovich smoking, me still sitting in the chair opposite his desk, the babies' baskets at my feet.

She corrected the pussy bow on her blue shirt, unnecessarily.

'Your next appointment, Comrade Lekovich,' she said, looking in my direction. It was an obvious way of checking if he wanted to end the meeting. Pretence – making sure that both sides are aware of it – was part of the strategy; she was offering him the means to humiliate me.

'Not now, Comrade Manya,' Lekovich said. 'Let them wait. And please bring us a couple of glasses of the President's vodka.'

His lips spread in a smile, a proper, wide smile. She mirrored it with one of her own.

'I've heard so much about you, Comrade Urbanska,' she said to me.

'I am sure you have.' I smiled too.

She returned with a huge silver tray, bearing two tiny glasses frosted with ice and a vodka bottle so heavy that she had to hold it with both hands to pour. Then she left the room, walking backwards.

Lekovich raised his glass. I took mine and I felt my fingers sticking to its cold sides.

'Happy New Year, Rastislav,' I said. The New Year was two weeks away, and there was still the English Christmas with Jason to live through, but the Western Christmas didn't figure in my homeland's embassy any more than it featured in what remained of its religious calendar.

And I couldn't imagine anyone other than his long-dead mother calling Lekovich by his first name, but he took it from me without flinching.

'Slava, please, Mina,' he said and downed the vodka in one.

'Touché,' I said. Only my father had ever called me Mina, and even he stopped using the nickname when I was eight, because Mother hated its rustic sound, preferring the operatic Mimi instead. This man was equal to every move I made, I thought, but that was just as well. He was my ally now.

If Lekovich's assistance had a price, I wasn't going to foot that bill. Father was. Everything would be exactly as I wanted it.

Chapter Twenty-Seven

Return to Zenda

1987

> I will set out and go back to my father and say to
> him: Father, I have sinned against heaven and
> against you.
>
> Luke 15:18

I locked the door of our rental flat behind me, put the key
in an envelope with Jason's name on it and stashed the
envelope in my pocket. Everything I wanted to take back
with me was now on the landing between the doorway
and the bathroom. I carried the rucksack and then the
pram downstairs, then went upstairs one final time, to
carry down the most precious luggage I possessed, one
cot on each arm.

The boys did not feel heavy at all. Being a breadwinner
and mother in Britain had made me much stronger than
I was before.

I didn't want anyone to see me. The flats in the building belonged to yuppies who worked all day in the City,
but you never knew. Someone on extended New Year leave
might step out at the wrong moment and then my

departure would be witnessed. Inconvenient, but not the end of the world. Even Will might be downstairs in his basement lair, I thought, but, if so, he was likely to be sleeping off the festivities in his hall of mirrors at the back of the house. I had a story ready for him too: I was joining Jason, who was away on business. I was sure that Will would find the idea of Jason's 'business' both funny and sufficient. He wasn't a naturally inquisitive man. He was hardly going to ask where exactly I was travelling to. Two years after we first met he still had no idea where I came from.

Jason had left on Sunday evening. The day of my departure from England was supposedly the second day of his recording session in a studio on the Derbyshire estate of the Earl of Cleigh. Tiptoeing into what Jason called the brave new Thatcherite world, the BBC had outsourced the production of *The Argonauts* to an independent company belonging to Apollo, Artemis's little brother. I jest. The boy was called Hugo, Jason had told me so himself. And there was no question of nepotism involving Hugo, either. He had the best recording studio this side of the Atlantic, and had produced an award-winning series of rare bird sounds for Radio 3: recording Jason would be a doddle.

My husband did not know, still, that I knew Artemis was his mistress, but that no longer mattered. What mattered more was that even Derbyshire did not seem far enough away. He might disengage his penis, return suddenly, find me as I prepared to flee, try to stop me. That was my only remaining fear.

The gods were on my side. There was a banging of pots and pans behind one of the doors, but no sighting as I went past it five times: down-up, down-up, then finally down again with the boys. The babies made no sound other than suckling. I had acted against my own best principles and given them dummies dipped in honey. Slava Lekovich, who was once rumoured to have smothered an infant that threatened to give away his partisans' whereabouts to a German patrol, would have been proud of me.

I closed the front door slowly, locking it behind me, then added that key to the envelope and pushed it through the letterbox. There was, now, no way back.

'Going back home. Please don't try to get in touch. I won't answer. M,' the parting note in the letter said. Unlike Artemis, I had added no doodles.

I was too wearied by practicalities to consider the poignancy of the moment, if indeed there was any. I still worried that someone would stop me at Heathrow, try to keep my babies in the country. Lekovich assured me they couldn't. Two near-identical faces stared at me from the last page of my passport, round, satisfied, already sporting silky little locks of that Connor copper-blondness that looked white in the pictures. It was not mandatory to have baby pictures in the passport, but I wanted everything to be doubly safe. I had had them photographed in a corner studio the day before I took them to the embassy. Nicholas and Philip Urbansky, sons of Milena Urbanska: you could travel unnoticed with those names, even in 1987.

It was raining when I pushed the pram down Shepherd's Bush Road. Leftover Christmas lights blinked forlornly in the drizzle, the early January morning almost exactly matching the December afternoon when I arrived two years and some small change of days earlier. The embassy car was waiting for me at the prearranged safe distance, on the corner of Netherwood Road, without Lekovich in it, as I wished. The man had no small talk and I couldn't imagine him being capable of companionable silence.

We were helped into the car and set off, passing Brook Green, then Hammersmith Library. By the time we got onto the motorway ten minutes or so later, everything in London had already begun to seem like a mirror image of my arrival. The years were like something I had dreamed, in spite of the very real children I was taking back with me. Misha, dead, seemed more real to me in that car than Jason, still very much alive, I assumed, somewhere in Derbyshire, on the Cleigh estate, and maybe on Artemis as well.

The plane would break through the clouds and I would never see him or this city again.

I was not a *nepovratchik* after all, Lekovich said while raising his glass in a toast – not a one-way defector. He had always known that would be the case, he said. He had every confidence I would see the truth about the English.

'I repeated that in every report all along,' he said, like a headmaster praising his head girl. 'She's an Urbansky. She will see the truth.'

It was mere politesse. I knew people like Lekovich did not permit repentance, or forgive errors, but I also knew that my still unshaken hereditary privilege trumped that: I was forever Daddy's girl.

I was wearing the same thick winter coat for the first time since my initial days in London, and I was feeling too hot inside the car. I would need it again, for at the other side

it was minus sixteen and snowing. I had missed the whiteness, I realised, the crispness of proper dry cold, not the
persistent mushy chill that was the best London could
offer in place of snow.

The boys were also wrapped up well and their little
faces were red. I lifted them out of their cots, one and then
the other, trying to soothe them by cradling each against
my shoulders. Nicholas reached out to try to touch the
misted window behind him. Philip just pushed his skull
gently into my cheek. It was strange to think that they
might be seeing London for the last time without really
seeing it, without knowing the city at all.

The boys' kit aside, I was taking back much less than I'd
brought over. I had left behind most of my clothes and
books, and all the knick-knacks I had acquired while in
Britain, in order to travel as light as possible. Jason would
have to throw it all out, even that copy of *Orlando*, if he
wanted.

I had left the second photograph – the close-up –
together with the last, thousand-Deutschmark note, the
wedding gift from my parents, under my signed copy of
The Argonauts on the kitchen table. The money had never
been exchanged because I had always kept it for an emergency. It was ironic, when that emergency arose, that I did
not need any cash. Our travel, one way only, was arranged
by Lekovich exactly as I requested. I liked the idea that I
was, after all, paying Jason off. I knew that he would figure out what it was saying – that he might need the money
more than I would.

I took the first photograph, the street scene, with me,
tucked inside my almost empty wallet. It would remind

me of London. If you didn't know what to look for in it, the image was inconspicuous enough, even charming.

It occurred to me only then that I wasn't sure, and that I did not care, how – if he wanted to marry Artemis; and, less likely, if she wanted to marry him, gluing her ambition to his limited success to date, instead of simply fornicating with a pauper poet – he would go about divorcing me.

Terminal Two was almost empty, and the check-in for our airline completely deserted. I had to wait several minutes before someone came over from an Alitalia desk to serve me. I showed him my passport and the ticket. The man looked at the babies, flicked to the last page of the passport, saw the photos, smiled in that way that only Italians smile at babies, printed out the boarding pass, reeled off the guidance about travelling with infants and the complexities of having two, weighed my rucksack, tagged it, then finally pressed a button. I watched as the rucksack was carried away. He explained how to present the pram for boarding, tagged that too and wished us a safe journey. In all that time, no other passenger joined the check-in queue.

'There's turbulence over the Alps,' the man added as an afterthought when we set off towards Departures. 'I hope they are good sleepers.'

We went through. Leaving Britain was much easier than entering it.

The plane was almost empty too. There were more crew members than passengers. They fussed with the boys, and pretended this time not to know who I was. It must have been easier that way. They ignored my boarding pass and gave us the best row of seats on the plane.

The boys started crying when we took off and cried until we reached the cruising height. I was surprised to be told we were somewhere over Belgium already. Britain seemed smaller than when I arrived.

'It's their little ears,' a hostess soothed. 'The pressure. They will fly more happily in a year or two.'

I fed them over Germany, one and then the other, watching the European landmass whisk itself into higher and higher peaks. Then they finally slept and I prepared for the turbulence ahead.

The plane descended into whiteness. I set my watch three hours ahead. When we landed, I waited until the handful of other passengers had disembarked. The piles of ploughed snow alongside the runway were as high as the wings. I watched my handful of fellow travellers out of the window, gripping the handrail, walking gingerly towards a waiting bus to transfer them to the terminal.

'We are waiting for the final instructions on disembarkation. When we get them, we will take the pram downstairs for you,' the hostess said. 'The pilot and the co-pilot want to take the boys downstairs themselves. It will truly be an honour.'

I sat and watched the snow outside. Two years since I'd seen snow.

Then I saw a familiar black car drive down the runway towards us and right up to the plane. These were the 'final instructions', I realised. I knew I wouldn't encounter any passport controls here.

*

My father did not step out of the car to greet me. The driver opened the door. I got in and watched the pilots in their blue uniforms come down, carrying the cots with even more care than they had flown the plane. I watched them salute Father. The driver placed the boys' cots on the folding seats in front of Father and me. I had forgotten how vast the car was, forgotten the smell of leather and tobacco inside it, the warmth behind its darkened windows.

Father looked at the boys, looked at me and said nothing. The car started slowly and, as we passed through the airport perimeter gate, two motorcyclists switched on their blue lights and went ahead. I could tell from the play of light in the car that there were two more behind as well. This, in Father's world, passed for very low key.

We joined the motorway. There were vast empty lanes ahead, and I expected the car to pick up speed. It didn't.

For the best part of an hour we glided through the white fields. There were mountains in the distance; I recognised every shape. Village houses came into focus for a moment, when the blue motorcycle lights shone upon them, then disappeared. We drove through the city streets, past the Manezh, past the Praesidium, then through the residential areas and finally along the familiar lane in the woods and up the gravel driveway, where the car stopped.

The driver stepped out and held open the door. The brilliance of the snow outside, the sharpness of the cold, took my breath away. I could see Mother, who had obviously been denied a place on the reception committee, coming out of the villa in her enormous fur coat and, in the doorway behind her, Dara, waiting, in the same brown suit she always wore. She raised her right hand as though about to wave, but held it to her heart instead. I turned to Father and he surprised me. There were tears in his eyes.

He put his hands on Philip's and then on Nicholas's head, as if to bless the boys. Philip opened his eyes but did not cry. Father lifted him from his cot, pressed him against his shoulder and, still, the boy did not cry.

'Welcome home,' he said – to Philip or to me, it wasn't clear. 'I knew you would come back.'

I picked Nicholas up, inhaled his milky smell, felt his already-cold cheek. I may not have had much choice, I thought, but I felt powerful again. My power was the power to hurt Jason and that was all I still wished for.

Without waiting for the driver to do it, while still cradling the baby, I found the handle with my left hand and started to open the armour-plated door. It required a bit of strength at first, but then it moved under its own weight. The snow path before me sparkled and the cold was so sharp that my lips tingled.

'I don't want him, ever, to come here, Father. Please promise me that,' I said.

'He won't, Milena,' Father said. 'He will never enter this country again.'